HIDDEN
CONSPIRACY

HIDDEN CONSPIRACY

JOHN BERTUCCI

First Printing: February, 2022

ISBN: 978-1-955541-03-9

Library of Congress Number: 2021923444

Cover and Interior Design: Ann Aubitz

Published by FuzionPress
1250 East 115th Street, Burnsville, MN 55337
612-781-2815

TABLE OF CONTENTS

HIDDEN CONSPIRACY 7

Chapter 1: The Upper Peninsula of Michigan 9

Chapter 2: The Teacher 17

Chapter 3: The Problem 37

Chapter 4: Friends and Enemies 45

Chapter 5: Inside and Outside of the Bunker 54

Chapter 6: What to Do? 69

Chapter 7: The Accusation 91

Chapter 8: Wyatt and George 99

Chapter 9: *Me-Too* Works 132

Chapter 10: Search for an Answer 142

Chapter 11: Where are Joe and Ron? 165

Chapter 12: Missing People 197

Chapter 13: Missing Property 221

Chapter 14: Time Flies 225

Chapter 15: The FBI 243

Chapter 16: On to Traverse City 272

Chapter 17: Chicago 279

Chapter 18: Heading South 285

*To my brother, Joe, who left us too soon,
and to Ron, my best friend and colleague*

"Then it don' matter. Then I'll be all aroun' in the dark. I'll be ever'where—wherever you look. Wherever they's a fight so hungry people can eat, I'll be there. Wherever they's a cop beatin' up a guy, I'll be there. If Casy knowed, why, I'll be in the way guys yell when they're mad an' —I'll be in the way kids laugh when they're hungry an' they know supper's ready. An' when our folks eat the stuff they raise an' live in the house they build—why, I'll be there. See? God, I'm talkin' like Casy. Comes of thinkin' about him so much. Seems like I can see him sometimes."

Tom Joad, *Grapes of Wrath* by John Steinbeck

"Injustice anywhere is a threat to justice everywhere. We are caught in an inescapable network of mutuality, tied in a single garment of destiny. Whatever affects one directly, affects all indirectly."

Martin Luther King, Jr.

"Our struggle is not easy. Those who oppose our cause are rich and powerful and they have many allies in high places. We are poor. Our allies are few. But we have something the rich do not own. We have our bodies and spirits and the justice of our cause as our weapons."

Caesar Chavez

ACKNOWLEDGEMENTS

I would like to thank my editor, Connie Anderson, *Words and Deeds, Inc.* for the hours she spent reading and rereading—and for her excellent questions and help. She was invaluable in this process. Thanks also to my publisher *FuzionPress* and Ann Aubitz, whose help with this novel made it all possible.

I appreciate my teachers, my teaching colleagues, and my students from Michigan, Wisconsin, and Minnesota who helped shape me as a teacher. However, it is without question that my greatest influences have come from my family, especially my amazing wife, LaVonne. Without her support, I would not be at this point today. I would also like to give a special shout out to my children, John and Christina, their spouses My and Bobby, and grandchildren, Bella, Noah, Elijah, and Clara, who inspire me daily.

I would like to acknowledge my parents, Jack and Teresa Bertucci, who worked so hard to raise a family of fifteen children and who were positive role models to follow. They believed that everyone should be treated kindly and with respect, and they instilled these values in their children. Thank you to all of my brothers and sisters, and to Grandpa and Grandma Valela, bright lights in my life.

Finally, thanks to Emil and Recarda Carlson, my father-in-law and mother-in-law, who supported me and my writing when it was so important.

CHAPTER 1: THE UPPER PENINSULA OF MICHIGAN

What type of people live in the Upper Peninsula—and why would a person want to live there? It's a place where winter can start in September or October and end in May or June. If you have ever witnessed a lake-effect snowstorm, you could tell some interesting stories to make the listener glad he never did! Yes, it's a place where one can get eaten alive by mosquitoes on a summer day, get lost in the woods in one's backyard, get chased by a bear or meet up with a wolf or mountain lion living next door, or maybe even get swallowed by a wave on the great Gitchee Gumee, Lake Superior.

Residents, called Yoopers, can have whatever level of privacy and life in the wilderness they wish, and no one comments. Living in the U.P. can be challenging and trying...but it is also wonderful if you love being around good and hard-working people or prefer to live in a run-down cabin in the wilderness.

In many places, the people of the Upper Peninsula want to keep things as they were. Many make their living off of the land and water. You will find loggers in every part of the vast area, miners, fishermen, hunters, farmers, tour guides, conservation officers, and, of course, you will find those who work the service or white-collar jobs, such as teachers, police officers, doctors, lawyers, politicians, but in more remote areas, even people providing those services are scarce. In the many small communities, the Yoopers hope to always keep it just like much of it is—primordial and untouched by humans, machines, and technology—anything that represents the "outside world." However, Wi-Fi has crept into the area, adding much joy to the outreach of the younger residents.

You cannot mistake real Yoopers because they have their own dialect—and way of thinking about friends—and outsiders. They sound part Canadian, Native American, Scandinavian, and some sound backwoods, although you do not want to make that a general classification.

The Upper Peninsula of Michigan is quite grand and spectacular to those who live there. It is almost completely bordered by three of the Great Lakes: Superior, Michigan, and Huron. Because of its location, when speaking about Michigan, it can sometimes be overlooked and forgotten by people, especially those in the Lower Peninsula known as the Fudgies or Trolls. Even the national news once referred to the Mackinac Bridge, separating Upper and Lower Michigan, as the International Bridge, thus giving the U.P the astute honor of being part of Canada. In fact, many Yoopers love the Canadians.

Yet, looking at the area, the U.P is East-to-West over 320 miles long and North-to-South about 125 miles. One is surprised by the sheer size, from Detour to Ironwood from Marquette to Menominee, it covers 16,377 square miles of tree-covered forests, lakes, wetlands, and small communities, and that's more land than nine U.S. states.

The population is just over 310,000 residents, and the largest city is Marquette, located on Lake Superior and almost in the middle on the northern edge of the U.P., with just over 21,000 inhabitants. It is home to Northern Michigan University (NMU) also on the shores of Lake Superior where NMU has constructed a dome—The Superior Dome—made completely of wood. All spread from east to west, this area also hosts Michigan Technological University in Houghton and Lake Superior State University in Sault Ste. Marie, Finlandia near Hancock, and five community colleges. For a place with fewer than twenty people per square mile, that's a lot of access to learning, but access doesn't always translate to being able to get an education.

With all the vast areas of plain wilderness, most of the people who live there like to take advantage of nature. Many Yoopers do leave for jobs or a taste of something different, but they *are and will always be* Yoopers. Many of them usually own hunting gear and an ATV to get where they need to be to enjoy the outdoors and take advantage of the many hunting, fishing, and hiking opportunities that exist. For natives, this includes the four seasons. Since many areas have dirt or no roads, it makes it interesting from season to season. You can't get to many places without a four-wheeler in the summer or a snowmobile in the winter. In some areas getting a signal for a phone is almost impossible. Some places are better suited for cell phones since Northern Michigan University has been working on improving Wi-Fi for many areas. Other areas have similar projects, yet progress is slow there.

Many of the people in much of the U.P. do not have six-figure incomes. Many don't have incomes that would place them above the poverty line, but this doesn't bother some of them because they are happy with what they have. Their houses are not the mega-sized homes that you might see in a typical suburban neighborhood today, but they are pleasant and comfortable.

So, these insights into the residents of the U.P. are why something like this could easily happen in the Upper Peninsula, especially in a remote area where law enforcement—or even "common law"—is not very present.

Welcome to Colewin, 2019

Colewin is a community located somewhere between Lake Superior and Lake Michigan, nestled among woodlands of pines and maples deep in the center of one of the U.P.'s great forests. Anyone planning on visiting Colewin had better plan to go off the beaten path because very few paved roads lead to this remote area. Well, there are some roads like M-28 and US-2 to get people east and west, and in some spots, they can get north or south on paved roads, but after that, most are on their own.

Colewin in the U.P., Saturday, June 1, 2019, early afternoon

Every town has a mayor, and Colewin's mayor is Don Palin. A nice guy, he knows everyone in Colewin as well as anyone in a 10-mile radius of Colewin. He's well-liked and friendly, and no one calls him mayor. They call him Don.

"Hey, how you doin', Don?" Bud asked. Bud was a tough character who made his living in the woods cutting trees and hauling logs.

"Not bad. Had a small bout of the hard-liquor flu."

"Out too long, huh," Bud laughed.

"Man, I'm not getting any younger."

"You been hanging around the Sportsman's too much. But hey, why not? Good cold beer and the best pizza in town. Well, the only pizza, but who's counting?"

"Hey, Bud, have you seen that new guy up on the ridge near the old hunting shack? Haven't seen anyone in that area for a long time, 'cept for some of the women blueberry picking. I think he set up camp in the old shack."

"Yeah, I heard something about him, but don't know much. He must keep to himself. I did hear that Tommy's Uncle George got into a bit of a scuffle with him, but that's all I know."

"How's the family?"

"Good. Aside from the skeeters that keep ransacking the place, we're all doing fine."

"Hell, yeah, nothing like the mosquitoes this summer."

From the gas station across the street, a tough-looking guy with a crooked nose and a jaunty style yelled, "What you two jibber-jabberin' about anyway?"

"Hello, Gunnar!"

"The new guy on the ridge," said Don.

"Oh, yeah, met him the other day. He's a decent type. Ex-marine. Got some crazy huntin' sticks. Who needs those things anyway? AK-47, M-16, AR-15 and a bunch of other smaller stuff. He has all kinds of old Marine equipment. Not sure where he got all of it, but he's a decent guy. Think he might be a Troll... at least he's not from around here. Someone said he might be a Yooper from the west end. He doesn't say much 'cept to talk about his arsenal."

"Hey, see you around. Got to get to the bar." Bud waved and turned to go.

"You get your 200 sticks already?" Gunnar asked. In U.P. terms that's the eight-foot-long logs that loggers cut to load on logging trucks. He knew that to make ends meet, Bud had to cut around 200 logs a day, each just over eight feet.

"Naw, bad day. Too many damn mosquitoes, and I cut my hand a bit. Had to stitch it right there. Going to get something to ease the pain," Bud added.

"How the hell d'ya stitch it out there?" asked Don who was concerned. "You must be working alone again. You gotta stop that. You're getting too old. What about your boy? What's he up to?"

"Can't get him to go with me. He's too stuck on that woman of his who wants him to stay close to the house. How the hell is he going to get a job doing that? Have a good one you two, less you wanna come an' spend some time with me curing my hand."

Gunnar was quick to respond, "Sounds good to me. What about you, Don?"

"Sure, why not?"

So, passing time in this small town of Colewin isn't always exciting, but it isn't as bad as some might think. As noted, the pizza is good and the beer is cold, and there are all kinds of conversations to keep one happy. Some people might not like these guys, but they are very good people: family men, hard-working, honest, tough, and opinionated. If they were neighbors, they would be instant friends because they would do anything for a neighbor, and, on top of all this, they are sneaky smart.

Earlier that morning, 10 a.m.

As Wyatt lay out his trap and suet, he stopped suddenly and looked through the trees. It was a hot summer day in the woods, and the mosquitoes were surrounding him, but thanks to his mesh mask, he could still see that someone was heading his way. Wyatt was very wary from too many military tours in Afghanistan. He'd been shot at by someone quietly sneaking up on him more times than he cared to think about. This person obviously was not sneaking up, but he—no they—were being awful cautious. What were they doing on his land? He'd have to check if he miscalculated, but anyway, there they were. He raised his AR-15 and looked through a powerful TAC Vector Optics Tactical scope which he used as both a hunting and target practice piece.

Far from town, in very thick green woods

The two men walked slowly and cautiously, carrying something. "Be careful, Tommy. We don't wanna scare off any critters that might be heading to the bait pile. We'll just throw this bait down and get the heck out." George grumbled as he moved ahead, moaning quietly, "My back is killing me."

George was a quiet, hard-working man whom everyone liked and who had carved out a living in the area by giving guided tours to individuals, usually Trolls, who wanted to come up to the U.P. and hunt for bears. Black bears are very common in the area and could be lured into the open with a good stock of suet and other goodies that he could find—some of it from his own hunting. George was a nice fellow who could charm the people he guided through the woods that he knew so well, having been raised in Colewin and never having left. Ever.

"OK. Let's get this done and get outta these skeeters."

This was his life, and George was getting to the age that he figured it was time to pass on his skills to his young nephew, Tommy, especially now that he was about to graduate. George had helped raise Tommy from a little guy, but not so little anymore, Tommy had grown to be 6'2", 210 pounds. He was strong, fast, and agile. Perfect for the life he revered. His life in the woods had kept him strong and healthy, and he had no desire to leave Colewin either. He adored George and wanted to learn everything he could.

Decked out in their best camo, they quietly floated through the thick foliage as fast as they could. Once in their spot, they would deposit the suet and meat in neat piles around the area in a way that they knew would attract the biggest black bears they could find. Now most people would have never seen or heard them, they were so expert in getting in and out of an area like this. Except, on this day…

"OK, Uncle G.," Tommy said quietly. "But why don't we just go in from the other side where you have your blind? It's easier and open."

"I would, but this is quicker, and I'm in a hurry. I want to get to the other blinds and get home 'cause I got a lot to do on the new cabin."

Suddenly from nowhere came a voice that startled them.

"Hey, what the f##k you doing there?" Wyatt yelled.

Startled, George and Tommy stopped in their tracks. "Whoa, who said that? What's the problem?"

"You two!" Wyatt hollered.

"Where the hell are you? I can't see you through this thick brush."

"Doesn't matter! Get the hell off my land."

"Your land? This isn't your land. I been workin' these here woods for years. Never have seen anyone here before."

"Yeah, well you have now. So, get the f##k out of this place before I shoot. These hollow points would put a nice hole in your chest."

"Hold on now. You got a gun there?"

"AR-15, if you want to know."

"We don't mean no harm. Just doin' our job. Ah, that's got to be you—the guy who lives on the ridge. New guy, right? Troll. You don't talk like a local. I still can't see you, but why don't you put down that weapon and step out to talk this over."

"Talk what over?" snorted Wyatt.

"This land here. You know!" George was getting mad now. He heard it in his voice. He knew the man wasn't going to talk, and the guy didn't like him from the start.

At that Wyatt thought just one thing. Shoot and ask questions later. Wyatt quietly said, "Here you go. I could nail you both right now and nobody would know out here." But he didn't. He only yelled again, breaking the lonely silence of the trees, "Get the F##K out now!"

CHAPTER 2: THE TEACHER

Two miles away, 2:30 p.m.

School had just ended the past Friday, and except for graduation, Joe was almost finished wrapping up this school year. He had decided to work on a new class for next year since everything was fresh in his mind, and because his wife was out of town for the day. He was finishing up his work on the lesson plans that he'd made for the new course. He was planning on making a course in which students read every day, then wrote about what they read. He wasn't sure it was going to be accepted by the principal and school board, but he had a great idea he wanted to try, so he was going ahead with it until he got the OK.

He looked up and saw it was already past noon. He'd been at it a while. Working in a rural community like Colewin with about 600 people was not his ideal, but he loved the kids and he loved being in nature. He built a small log cabin not far from Colewin, about midway between Colewin and Poplar. Poplar was much smaller, about 350 souls, but it was a great place to fish and hunt when he could.

Joe was a Yooper, and he was once part of an elite civilian group that worked on clandestine operations for the military—but that was a long time ago. His best friend, Ron, was always with him in these operations. He was not a Yooper; he was from Norfolk, Virginia. Now they were just ordinary citizens, but because they had once operated in these circles, it made life difficult. Yes, they had created a lot of enemies along the way. They had spent too much time working against the wrong people, but they were always intent on making a difference. Now, they both just wanted to disappear into regular lives.

"Darn! It's already late," Joe exclaimed. "Maybe I can still get out there and have a little fun. Guess I'll try some fly fishing at the bend in the river." Joe didn't often talk to himself, but this day he felt the need. He had been quiet too many hours. He usually liked to fish early, but today he had to complete his work.

He left the house, grabbed his gear and jumped on his four-wheeler and roared off. He drove for about thirty minutes on rough trails and through some wetlands, up and down, swerving around trees and spitting mud everywhere. It was quiet. The sound of the ATV was the only thing he could hear, until BOOM! Joe was stunned and swerved uncontrollably and almost hit a tree. "Holy, Mother of God! That was loud. What the hell? What was that anyway? Was that a bomb?" He was frozen in place.

His first instinct had been to dive on the ground, but that wouldn't have been too smart. Then shortly after he recovered from his daze and got his breath back, the boom was followed by a thump and another BOOM! Joe almost lost control of his ATV again; it startled him so much, but he recovered quickly and stopped on a dime. He thought it came from the river. "What the heck!" he yelled. He slowly crawled forward, afraid to head into whatever that just was. He thought he should investigate a bit—until he heard more loud noise. This time it was a volley of rifle shots, but that was it. It stopped suddenly. He stopped and listened. Nothing. Again, he yelled, "Who is shooting at this time of day and out of season?" His first thought was to do some investigating and skip the fishing trip.

After an hour, Joe had found nothing, and he decided to go back home. He thought *that must have been that new guy again. That's the second time he scared the hell out of me, ummm, or maybe the militia is at it again; it's been a while. Somebody's got to do something about this. These are sounds that should only be heard in war zones!*

Deep in the woods near a river, earlier that afternoon, 2:00 p.m.

"Stand at attention and then we can begin. We might as well do this right. If we're going to be an elite outfit, we need discipline."

"Aw, for cripe sakes, Charlie," whined Sam.

"Shut up, and just do what I say."

"OK, OK, I's just sayin'."

"The rest o' ya stand at attention."

This is the Eastern U.P. Militia. Twenty strong right now. Thirteen men and seven women. All in camo gear and toting some form of an assault rifle. You would think this is just fun and games—but it is not.

"Let's do as Charlie says," barked Betty, a petite blond of 33 who has lived in the U.P. her entire life. She is a tough cookie, as they say. She has worked her whole life, mostly farming. Shake hands with her once and you'll get the idea. Like sandpaper! Don't cross her.

"If we're gonna be successful, we got to stick together and get organized. We know they will be," added Lane. Lane is Betty's close friend, and they share the same philosophy.

"The politicians keep taking our freedoms," Betty snarled and then she spit a big gob on the ground.

"Right on," yelled the rest of the troops standing at attention as they formed a line.

Zooooom, crack, and a loud whining sound. Charlie quickly realized it was an ATV traveling extremely fast. "Hit the ground!" he screamed. "Prepare for engagement!"

Charlie ordered his troops again. "Be sharp!" Soon bodies were dropping everywhere, looking for cover as they pointed their weapons in the direction of the sound.

Out of nowhere a dirty old black-and-green ATV stormed into their camp. Pulling up to a sudden stop and sending dirt and sticks in all directions, Wyatt stood up on his machine and yelled: "What you all doing? Looks like you're ready to kill someone. Hey ya, you troops! Can I join in?" Then he pulled out a canteen and took a long swig. "Who the hell's the boss anyway?"

Charlie stood quickly while keeping his M-16 pointed right at Wyatt's head. "Who's askin'?"

"Wyatt A. That's all you have to know."

"Yeah, well, maybe we do and maybe we don't. We heard about you up on the ridge. How'd you get that place anyway—it's been empty for a long time."

"Who cares about that? Can I join up with you? I think we might have similar ideas about this country. That's really why I'm here. Tired of all the BS going on in this country, and I need a break, plus I like to be where people don't much care if I carry a gun, and what I do on my own time."

"And who says we're tired of the BS?"

"Just heard," snorted Wyatt.

"Well, that part is right, but we really don't have nary an idea who you are, 'cept you bought the old place on the ridge."

"Let me tell you then." Wyatt didn't say much, but he did let them know his experience in the Marines, his life the past few months, and how much he could help them. He told them about his plan to become a bear hunting guide, deep in the woods, so he could get away from it all. "I'm tired of taking orders from bozos. So, what do you say? I've got a lot of experience and loads of weapons. Ever have any bazookas and mortars?"

"No, we don't. But we also don't know who yer working fer," snarled Jim. Jim was antagonistic, contrary, and cynical by day, and with that same attitude, he worked for a pipeline during the evenings. He watched dials most hours, and he read the rest of the time—mostly militia stuff.

"I get it," answered Wyatt. "I guess, you'll just have to take me at my word. Anything I could do to convince you?"

"Not really," chimed in Charlie. "Anybody that has them types of weapons, we're a little suspicious of."

"Yeah, well what if I show you how to get those and a lot more." Wyatt looked at the startled men and women around him. He had a number of interesting pieces of equipment. From a huge bag on the back of his ATV, he pulled out a small plastic bazooka rocket launcher.

"Where did you get that thing? And why did you bring the damn things here? You ain't supposed to have those. And why you driving crazy with those explosives? You dumb shit," Charlie said.

"Yeah, well you asked for proof, and to show you I mean business, here you are. Would I show you these if I wasn't serious?" Wyatt unloaded a small M72 LAW rocket launcher and an M224 60mm mortar which he had secured with bungie cords to the back of his vehicle. It was a risky move, driving the way he did. Everyone hit the dirt once again when he launched the rocket. BOOM! The troops could see from the top of the hill that he had just blown a large maple out of the ground, leaving a crater about the size of a large pit about a quarter mile away. Then he proceeded to set up the small mortar and lob one right into the same hole. Thump and BOOM! The shock waves rang in their ears, and they all looked rather shaken.

"Hey, they gonna hear that in town if you ain't careful. We'll have the mayor out here asking questions again. Take it easy."

Late afternoon, 3:30 p.m.

Joe drove back home thinking about what he had heard. Those loud booms had to be heard in town just a little over two miles away. That first boom sounded like a rocket. Couldn't have been. He knew from his military experience that one of the sounds was a mortar.

"Who the hell needs mortars or rockets anywhere in a civilized country? Well, it's civilized here, isn't it? I need to talk to someone."

When Joe arrived home, he parked his ATV in the lean-to shed and then went inside.

"Hello, you home?" he yelled.

"In here."

He heard his wife's voice in the kitchen. "So, you're back. How did it go?" Joette was very smart and was also an excellent reading teacher. She was also a tough one since having to live with Joe—who had often been absorbed in his old job involving some serious drama and much time away, which meant she learned a lot of skills regular people often didn't. She was an excellent shot and was adept with a compound bow. She often hunted with Joe, as well as on her own when he wasn't around, often bagging big trophy bucks. She was also a top-level pianist and a ravenous reader—so much so that she would probably have been great on the "Jeopardy" TV game show that she watched religiously.

"Not bad, we were able to find a good washing machine for Cathy." Cathy was a friend of Joe's wife, a constant companion who also taught fifth grade at the school. "No dryer though. She thinks they can do with the old one for a while."

"Well, good. I'm glad you had some luck. How was Petoskey?"

"OK, but we had to go to Traverse City. I like going there, but I sure liked getting home. How was your day?"

"I finished a lot of the course I'd been working on for next year, and then I tried to go fishing for a while, but ran into something strange." Joe waltzed into the kitchen and gave his wife a peck on the cheek. They'd been married for forty-five years, and had moved to Colewin several years ago to slow life down a bit. They were both past retirement age, but they loved what they were doing, so it really wasn't work. Since both worked in the same small school district, they enjoyed their jobs and took them very seriously, which meant they were involved in everything.

"What kind of strange things, Hon? Weird fish, funny bait…"

"It really isn't funny. It was a very loud noise, like I used to hear when I was in the military. Did you hear anything?"

"Not sure, I've been here for only forty-five minutes, and I've had the music on all the while."

"Anyway, it sounded like rockets and mortars."

"Rockets and mortars! What are you talking about? Do people hunt with those? Besides, you own three guns yourself."

"Yes, my antique 8mm Mauser and my Winchester .30-30 make a lot of noise, but nothing like that."

"Well, then what was it?"

"I'm not really sure, but I am going to find out."

Heading into early evening on the same day, 5:30 p.m.
George and Tommy sat quietly in George's home, which was a rather large trailer with all the amenities of life. George certainly didn't have any famous artworks, flowing drapery, or fancy knick-knacks here and there, but his home was pure comfort.

"Man, I was scared today out there, Unk." Tommy always called his Uncle George "Unk" since he was a little child.

"You know, I guess I kinda was too. That's one scary, crabby Troll. Not sure how he got here or why he's here, but he's tryin' to take our business and mess around with it. Seems like he's trying to move in on us." George leaned back in his recliner and took a long slug from his beer, chugging it quickly. He scratched his scruffy face and burped a long, hard one. "Son of a bitch."

"Yeah, that land's been ours forever. How can he just jump in there and take over?"

"It really don't belong to nobody. We always worked it 'cause it was thar and no one ever cared none for it."

"I know," choked Tommy as he coughed drinking his root beer. "But he really scared me because I know he has all kinds of guns and stuff, and he said he had an AR-15 with hollow points aimed at us!"

"Sure enough. I don' think he would use it though. He ain't stupid. We all know the law around here, what little there is, and if he gets ornery, we can just go to Daryl and tell him to let the man know he ain't wanted around here. That should take care of it."

"I don't know. He seems a little crazy."

"Well, from now on, we'll take our guns on every trip out to the bait piles or when guiding da Trolls on a hunt. He's not the only one with a gun."

"I think that's a great idea, but I really don't want any part of that. I just want to learn to do what you do so well, so I can make a living someday like you do. I graduate this coming Friday, and I'll need a job. Mr. Joe keeps telling me to go to the community college in Escanaba, but that's not for me."

"Yeah, don't worry. You will. This will all pass, but we are going to be prepared. Besides, I think the man is a lot of bull. He talks like he's got an army with him."

Evening that day, 6:00 p.m.
At the bar, it was very busy and talk was loud. Saturday afternoons can get kind of rowdy at the Sportsman's Pizzeria and Bar. Several men and a few women sat around at tables talking about life and

having a few laughs. A slow country song played in the background. The bar had the same patrons that it had most days at this time. It was a way to pass the time and forget one's troubles or just to sit and visit with friends. Don, Bud, and Gunnar were sitting in the corner quietly shooting the bull over the music and noise.

Don asked, "Bud, so things are tough, right? How you doing with everything?"

"Not too bad. Wished I could get some help, but I can't afford to pay anyone right now. Getting a load is getting harder and harder each day. I need to do something. Pay isn't what it should be, and I'm getting older. A man can hardly make a living these days. Now I don't need much, but I need something a little better."

"Yeah, been a few tough years. Never did recover here after the turndown. A lot of people are doing better, but it doesn't always reach us. Damn shame."

"For sure," Bud agreed. "Think of all those big wigs getting all that money for doing little-to-nothing but sitting in meetings all day. I been working my tail off for years and am still paying off my equipment. I saw in the paper that some guy got a three-million-dollar bonus for sitting on his ass. I mean that was *a bonus*. Wonder what he gets in a year?"

"I read that CEO's pay in some of the big companies came to about nineteen million bucks. Some of them have salaries more'n that. How is any man worth so much when we have people here making twelve thousand dollars a year, and trying to live on that?"

Bud yelled, "That pisses me off! I often wonder why we all put up with it. I guess that's why those fellers and some women joined that militia thing. They think they can change somethin'—but it's never going to happen."

"Whoa, Bud, take it easy," Don said.

Gunnar had been quietly sitting listening to them. You could tell he was upset too. His face was red, and he was the picture of angry. Finally, he spoke, "You both talk the truth. My farm is about to go under, and I have no way to save it. We have worked our butts off trying to make it, but we just keep getting farther and farther behind. If we had a big farm, we could probably get government help, but that's just for the rich. They get money not to farm for Chris' sake—*money not to farm.* And how about the rich oil people who get money for nothing, just because it's oil. They get handouts, but they complain about people who need a little hand-up once in a while. They don't care! I heard that a lot of the politicians are millionaires. What do they know about us poor folks trying to get by on a buck and a quarter?"

"Son of a bitch. You're right, Gunnar," Bud spit as his words flew out, he was so upset.

"You know, I think Charlie and that bunch might have something. I'd join but I can't afford to spend time playing war games. No one's going to give me a bonus or help me in the woods. They gettin' purdy serious, I guess."

"You guys want another round?" asked Todd, the owner of the Sportsman's. He was a friend and neighbor too. He hung by as they reacted to his offer.

"Naw, I gotta get goin'. It's getting late," Gunnar said.

"Me too," agreed Bud.

As Don stood up, he said, "You boys take it easy now." Then he whispered, "Let's get together and see if we can do something to help out here. After all, we've known each other for years, and we're neighbors who take care of each other."

"Thanks, man," said Gunnar, "but I'm guessin' we're too far along for that."

"Yeah, who knows what the hell we can do?" said Bud.

Todd said, "You have a good day. If there is anything I can do, let me know. I agree with Don that we can help with whatever it is."

"Thanks," came quickly from both men as they left.

Earlier, around 5:45 p.m.

Joe left home and drove into town looking for Daryl, the local law enforcement. It was always tough to find him. He worked out of St. Ignace, and so could be fifty miles away. He headed for the town hall hoping to find the mayor and get the lowdown on what was going on. Don would know where Daryl was. He pulled up and saw that the town hall was dark. His next instinct was the Sportsman's where Don did a lot of his business. Don was an insurance agent, and found that on most days, the Sportsman's was not loud and crowded, and so he could work there and meet with people who needed his help. Just as Joe was heading to the bar, out walked Don with Gunnar and Bud, each going his own way. As Don walked to his car, Joe intercepted him.

"Hey, Don," yelled Joe.

"Howdy, Joe, how's it going?"

It's interesting that when you move to a small town, you get accepted right away, but you never quite fit in with all the locals. Most people are very accepting and welcoming, but a few harbor nasty thoughts that they sometimes let you hear. They know you moved there, and they have suspicions that you will not stay and that you are not who they are; yet, they are very polite and accepting if you act like you belong. So, Don was kind and always offered to let Joe in.

"OK. I just have a question for you. Did you hear the booms today out northeast of here?"

"Booms?" asked Don.

"Yes, about a couple of hours ago."

"Man, I was in the bar most of the afternoon. Didn't hear a thing."

"Well, there was one really loud boom like a bomb or rocket, followed by a thump like a mortar—sounds I have not heard since 'Nam."

"Could have been Charlie and his gang out there in that clearing up on the hill past Poplar. Is that where you heard it?"

"Yes, I think so, but I've often heard small rifle fire, but I never hear anything like that. Who knows what it might have been or if anyone is hurt! Shouldn't we have Daryl check it out?"

"Well now, Joe, don't get so excited about these sorta things. You know this is God's country, and people do just about what they want. Might be someone goofing around with some dynamite out there."

Joe felt like he probably wasn't going to get anywhere with Don. He had learned with his time here that some people did not want to get involved with other people's business when it came to activities like this. Yet, he felt he had to do something.

"Do you think we could, at least, have Daryl check it out?" asked Joe.

"Sure, sure, first thing in the morning. Ah, no, tomorrow is Sunday, so he'll be at church. Maybe Monday morning."

"Whatever, as long as he checks it out. That noise scared the heck out of me, but I couldn't find anything. Although, who knows for sure if I was in the right place. There are a lot of woods and land out there, and I didn't get as far as the clearing where those militia practice. Those guys worry me. They all run around with assault rifles and expend a lot of rounds. For what reason, I'm not sure."

"Oh, they're all right. They want to change things—and they feel like they have to be ready when the change comes," said Don.

"That kind of change we can do without. If you want change, do it peacefully."

"Yeah, well *that don't work most times*," said Don forcefully.

"I guess that's a matter of opinion, but I do know what you mean," answered Joe. But Joe was thinking just the opposite. He felt like these guys were wrong, and a lot of them were just bullies who never quite grew out of their early adolescent habits—using force and pushing around those who don't agree. "Let me know what you find out on Monday. Guess I'll head back home."

"Right, see you later." Don was pissed. He hated these people, especially some teachers who move in and think they have all the answers—and on top of that, get paid well and get the whole summer off! Who the hell gets to take time off and still get paid? What a little prick, probably never worked a day of hard labor in his life. All book learning. I suppose I better call Daryl or I'll never hear the end of it. Don checked his cell phone and once again noticed no service. "I don't know why I have this damn thing!" he exclaimed. He decided instead to go back to his office and make the call.

"I wonder if I'll even get him at this time of day." Don called the number, and it was picked up on the first ring. "Hey, Daryl, how you doing? Good, yeah, you hear anything about loud noises in the area? No? Well, that teacher, Joe, said that he heard some loud booms out there past Poplar. Maybe in the clearing. Wonder if it was the militia out again. They do some crazy things out there. Can you check on it? No, not today. When you get a chance. Probably nothin' anyway. Could be some kids fishing with dynamite again. We gotta stop that, or someday they're gonna get hurt. Remember when that kid blew his fingers off a few years ago? Yeah, so good, you'll check it out. Yeah, talk to you then. OK. See ya."

Saturday, 6:15 p.m.

Daryl hung up the phone and said out loud, "Damn! That stupid shithead shot that rocket and never thought of what it might cause." He was a little nervous because he had been there. He thought for a minute, and then realized he'd have to go out to the spot where it happened just so he could tell Don that it was some guys playing around with some big toys. What the hell. That Wyatt is going to mess everything up. We're getting close to being ready to join the boys from Escanaba and downstate to do something big. Something like the Oklahoma bombing in 1995, but this time we'll make sure there is very little collateral damage. That event set us back and hurt our image. Most of the guys dropped out back then, but we finally have the numbers up again. We need to keep everyone. We could join with other groups who think like us—and make it even a bigger event. Daryl thought he should call Charlie right away because he should handle this.

"Hello, this Charlie?"

"Yup, who's this?"

"Hey, Daryl here. You know what happened today with that new guy. Well, Don is checking around and wondering what happened. I guess that school teacher was at it again snoopin' around our territory. No idea what he saw or found, but we need to fix that."

Charlie sighed, "For sure, but we can't just take 'em out."

"Don't need to take him out. Just got to get rid of the teacher somehow."

"What's that mean, Daryl?"

"He just needs to find out that it would be to his advantage to move out of the area, know what I mean? Like we did with that other teacher that kept askin' questions several years ago."

"That worked once, not sure it'll work with this guy. He's older and ex-Army. Been to 'Nam. Kind o' set in his ways, and the story goes that he worked undercover for the military or something like that."

Daryl understood. "I know all that, but yeah, that might be different—but it makes him a real threat."

"Maybe we don't got to do nothin'. We could just lay low for a while."

"Not with that nut Wyatt around."

Tuesday, June 4, 2019

George and Tommy had worked together to fill the truck with suet they had gathered from the meat market in Colewin. They had also traveled around to get fresh leftovers from a few other friends and neighbors who did a lot of hunting and fishing on the side, and from their buddy Nick who set traps for a living. He had good stuff and usually plenty of it for them to build their bait piles. The fishermen on Lake Michigan usually had a bucket or two from their days cleaning the fish. George and Tommy had been at it all day, and now it was time to get out and fill their blinds with all the bait before dark.

After loading the last of it from Nick, they said thanks and were on their way. First stop was George's most prized spot, not far from the old city dump where people had driven their garbage to an open hole in the ground outside of town. It was a good spot, and he had several big bear trophies to show for it. Well, he didn't have trophies, but he was a part of getting several big bears for his clients.

"Let's take a ride to the old dump first," said George.

"Think we'll be lucky and get some good ones there this season, Unk?"

"Sure, this'll be a good year, and that is a great spot."

They drove for about twenty minutes on a paved road, and then cut into the woods on an old road that had been in fairly good shape before they closed the dump. They drove for about a half a mile and then turned onto a two-track road with big potholes and washed-out sections. This would get them closer to the bait pile.

"Tommy, look straight ahead. You see it, a mama and her cub. We'll sit back here a bit and not disturb 'em, else we could find ourselves in trouble if the mama bear comes after us. Get your gun ready just in case when we drop off the bait."

It was a while before they began again as the mother bear and her cub walked lazily down the road, luckily in the other direction.

"Most people probably have never seen a bear attack, and they are lucky if they haven't. It was no fun last year when we almost got caught by that one over by Poplar."

Slowly, George put his foot on the gas and crept forward. "When I stop, grab that box of suet we got from the store today. We'll put that here and hope for good luck again. But don't get out of the truck until I tell you."

"OK, Unk," said Tommy.

"We got to stay away from that new place we had been stocking 'cause the DNR is hot after people not following the rules. I don't wanna get caught again. Last year, Leonard, the DNR officer, gave me the business and told me I better be careful or he was gonna throw me in jail. Shit, that made me nervous. You know we can't bait legally until sometime in early August, so we got to be careful, but I like establishin' a place that the bears know will be there come hunting season."

"I heard that baiting isn't allowed in most places in Michigan," Tommy said.

"Right! Only in some parts of the U.P. We are lucky that we have a few months to make some good money. I always like to start about this time of year. The rest of the time I get to cut a little wood on the side. Don't make as much as I used to though."

"Whoa, Unk, there's the DNR's truck up ahead. We gotta get outta here!"

"Shit, he'll see all this stuff and know what we're doing."

George turned the truck around hoping he would not get stuck moving off the road, and this time he was lucky. He turned around and headed for the dump road. Once there, he turned right.

"We gotta head up north a bit and get away from him. We can put most of this up near the old cabin. See if we can find a good spot. Maybe make a new pile. This'll make our fourth one."

"Yeah, but Unk, we're gonna get close to that Wyatt guy."

"Better than getting caught by the DNR. I'll sure go to jail this time."

"OK, we can unload quickly."

But before they could get to where they wanted, out of nowhere a green and black four-wheeler came blasting through the brush.

There he was again. *What now?* George thought.

"Eh, you two, why are you down this road? You don't have any business here."

"Just taking a little stroll," answered George.

"Yeah, well looks like your truck is full of bait. You know it's illegal to bait this early."

"You should take your own advice."

"Don't get smart with me, you old fart," hollered Wyatt.

"Just statin' a fact, buddy," George threw at him.

"Smart ass. Always a smart ass. One day you're going to regret all that high-and-mighty talk."

"Says who?" George said with an air of indifference.

"Says me. See this?" Wyatt pointed his favorite German Nazi Luger at the truck. "This is my best Luger. I collect them. Got about five now, and this one works real fine. Hee, hee."

"Put that thing away. You wouldn't want the DNR here. They're right up the road there just waitin' fer some guy like you to do somethin' stupid."

"You calling me stupid?"

"If you shoot that gun—that *would be stupid*."

"I hate your guts. Just get out of here."

"Get out of our way and I will."

Wyatt backed his four-wheeler off the road and sat there with the Luger still aimed right at the truck.

George yelled as he pulled ahead, "See you around," and quietly whispered, "dipshit."

Wednesday, June 5, noon

Joe headed to the school in Colewin to do some work to complete the year they had just finished when he ran into Theresa, the secondary school secretary. "Theresa, how you doing? Lots of work to complete the school year, I bet."

"Always." Theresa was a very kind person who had lived in Poplar most of her life. She loved it there. She was a good confidant when you needed one—and Joe needed one right now.

"Theresa, I have a question for you."

"Shoot. I love questions."

"It's kind of personal, and I'm not sure I should even ask, but…"

"Oh, you know me. Ask anything, and I'll give you my two cents. Like it or not."

"True, and I appreciate that. Here it is. I was talking to Don today about Charlie and those militia that train on the hill out north. He listened to me, but I got the distinct impression that he wasn't really listening, and the tone of his voice was something like—well, get lost or who cares. You know what I mean?"

"Sure do. That's Don. He loves it here and thinks he owns the place, and he doesn't like people who weren't born here. You know the type. There are a few others like him, but most of the people around here are very warm to outsiders because it makes our home that much better, and we love teachers like you who make a difference."

"Well, thanks. I know I touched on a sensitive spot with Don when I mentioned the militia. I'm not sure how he feels about it, but I know most of the people who are in it are his friends."

"Oh, yes, I'm not certain that he's in the group, but I get a sense that he wouldn't stand in their way either."

"Good to know because I asked him to call Daryl and have him check out that loud boom today."

"Yes, what was that? Some of the people at the restaurant said it was kids fishing with dynamite again, which they've done for years. Where do they get that stuff anyway?"

"I sure don't know. I hope that's all it is. Don said Daryl would check on Monday, but he hasn't gotten out there yet according to Don when I called today, and it seems like whatever went on will be covered up by now, so I'm going to check it out today."

"You be careful there, Joe. Don't get yourself into any trouble. A lot of crazies are out there with guns and stuff."

"Will do. Thanks for the talk. I've got to get my grades and paperwork wrapped up before I can leave here to check it out, but hopefully it won't take too long. Also, I've been working on that course I told you about for next year. Hope it gets the OK. See you at graduation Friday. I still cannot figure out why they have graduation a week after school is out."

"See you there, and good luck with it all."

Joe went straight to his room and finished the work he had left last week. He felt a little better talking to Theresa, but he wasn't so secure in what he thought he had heard. Maybe that is all it was—a bunch of kids doing crazy things. When he finished at two p.m., he quickly headed out the door to the old truck he had borrowed from Cathy's husband, Wayne. It was black and very rusty and beaten up, and the back window was knocked out when he and Wayne were loading wood, and Joe threw one too hard and smashed the window. Wayne said he owed him a case of beer for that one. "Oops. I think I still owe him that," said Joe, and he jumped in the truck and started it up and vroom, off he went. He made a quick stop at the post office before he went directly out north to the hill where he thought he might check today since he didn't check it out last weekend.

As Joe pulled away in the black truck, a new dark camouflage four-wheeler came around from behind the post office and made a beeline to follow Joe as he was heading north out of town.

CHAPTER 3: THE PROBLEM

Wednesday, June 5, 12:15 p.m.

Don, Charlie, and Daryl were huddled in a quiet spot in the woods just outside of Colewin. They decided to get together to discuss what had happened, and Charlie filled Don in about Wyatt and his entrance into the camp.

"The dang guy just came tearing into the camp out of the bush and scared the hell out of everyone—and he had explosives on his machine! He's lucky that he ain't dead. Now we have sentries at both roads into the camp, so we shoulda had 'em before, too."

"OK, is it safe to have that guy with us?" asked Daryl.

Don added, "Pretty much I think you guys are all nuts, but he's the nuttiest from what I've heard. I talked to George about him—and he's constantly harassing George."

"Well," Daryl said, "George doesn't have much respect for the law, you know."

Don thought Daryl was a bit hard on George. "Oh, he's harmless, just trying to make a living. It's tough out there these days, and you got to do what you can to earn a buck."

"True, but he could do it legally."

Charlie gasped, "Legally, since when does that matter? If we did things legally, then we'd all have to go home and kiss our wives and become some kind of couch potato who gives in to the rich SOBs and those damn politicians who make all da crappy laws we follow."

Don finally interjected, "Why didn't you tell me about Wyatt sooner?"

Charlie spoke here, "Well, we had ta think about how you would behave to what we were going to tell you. Ya sometimes get a little ornery about these things."

"What do you expect? We got a town to run. It's small, but it's our home, and we have to protect it."

"If you're going to protect this town, you got another problem then, and you got to fix that."

"What problem is that?"

Charlie let him have it. "You got a man snoopin' around our area out there, and he could make a lot o' trouble. We're hidden purty good, but he's gettin' on to us."

"Who the hell you talking about?"

At this, both Charlie and Daryl blurted out, "That damn teacher!"

"A teacher. You guys are afraid of some teacher. Holy catfish, shit. Are you turning into a couple of wimps?"

"No," yelled Daryl. "We're just trying to figure out what to do with him if he gets too nosey and butts into our place. It could mean real trouble."

"You got enough trouble with that Wyatt guy. Take care of that first."

Charlie sighed, "We can take care of him. He has a little wild side, but I think we can tame him a bit and get him in on the plan, so he's no concern right now. But if that teacher Joe finds out what we're really doing out there, it'll be trouble for us. Escanaba isn't gonna like it."

Daryl spoke up, "I got a man following that teacher right now, and if my deputy doesn't learn anything, then we don't have to do anything, but that teacher's trouble. He's the kind that's filling our kids with all kinds of nonsense."

Don interrupted, "Nonsense? What do you mean? I really don't like him either, but he's a decent person from what I can see. I just don't like that he isn't from here, and I think he thinks he is better 'n us. But the kids really like him—and there's your problem."

Daryl cringed. "So the kids like him, why, and who cares about the kids? They're all nuts these days. See that girl with the green and blue hair, and what about those kids that wanted to walk out last year? What the hell. Our tax dollars pay for them to screw around these days. Next thing you know, they'll be complaining about the police like the rest of the country, and some schools even calling for their courses to include stuff like gay rights. Gay rights…we need rights for everyone. This gay stuff is crazy. Our country is going to hell. Everybody wants this and that—welfare for some, billions of dollars for the rich. Christ, we don't stand a chance."

Charlie was not happy. "Watch who you're talkin' about. My brother's son is gay, and I have known him for years. My nephew's a nice fella and wouldn't hurt anyone. I don't agree with his life choice, but we all have to live with the hand we were dealt."

Don kind of chuckled, "Daryl, do you even know what you want and what you're talking about? Stop the bitchin' and watch how you're runnin' your mouth. Yeah, a lot of points you make I agree with, but you need to back off a bit. Let's get back to your problem with the teacher, Joe."

Charlie vented, "Yeah, Daryl, but I do agree with some of that other stuff. You have to agree that paying people millions of dollars for their work is wrong, when we make just enough to keep going. What the hell. How can you ignore that?"

"You're right, Bud and Gunnar were saying the same thing the other day. What can we do? They have all the cards in the deck, and we don't have any. We need to keep busy working each day to make it. Damn shame when most of the people runnin' the country are millionaires who don't understand the little guy."

Sheriff Daryl agreed, "That's it. They don't understand."

Don decided to change the subject, so he said, "Let's get back to why we are here."

"Eh, yeah, that teacher guy," chimed in Charlie.

Daryl interrupted, "All right. We might have to get rid of him."

"What!" snorted Don.

Charlie agreed, "We might, Don."

"Holy, hallelujah! You guys are nuts."

Charlie blurted out, "We could have him fall down the hill into that deep pit now that Wyatt made it a bit bigger."

"Can't kill someone like that. Next thing you know we'd have the state police, FBI, and the governor, the whole bunch after us. Sweet Jesus! We would have to do something legal."

Daryl thought for a minute and then added, "If he does get too much information or even before he does, if he keeps snooping around, we could get him fired."

"Nice idea, how you going to do that?" asked Charlie.

"I think I got an idea. I read about this teacher downstate who got fired because they thought he was dating a girl in his class. We could set up something like that, and I think it would work 'cause we got a real conservative board of education."

Don was still doubtful. "Yeah, but a lot of people in Colewin and Poplar like the guy, especially the kids, as we said before. My niece swears by him."

Daryl was pensive. "You know, as the local law enforcement, I think we could arrange something. Let me see what my guy finds out. He's following him around all week. I got him assigned to this case about the loud noise to satisfy everyone. If that teacher snoops too much, we'll catch him, and then we'll spring a trap and get him fired."

"I don't like *any of it*," Don finally blurted.

Afternoon of the same day

Joe was headed north along a primary road out of Colewin, and then turned right onto an old dirt road that would take him to within a mile or two of the road that he was really intent on finding. He knew that the noise he heard on Saturday was not in the area he had searched previously, so he decided to head for the hill north of town. He knew that the militia was active in that area, so he thought he might find something.

"Hope this isn't a wild goose chase," he mumbled as he avoided a huge pothole in the road. He actually had to stop for a minute and back up to get around it. It looked deep and filled with water so he didn't want to take any chances. As he backed up, he noticed in the rear-view mirror what looked like a flash of light. "Was that a vehicle heading off the road? Might just be someone out for a ride, but I can't be sure," he said out loud in a rather gruff voice. "If it's militia, those sons of a guns might have me followed. I better be careful."

Down the road about a quarter of a mile, Deputy Jason slipped into a grove of trees. "Shit!" he exclaimed. "I hope he didn't see me. Damn, I got too close. I gotta be more careful."

Joe sped up as much as he could, and then he pulled off the road in an abandoned logging trail and hid the truck behind some thick cedars. The trail had enough tracks in it that he knew that if someone were following him, he would never know he turned off, so he just sat and waited.

"I'm gonna wait here a while and try to catch up," said Jason. "Wonder why Daryl is having me follow this guy anyway. Seems like a waste of time."

Five minutes later Jason fired up his four-wheeler and headed onto the road again. Joe sat quietly in the truck and waited. Joe knew if someone were following him, that person would have to wait a bit, but not too long because then whoever it was would risk losing the truck, so he was patient. Sure enough, several minutes later he saw the vehicle again. This time it was going slowly, but steadily moving up the road. Once it passed Joe, he knew that he was being followed, and he recognized Jason, whom he had seen in town a few months ago. Joe wondered…*why was he being tailed by the law?* The scary part was the deputy had a rifle in a holster attached to his four-wheeler and a handgun on his hip.

Joe knew that two roads led to the hill, but he wasn't sure how to get to the second one from here, so he decided to turn around and head back home. He'd have plenty of time to check this out tomorrow morning before most folks were up. He could leave in the dark and probably avoid anyone who might want to follow.

Jason kept driving on the dirt road leading to a two-track road, but one that was in fairly good shape compared to the one he just left—this didn't make much sense to him. He had been driving for twenty minutes and hadn't seen anything. "Did I take a wrong turn and lose him?" he muttered. "Daryl will not be happy." Worried he might enflame his boss, he kept moving forward and drove for another thirty minutes, hoping to catch sight of the truck. He didn't have any luck, but it brought him to the bottom of a hill with a steep incline and a road. He wondered if he should take a chance and move ahead. Of course, he knew he would be in trouble if he didn't find the truck and figure out what that guy was doing.

Joe was back on the main road and headed home. He was satisfied with his decision, but he was also wondering about why someone was tailing him because that is exactly what he thought it was.

Jason put his four-wheeler in gear and headed up the hill. It was steep and long, but when he reached the apex, it leveled out and he drove for a few more minutes until he came to a chain-link fence with a locked gate that was about six feet high with razor wire on top.

Jason got off his ATV and complained out loud, "Now what the hell do you think this is doing here? I wonder if the fence goes a long way into the woods," but he couldn't tell from where he was, so he decided to inspect the area on foot. There was no sign of the truck, and he wondered: what if it was inside the fence? Jason reached the gate and pulled on the lock. It was a large sturdy chain that loggers use on their load plus a massive lock, and he had no way to get it open, so he started walking along the fence looking for a way in. He was rewarded several minutes later after fighting mosquitoes and walking through tangles of branches and roots that had been exposed. He saw that the fence actually ended, so he walked around it and headed back toward the gate.

On the way home Joe kept thinking about what just happened, and he realized that he might be getting into the middle of something or nothing, but he knew he could not continue doing this by himself. He had had too many situations like this in the past when he needed someone to watch his back… or "watch his six" as they say in the military. "And I know just the person to do that," he muttered as he pulled the truck into Colewin.

Jason was almost to the gate when a sudden flutter from the brush up ahead made him stop in his tracks. "Holy shit!" he blurted. "What is that?" As he looked up, he saw a partridge flapping through the trees. Relieved, he began to move more cautiously down the fence.

Joe pulled up at home. It was late afternoon now, and he knew Joette would be making supper, so he went inside. The first thing he did was check his cell phone. No service, so he used the landline. "Yo, Wayne, how's it going, my friend? Good. Mind if I keep the old truck for another day? Sure, all right, I will drop it there tomorrow night. See you then, and thanks again."

Jason moved slowly because the brush was so heavy here, but he did make it back to the gate. Once there he could see the road was in good shape, so he slowly walked forward. He walked for some time, but he wasn't sure how long when he reached what looked like an opening. Once there, he walked to the middle of a big empty field with trees on all sides. What he could see, made him wonder. On one side were silhouettes that were riddled with bullet holes. On the other side, inside a tree line, were what looked like dummies on poles. He walked between these as he headed for the edge of the hill, and when he got there, he could see that something had happened. In the ravine below was a hole with a lot of trees and dirt spilled all over the place, like a bomb had gone off.

CHAPTER 4: FRIENDS AND ENEMIES

Late afternoon

Joe and Joette sat at the kitchen table as they enjoyed his favorite meal—homemade pizza. He had received a package of Cudighi, Italian sausage, from his brother in Ishpeming, and he and Joette liked it piled on. It was the best, with loads of cheese, pepperoni, green peppers, and mushrooms. After supper he told Joette he would take care of the dishes.

"Oh, thanks, do you mind if I play the piano while you do that? It relaxes me and I haven't been able to play for a few days."

"Go ahead, I'm going to call Ron in a bit to see if he can help me with any of this stuff that's going on." Joe knew if he were going to follow up on his plan, he needed someone capable that he could trust, and someone who thought like he did. If he were being followed, he'd need help, and he didn't want to involve anyone who did not have experience with the types of things he was thinking might be a bit complex.

"OK, say hello, will you?"

"Sure." Ron was an old army buddy who was very dependable and knew a lot about explosives and any kind of munitions, including rifles, bazookas, and artillery. He often visited Joe during the summer so they could catch up. Ron had remained in the service for over twenty years; then he became a teacher when he got out. That's when they teamed up on the clandestine operations for the military. They knew each other well and worked smoothly together, and they had remained close friends. When Joe finished the dishes, he decided to call Ron right away, "Hello, Ron."

Ron was enthusiastic, "Hello, Buddy, how you doing? Great to hear from you!"

"Nice to hear your voice too. Been about a year. We're too busy."

Ron and Joe had spent over a year in 'Nam together. They were both in their sixties now, Joe, 69, and Ron, 68, but they were still teaching and keeping active. People think when you turn this age, you're done, but staying active had kept Ron and Joe in great health. After 'Nam, they had gone their own way for a bit. Joe went to college; Ron stayed in the military and reached the rank of Master Sergeant. Ron completed much of his college work in the military, finishing after leaving the service. The two of them visited in '74 when Joe left the service, and they and their wives had been meeting once a year since.

"Say, any plans of coming this way this summer? You and your wife are welcome anytime. I have an interesting situation that I'm investigating and am wondering if you would like to join."

"Ohh, sounds intriguing, I'm always in. Just as long as you don't get us both hurt like that last escapade we went on."

"Ah, last time, remember that was your idea."

"Mayyybeee, it was. Did I tell you *sorry*?" And at that Ron began to laugh a great big laugh that sounded wonderful.

Joe couldn't keep from laughing either; they both roared, thinking of the times they'd gotten themselves in crazy situations.

Wednesday, June 5, 4:30 p.m.

George was tired. "We never filled our bait piles yesterday, and today we won't have a chance to do anything because we need to do some cutting in the woods. Seems like we have to do more and more of that, and we get less and less for a load," he said to his nephew.

Tommy agreed, "We cut more 'n enough for a load today. I think we got a load and a half. With the price of wood today, you'd think we woulda made enough to cover what we're doing, but no luck."

"You boys should just devote your time to cutting wood, and you would make more in the long run," added Sherry, George's wife.

"Sounds good, but there ain't enough to cut anymore. Too many laws and regulations are keeping us out of areas or are telling us how to cut, or big companies are buying up the timber and clear-cutting huge plots of land. Just not worth it."

Tommy added, "Yeah, we make less and less per load. We do like hunting bears and taking people on tours to get theirs, too."

"We should probably get out and check everything. I don't know what that idiot Wyatt is doing, but we need to get established for the season."

"Let's go then. I'm ready, Unk."

"OK. We can drop that bait off or at least what is left of it. We got until around nine 'til it gets too dark in the woods. Let's get at it."

"We better be armed from now on like you said," Tommy added with a bit of fear in his voice.

"Yep, get my .30-30 outta that cabinet and give me my ammo belt. You take that Winchester 70 with the scope and that box of shells below in the drawer. Make sure you take the ones for the 70. That way we don't have to worry about that guy pointing guns at us. We'll point right back."

"Don't forget though, he has those assault rifles with those huge clips. Looks like at least thirty rounds."

"Don't matter if he doesn't get the shot he needs or we shoot first. Hope it never comes to that."

"For sure."

Sherry didn't like the situation they were in with this guy Wyatt. "Like I said, you should stick to the logging. No one is shooting at you when you do that. This baiting since that Wyatt got here has been terrible."

"Don't you worry none there, woman. We got this!"

George and Tommy took their rifles along and headed out to the truck. It was a nice afternoon, and they felt good about how things were going, but neither one liked the way they had to do things these days. Baiting early is one thing, but Wyatt was another.

George and Tommy drove around to the three piles, well hidden from anyone who might be looking. It took them several hours to complete the rounds, but they were satisfied when they headed back home with no sight of Wyatt and no DNR or other problems.

"Good day today, Tommy."

"Yep, Unk, I wish all days were like this one. This was really fun. It's exactly what I want to be doing."

"You and me. Let's get home and have a beer."

"Oh, I can't stay too late today, and I shouldn't be drinking. I have a date lined up for later. I asked Wendy if she would like to watch a movie at our house tonight. My mom is going to make popcorn and treats, and she said she'd let us watch in the living room—and she wouldn't bug us too much."

"Good for you. I hope you have a good time."

7:33 p.m.

Deputy Jason wanted to call Daryl to tell him where he was and that he could not find the guy he was supposed to follow—but that he had found something *very interesting*. It was getting late, and he did not want to end up in the woods in the dark. It was tough enough getting here in daylight, he thought. Up on the hill, he had a few bars on his cell so he made the call.

"Daryl, hello, you there?"

"Yes, got you. What's up? Did you follow him?"

"I did, but I lost him, so I kept tracking, and it led me deep into the woods near a hill."

"Well, then, just head back."

"But I went up the hill where I found something weird."

"What, you went up the hill? Are you calling from there now?" Daryl immediately was angered.

"Yes," Jason answered.

"Get the hell out of there *now* and hang up that phone. You can be tracked right to there."

"What?"

"Hang up NOW!"

"Geez, what's up with him?" Jason was upset, but ready to do what Daryl told him. As he turned around to head out, he noticed something on the far left in the trees that looked out of place. As he got closer, he realized it was a building. The closer he got, the more curious he became, so he walked into the woods just to get a peek. "It definitely is a building. Looks like they built it right into the hill. Wonder what that's about." Then he walked toward the gate, around the fence, and headed to his four-wheeler.

Later that day

It was getting late, but Daryl and Charlie were still at it when Daryl got the call from Jason. They had said good-bye to Don and had decided to find a quiet place to talk to try to solve their predicament.

Daryl was agitated. "I didn't think that Jason would go into the fence. We need to secure that place better. If he had his cell phone there, he could be traced to the place. Where were your sentries?"

"They're only there when we have training, and that's why we say no electronic devices on the hill," moaned Charlie. "The place has all kinds of communication stuff, but Bates only uses them when we need 'em, especially to connect with Escanaba and some place in the Lower Peninsula."

Daryl moaned, "He could have opened us up to all kinds of people using his phone there."

Charlie was mystified. "I don't know much 'bout that stuff, but I can't see that one little call will ruin the whole operation."

"Hope not. But I have got to get Jason off this mess. He's too young and inexperienced, plus he doesn't know anything about what's going on up there. That's why I thought he'd be good to follow the teacher, so I think we need to keep this among the people who are already involved."

Charlie responded, "I kin get some of the troops to follow the teacher. We got twenty that would be glad to get involved."

"Just be careful who you choose. We can't have people talking about what's going on here especially that one woman you've got who's always talking, and that guy, Sam. He's the worst. Always shooting off his mouth like he's somebody."

Charlie agreed, "Yeah, he's a problem. Always questions what I have them do. He don't got a lick of sense. Won't be him I'll be choosin'."

"And for God's sake, keep that Wyatt out of the loop. He's bad news. I think he's suffering from PTSD, for sure. Shouldn't have let him join up."

"He kinda invited hisself. Ran that ATV right into the camp. Gate was left open for the guys who were late. Big mistake. No one closed it after they arrived. That's on me."

"Well, just keep him reigned in. No information for him so he can make a mess of everything."

"We kin use him though. He has a lot of contacts and can get us some real firepower."

"OK, let's just keep it at that then."

A few weeks later

Joe knew enough to lay low for a few weeks even though he was afraid that he could lose any clues to what had happened. Yet, he felt it vital to have someone to cover his back; yes, someone who knew *how* to cover his back—and Ron was the guy. Ron could take care of himself in most any situation as he was in great shape, and he was a lot to handle at 6'5", 240 pounds. Joe was on the smaller side, but well-built and in top shape for his age. Running five miles a day and hitting the weights at his place kept him that way. Together they were a formidable pair with years of working together on various projects that often got them into tight spots. No one knew about the situations they often faced, but then *no one had to know*. When Joe spoke with him briefly on the phone, Ron had agreed to come up north in July.

Later that summer, Saturday, July 27th

"Ron, good to see you. Shanice, nice you could come along too. Joette will be very happy to see you. It's been more than a year."

"Sure has," said Shanice. "Actually, thirteen months to be exact. It's difficult when we live so far apart."

"Yes, it's not like the old days."

"Hello, Shanice," came a voice from the front porch. "You guys come on in and have something to eat."

"And drink," said Joe.

"And drink," added Ron with a laugh so loud it resounded in the trees.

Joette had homemade pasta and sauce with meatballs, one of Joe and Ron's favorites.

Shanice and Joette talked through the meal, mostly catching up about children and grandchildren as the guys downed helping after helping of spaghetti and meatballs followed by some chianti. Once they finished and took a deep breath, they both sat back and joined the conversation.

"So, what's this all about, Joe? Sounds like you got yourself into a situation."

"I'm not sure I am yet, but I'd like to investigate a bit more, but I can't do it by myself. At least it feels like that, and the first thought I had was that Ron owes me big time when I saved his ass the last time."

"Saved my ass? You mean I saved your hide, and more than once."

"Maybe. Anyway, I think there is something serious going on with the militia here. You're so good with arms and munitions that I knew I needed your help. If they are doing what I think, then there may be some trouble, and we may need even more help."

"What are you thinking?"

"Well, too many people are joining their group here, and earlier I learned that Escanaba, the Keweenaw Peninsula, the Lower Peninsula, and northern Wisconsin are also involved and have cells. This is like the last time we got involved in this rebellion stuff on the East Coast near Virginia. That group is still going strong, but we helped knock it down a bit."

"How do we get involved in these things? We're school teachers—or are supposed to be."

Shanice jumped in, "Yes, that's what you guys are and should be. Enough of this chasing the bad guys at your age. You know you're both in your sixties."

"Don't even try to tell them anything, Shanice. They won't listen. I just hope they stay safe and eventually retire!"

"Say again, *retire*!" yelled Shanice.

At that, both Joette and Shanice got up and started clearing the table, and the guys went out to discuss the situation in Colewin.

CHAPTER 5: INSIDE AND OUTSIDE OF THE BUNKER

July 27, 2019, 8 a.m.

Wyatt was getting restless; he had been a part of the militia now for almost two months—and nothing had happened. Charlie wasn't the kind of leader he liked, as it always was train, train, train, but for what? They could all shoot straight and run around the perimeter, and who needs bayonets anymore?

He muttered as he drove his four-wheeler up the hill to see if he could get Charlie to act, but when he got there, the gate was open, but no one was around. Wyatt yelled, "Hey, anyone here?" He parked his vehicle and walked around. Nothing. He checked the field, but it was empty, with no signs of any vehicles except for a small dirt buggy hidden near the woods. He thought maybe someone was in the bunker. He had only been in there once, and only for a second when Charlie had bumped into him in the doorway and pushed him out and shut the door. He also knew that they had a guy, Bates, who ran the communication system.

He walked up to the bunker and tried the door. Locked. He pounded on it. "Anyone in there? Hey, open up."

Bates saw the man on the hidden camera and recognized Wyatt. He opened the door quickly and stood there with an M-16 in his hand, locked and loaded. "What?" was all he said.

"Hey, take it easy, man. I don't mean any harm. Just looking for Charlie and the troops."

"All gone. Left a couple of hours ago. They didn't do much according to Charlie, not enough showed up to really do anything, and Charlie had some kind of appointment to get to."

"OK, you must be Bates. Heard about you."

"You did, huh. What'd ya hear?"

Wyatt half laughed, "Heard you're the key to the whole operation 'cause you run the communications. That's what Sam said anyway."

"Yeah, they don't know shit. Heard about you too, that you had a few tours in Afghanistan. Me too. Messed me up a bit. How 'bout you?"

"Naw, not me, I'm good. I'm a little bored, but I like what I'm doing, just not enough action. You know when you come back here from over there where you can shoot people and stuff. It's a rush, and then you can't do squat here."

"Why, you want to kill some people?"

"Don't know, just want some real excitement. You know how it is?"

Bates was interested. "I do. Hey, maybe the two of us can raise some cane around here. Not sure if there is anywhere to do it though. I just come and go from downstate as needed. Mostly just sleep here when I'm at it too long."

"We can go raise some hell at the Sportsman's Bar in Colewin. It's kinda slow and boring, but some women come in now and then, and we might be able to pick up a few."

"Hey, now you're talking. But it might be better if we go somewhere with more people where we won't be recognized so much."

"Good point, but who cares?"

"I was just about to leave anyway. Let's get out of here and see what we can find. I don't have to be back 'til morning anyway."

The same day at Joe's home, twenty minutes later
"That's the long and short of it, I guess," said Joe.

Ron was surprised. "Sounds like it might be a bit above our grade. If they have rockets and mortars, then they're thinking of doing something serious."

"I was hoping to find out what they really have, but as I said, I was followed last time and it made me a little jittery thinking about what they could do. This other teacher at the school is really interested too. He has one of those photographic memories and recalls all kinds of information, and he has kept me up on these militia cells around Michigan. He knows how to dig into the dark web and whatever other places they go these days on the internet. That's really what got me going."

"Wow, you'd think that in this place that you might not have very good Wi-Fi."

"Not much. But he has something he has developed and it works sporadically for the school, just don't get too far away."

"Let's talk about what we'll do to get started."

'We'll take tomorrow off and then we'll begin. We can all sleep in and rest up."

Sunday, July 28, 8:17 a.m.

Before anyone was up, Joe headed to town for some supplies for the trip he and Ron had planned. He hoped to catch someone at the general store before it opened. He knew he had just a few hours since the store only opened on Sunday from nine to twelve. When he got there, it was not open, but he saw Charlie sitting in his truck across the street, so he decided to ask him a few questions.

"Hello, Charlie, how you doing?"

"Fine, how 'bout you?"

"Good. Say Charlie, I know you guys are out there somewhere practicing for something. Just wondering how it's going?"

"Why do you care? Thought your type didn't like us parading around and carrying guns."

"I'm not exactly happy to see people 'open carry' in town, no, but I have nothing against using guns for hunting and protection, and I know that you and your people are good people. I'm just wondering if it is something that should be understood by everyone so we know what to expect."

"Nothing to expect 'cept keeping to yourself."

"Well, that's good. I know you're a good man, and that's why I know whatever you're doing, you're doing it for something you consider worthwhile. I hope it is."

"Yeah, thanks, I know you are a perty good feller too, and thanks for the help you gave my nephew a while back. He was goin' through a patch. I still don't agree with 'um, but he's my nephew and he's special to me."

"Nice kid. He has a lot to figure out yet."

"Listen, we don't mean no harm to no one. We just can't keep goin' the way we are. Politicians are taking all the money, scientists telling us what we can and can't do, can't even feel good about eating anymore. Police aren't allowed to be police. Country doesn't even look like it used to. Mexicans takin' our jobs! We even got religions we can't understand that are trying to take over. People who don't look like us are running the country. Can't own guns, can't hunt when we want, taxed to death, yet millionaires don't pay no taxes, on and on. The gov'ment tracks every move we make. That's why we try not to use all this new technology they say is so great. I just don't know."

"I hear you. Not in agreement on all of what you said, but I hear you." Joe stepped back a bit and took a deep breath. The tone in Charlie's voice was almost horrifying, and Joe pondered, *wow, it's worse than I thought*. He could see that Charlie had a few good points, but he was surely misled by all the media out there. A lot of his ideas bordered on xenophobia— seen by his dislike of people from other countries. Maybe he's just too sheltered to see the world as it is. It is different. I'm as guilty as anyone since I don't converse enough and exchange ideas with these people. That's got to be part of it: Lack of communication!

Just then Joe saw the lights go on in the store and said good-bye to Charlie, who also got out of his truck and headed for the store.

Sunday, July 28, 10 p.m.

The sun had set about twenty-five minutes earlier, and Wyatt sat at his kitchen table in his little cabin in the woods. He thought about all that had transpired lately. He was happy with what he had, and how things were beginning to play out. He had made some friends within the militia, although he didn't need friends since he was as content as he could be. His beer was cold, and by the six empties on the table, it looked like he really enjoyed them.

He had gotten away from the hassle of daily life and lived quietly—at least somewhat, except for the jerk who kept cutting in on his bait piles. He didn't need the militia, but he liked what it stood for, and he had a job to do. Joining it was the reason why he was there anyway. Not that he cared much, but there was now a man in charge who thought the way that they all did, and that would eventually make a difference.

Wyatt cleaned his rifles one after the other. This was something he did often and really liked doing. He would continue late into the night cleaning and organizing his cache as much as he could. Since he joined with the militia, he was even more focused because of what Charlie had said. He needed to make sure he had everything in shape just in case some day the call came, and he had to be ready.

He drank his beer and added his empty to the pile on the table, got up and grabbed himself another cold one, his eighth of the night. He looked around his cabin and realized he had kind of a comfortable place. Two bedrooms, kitchen, small living room with an old ripped couch, but comfortable, nothing fancy of course, and a bathroom with all the amenities: indoor toilet, running water, and a septic system that he had installed and that worked somedays. No hot water yet, but that was a luxury anyway. Suddenly, he yelled out, "Damn you, George, you're the only thing making this a bit of a mess. I really need to get you out of my hair and off my land."

He picked up his AK-47 with a banana clip, a piece he had picked up from a marine buddy. Wyatt aimed it out the window at a big yellow birch and let about thirty shots ring out. It blew the window out. It was already cracked anyway, and his volley just about split the tree in half. It hung there with the branches almost touching the ground. "There you go you motherfu##er. That'll teach you. Ha, what do you think of that?"

Wyatt slowly put the rifle on the table, to be cleaned next, and he quietly strode out the door. This time he took his AR-15 and three clips. He hollered again, "You might not like me, you old fart, but you're going to hear from me often until you stop trespassing and harassing me!"

He walked out to his four-wheeler and jumped on. He turned the key and moved out so quickly that he almost did a wheelie. He cranked the wheel hard and tore down the two-track path at an amazing clip, headed for George's place.

Sunday, 10:30 p.m.

George sat in his favorite chair as he and his wife sipped a beer and watched some tube. He loved cop shows, especially those live ones where they show actual situations, and loved those Alaskan wilderness shows. People making it on their own. His wife didn't much appreciate them, but she always went along with him anyway and enjoyed the time they had together.

"This is boring tonight, George," she said quietly, so as not to disturb him if he thought it was good.

"Yep, not good tonight, Sherry. Can't win 'em all. Let's have another cold one. We can see if there is anything else on the tube. I saw a good one yesterday about fishing in Canada. Man, someday I gotta do that. Talk about it all the time, but I never can."

Sherry got up and moseyed to the kitchen where she grabbed two cold ones. She saw a light flashing in the woods through the kitchen window and loudly blurted out so George could hear, "What the hell is that light down the road? It looks like it's heading here fast. Coming up the old logging trail. It's heading right for the trailer. Think it's some kids playing around, or are you expecting Tommy tonight?"

George didn't think much of it, and he yelled back, "There's always some kid messing around now that school is out. These young kids, they got too much time on their hands. You know that."

"I guess you're probably right, but the light is shining right at us."

11:00 p.m.

Wyatt just sat on his ATV and ruminated about all that had happened so far. He wanted to put a couple of bullets through the light he saw ahead, but he decided against it. He just drove very fast right up to where George's truck was and took out his bowie knife and slit both front tires. Then he jumped on his machine and drove like a maniac, so he was quickly out of the yard and into the darkness.

Sherry saw the car, or whatever it was, had stopped, not far from their truck. Then all went dark until suddenly she saw tail lights heading erratically out of their yard until they disappeared. "Well, whoever it was is out of here," she said to George.

"Good, nothing to worry about. Let's hit it. I'm tired from everything today and need a decent night's sleep."

"Sounds good." Then Sherry began cleaning up the place and shutting down the house for the night.

Monday, July 29

Joe got up early and loaded the truck. He made sure to have a few rifles this time and some grub, along with some cold beer. His plan was to search the area that he had left after being followed. He knew that whatever was going on had to be serious, just talking to Charlie gave him that feeling. He also packed two small pop-up tents just in case.

"Hey, Ron, you going to go with me today, or are you just going to keep eating?"

"I love these breakfasts your wife cooks. Fresh eggs, hotcakes, man nothing better!"

Joette was pleased. "I'm glad you're enjoying them, Ron. Some people are too busy to enjoy their food. They just shovel it down and run."

"He's the same way at home. I guess you just bring out the best in him with your wonderful breakfasts," Shanice added.

"It's still early so we'll have a good jump on the day. Just to let you know, we might be gone for two days. I packed food and gear just in case."

Joette protested, "You guys are crazy. You should take care of yourselves and not do silly stunts like this anymore."

"I agree," Shanice said very sternly.

"We are getting up there, but this shouldn't be too trouble-some. I'm sure we'll have this taken care of in no time," Ron said with a grin.

"Yes," chimed in Joe, "it's not like when we worked for the military. This is just a fun little get together to reminisce about the good old days and keep us in shape."

"If you *say so*," Joette snarled.

"You two behave while we're gone. None of those wild parties," Ron chuckled.

"Out here there's not much to do but party. We sure can't go shopping unless we head downstate," replied Joette.

At that Shanice said, "I know some real nice shops in the Petoskey area. We could take a ride and have some fun and eat at that neat restaurant on the pier."

"That sounds wonderful." Joette was thrilled with the idea. "Maybe we'll spend the night there and have a real party."

Joe got the point. "OK, OK, we get it. Have a good time and we'll see you when we get back. Hopefully, tonight. We'll be heading northeast into the hill area, but I'm not sure where it will ultimately lead us."

"Let's get going then so we can wrap this thing up in a hurry. We're just trying to find out what's going on—not making a stand and getting in trouble," noted Ron.

Joe added, "Hopefully, that's all it is, but I am not sure why I was followed and why the person following me was a police officer."

July 29, 10:00 a.m.

Charlie decided to head for the bunker to check on the cameras and to see if he needed any sentries or more fencing.

The hill was vacant except for Charlie and Bates. Bates was on a computer and making conversation with someone from Escanaba. They were in the bunker they had built into the side of the hill, and Charlie was checking the new cameras they had installed along the perimeter. Most of the equipment was made to work only when the bunker was in operation.

"How the heck is this supposed to work, anyway?" barked Charlie.

"Quiet, I'm trying to listen to our commander," said Bates.

"All right, I can wait."

Bates did not fit in. He was the type of guy you want on your side, but he was a psycho. He was not alt-right, he was just plain old psycho. He worked the communications part of the operation and was always on the web sending information and collecting it. He could only work in the bunker when it was safe to do so, and he did not live in Colewin, nor did he care to be in the bunker, but he did what he was told. His main job was to keep the communications center effective. It was only live when he was there, and there was a bit of a signal when he was not. They kept it this way so no one would be able to keep track of their activities on a daily basis.

Bates said, "Yep, that's what I'm thinking. The man said that this might have to be the time to do something because we can't trust the voting anymore. It's all rigged against us. Do you think we have everything in place? No, then we might have to wait a bit, unless the election goes the way we want it to go."

"What the hell you talking about an election for? That's a ways out there yet. We got to be concerned about right now. How can we change things?" Charlie asked.

"I told you to shut up, man. I have the commander on the line, and he's filling me in on the state of our movement. You just listen and shut the f##k up."

Charlie knew enough not to mess with Bates, so he just took a seat and decided to wait until the conversation was over. "All right, I'll shut up, for cryin' out loud."

It was unusual for Charlie to be in the bunker on a weekday because he usually was in the woods working, but he wanted to check out the cameras after what happened with Jason. He thought about what he was doing and decided he would come back next week when the troops were there and check everything out then. "I guess I'll head out."

Bates spoke into the mic, "One minute, I'll be right back." He turned toward Charlie, "OK, Charlie, but lock the gate when you leave so no one gets in."

"Who's gonna get in up here?"

"I don't know! Just do it; you old son of a bitch."

"Fine." Charlie headed out, but he wasn't happy. He was thinking as he left that these guys have really taken over the place, and it was never supposed to be like this. These guys are much different than his crew, and what Escanaba and the Lower Peninsula are planning is off the charts. Charlie decided to get back to work to forget about all this mess that he'd gotten everyone into by joining with these dudes.

Charlie had taken his truck all the way to the hill. It hadn't been easy, but he'd made it. He wanted to get more fencing to complete the security around the perimeter, but the chance of someone seeing him load six-foot-high chain link fence and razor wire wasn't in his plan. He knew he could get it from the hardware since two of his troops worked there, but it was still too much of a risk, so he just thought he would get one roll and say it was for his friend in Engadine, a town several miles to the west. "Been a lousy wasted day for me, I coulda had a hundred sticks in by now." He was off the hill and driving on the road they had improved.

Late morning

Joe and Ron were on their way. They had started a lot later than they wanted, but it was a nice day, and they were enjoying the time together.

"Sure we're going to find something, Joe?"

"Not sure of anything right now. We just have to find what's out there."

"Every time I visit you, I can't believe you moved up here, and you keep taking me to places that are deeper and deeper in the woods. What would happen if you got stuck out here? How would you get help? You said there's no way your phone works."

"That's the funny thing. Sometimes my cell even works when I'm fishing deep in the woods on the river. Not sure why."

"Let me see. Wow, Joe, I have a strong signal. When we left home, I had a very weak one, and I almost left my phone at your place, but now look."

"See what I mean, Ron. Something is off. I've checked everywhere looking into this and my friend Frank has too, but we have no clue what's going on, but he knows there is sometimes a strong signal from this direction."

They didn't say much for the next several minutes—and then there it was. A truck in the middle of the road.

"Who is that?" exclaimed Joe. "This is about as far as I got last time when I saw that four-wheeler. Now this truck." Joe slowed as the truck neared. As it got closer, Joe recognized the truck. He had seen it earlier at the store. "It's Charlie. What is he doing here? Could he be logging this far from home?"

They stopped about six feet from each other and just stared, both as amazed as the other. Charlie knew this is what he had been fearing the most. "That damn teacher is at it again, and now he's on our trail," he said to no one.

Joe turned to Ron, "I'm going to get out and talk to him. You keep me covered. I'm guessing Charlie is harmless, but you never know." Joe jumped out of the truck and yelled, "Hey, Charlie, what you up to?"

"What am I up to? You mean what are you doing?"

"My buddy and I are going on a little fishing expedition. Hoping to catch some trout out here where the river bends."

"You ain't in a very good place for that. You need to go back about a mile and take a turn north."

"Oh, maybe we will then. What are you doing?"

"I'm working. Got a spot that we might log next week, and I was here to check it out."

"Sure. Never thought of that." Joe did think of that, and he knew that Charlie was probably lying, but he had to act like it was the truth. "OK, well, let's just get past each other here and we'll be on our way."

"Who's the guy you got in the truck? Doesn't look like anyone from around here. Should we be careful?"

"What? What are you talking about?"

"You know what I'm talking about. Those guys can be trouble."

"Now that's just not true, Charlie. He's an old friend and a veteran. We met in 'Nam. He's a top-notch guy."

"Says you, but you're an outsider too, and I can't be sure about what you say. Why don' you an' yer buddy just turn around and head out afore you have some trouble?"

"Hey there, I was born a Yooper! But maybe we will turn back. Can't go forward or backward though unless one of us moves."

"Jes' back up a bit and you'll be able to turn around in that little clearing behint you."

Joe wasn't sure just what was up, but he wasn't willing to put his buddy in a jam right now, so he decided to take Charlie's advice and back up. He turned and walked to the truck, and then climbed in.

"Nice fellow," Ron muttered.

"Yeah," Joe agreed. "You hear everything?"

"Yep. Like I said, nice fellow."

"I guess we'll just back up and move out for the day. No sense taking any chances."

"I don't much care if we do. I'd like to get to know this guy a bit better, if you know what I mean."

"I hear you, but not worth it today."

They backed up on the dirt road about one hundred yards and sure enough, they were able to turn around. They began their trek back to Joe's place with Charlie right on their tail. They lost him on the main road into Poplar and continued to Joe's place. They had been gone a few hours, but when they arrived, they noticed the girls were still there.

"I guess the ladies didn't get a good start. Might be good. We can visit some since we'll have to wait until dark or until early tomorrow morning."

"Sounds like a plan," noted Ron.

As they pulled into the yard, both Shanice and Joette came out of the house. Shanice went right up to the truck as they pulled to a stop. She looked worried. "Ron, it's your mom. Your brother called and said she was very ill and to come home if you're able."

Ron had been half expecting something like this. His mother was ninety-five, and had been having some spells lately, but she had been a real active person up until a few months ago.

"What did Reggie say?"

"He thought you should head home quickly."

"Boy, I feel like I should, but I don't want to leave Joe in a predicament."

"No problem, Ron, we can pick this up later. There's no hurry about any of it that I can tell. Just trying to find out what's going on. Really, I don't have anyone's permission to do anything anyway, so maybe it'll be good to give it a rest."

"Are you sure?" Ron asked.

"Sure. I'll keep you informed if I decide to do anything later. Besides you need to be with your mom right now. Give her our best too. It's been a while since we've seen her."

"Will do. I guess we better get going right away."

Shanice said, "I've got almost everything packed already. We can be on the road in no time."

Joette was quiet up to this point, but she chimed in, "I'll pack you a good lunch and maybe a few extra sandwiches for the trip. Remember to fill up in Colewin because there aren't any gas stations 'til St. Ignace."

"OK. That's a plan."

Several minutes later, Joe and Joette waved to the couple as they drove down the road. They had quickly finished packing, eaten a sandwich, and accepted the lunch that Joette had made. After hugs and some tears and goodbyes, they were on the road in fifteen minutes.

Joe thought about the short time they had to investigate today, and decided he would wait some before doing anything else. He considered the situation and thought that, hopefully, Ron could return before school starts.

CHAPTER 6: WHAT TO DO?

July 29, late in the evening

"Hello, hello, Daryl, you there?"

"Just a minute. Who is this anyway?"

"It's me, Charlie."

"Why you calling me at home?"

"It's important. You need to meet me somewhere quiet."

"What? Why? What could be so important that we need to meet right now?"

"It's the teacher. He and some outsider are snoopin' around on our road."

"Really? OK. How about we meet at the old swimming rock on the lake?"

Charlie wasn't really listening, but thinking about what had happened. "Which one?" he asked.

"The only one I know is the one on Lake Michigan near the old sand mill. You know where they bag beach sand. Down the road from there."

"Oh, yeah. See you in a bit."

Daryl hung up the phone, curious as to what Charlie had on his mind now. He knew it must be serious. It took Daryl about thirty minutes to get to the lake. Charlie was already there, and he was frantic, walking back and forth, muttering to himself when Daryl found him.

Daryl jumped out of his truck and was agitated. "What the heck is wrong with you, old man?"

"That teacher's at it again. I caught him on the dirt road headin' to the road we fixed to the hill. He had some other outsider with him."

"Who'd he have? The law?"

"Don't know who he was. He was not from around here, and he was black. Sat in the truck while me and the teacher talked. I made 'em turn around, so I'm guessin' they are on to something—and we got to stop them."

"What the hell can we do now? We're all in this, and it could get bad for us if we're discovered. I could lose my job."

"We need to come up with something. Should I call Don?"

"That wimp won't do anything. We need someone who can come up with an idea that will send that teacher away for a while, like to jail."

Charlie thought that was a good idea. "How we gonna do it?"

Daryl's temper was on a short fuse. "I don't know, but I think we have to come up with an idea."

"That's for sure."

"We can't hurt the guy, but we might be able to set him up. Let's meet tomorrow and see what we can plan. Don't tell anyone else, especially Don or any of the troops or that crazy Wyatt."

"OK. Where should we meet?"

"Best place is the bunker. Be there after six tomorrow night and don't tell anyone a thing, especially if I'm not there. Bates won't be there, will he?"

"I have no idea because he comes and goes as he's needed."

"We got to hope no one is there."

"All right, see you then."

July 30, 2019

Daryl drove on the dirt road up the hill to the bunker. He was leery about planning anything with Charlie, but he had no choice. There just wasn't anyone he trusted these days who could get involved in this. He pulled up to the gate and saw that it was locked, so he got out to unlock the gate when he heard another vehicle coming up the hill. "It must be Charlie." Sure enough, before he had the lock off, Charlie's truck came bouncing over the road and into sight. "Good, he's on time."

Daryl hung the lock on the gate and swung it open. It was difficult because it leaned into the ground, so he had to push it with all he had. "Must have a broken hinge," he noted.

Finished, he jumped into his truck and drove it out of sight on the left of the road. Charlie did the same.

"Should we lock it?" yelled Daryl.

"Naw, no one's comin' here tonight."

"OK, let's get in there and figure this out."

Charlie took out his keys as he walked to the bunker and quickly had the door opened. "Here you go. I'll get the lights."

The bunker was fairly good-sized with a bathroom, bedroom, a little kitchen, and a large communications center. There was a door on the far wall that led to the armory. They had dug out a huge room in the hill that now was full of all kinds of weapons, vehicles, and other military equipment. They kept adding things as they acquired new ones.

Both men pulled up wooden kitchen chairs, not as comfortable as the one in the command center.

"OK, what we gonna do?"

"I have no idea, Charlie, that's why we're here. We don't have to decide on anything tonight, but we have to get started on something. Like we said before, we can't eliminate him."

"No, no. We can't do that. We just gotta get rid of 'em, both of 'em."

"You mean that other guy is still around?"

"No, I haven't seen 'im, but if he is, you know, we gotta get rid of that guy too."

"Shit, what the hell can we do? I can't keep coming here all the time. I have a job and need to be in a lot of other places, and this is keeping me around too much. Let's get an idea and get this done."

Just then the outside speakers picked up loud noises like vehicles racing up the hill. Charlie ran to the door and saw Bates first fly by to the parade grounds—and then Wyatt following. Both were tearing the place up, doing donuts in the dirt.

"Damn, those two must be drunk. What the hell! They been doing this for a while now, going downstate to party and then coming back here to sleep it off. I told Bates to stop, but you know him. They take Wyatt's truck and his four-wheelers, park at the lake, and then ride these machines all over the place."

Daryl was visibly upset. "We can't have those two involved. They're both crazy."

"They are, but they know how to keep their mouths shut when they're not drinking. Bad news is they drink a lot."

Bates and Wyatt parked their vehicles in the middle of the field and walked to the bunker. "Wonder why the gate was open," slurred Bates.

"Who cares, that was fun blowing through to the field like that. I think we tore it up pretty good."

"No sweat. The troops will fix it all up." They both roared at this and laughed all the way into the bunker.

Charlie was standing in the doorway, mad as hell. "What you guys think yer doin' anyways? You both gonna fix that mess you made."

"Hell we are," roared Bates. "Get the troops on it."

"You're a sorry ass of a human being, Bates," Daryl said softly, not to ruffle feathers too much.

"Yeah, well watch who you're talking to," said Wyatt. "He's my friend."

"What are you guys doing here? No one comes here at this time 'cept me," Bates roared.

"You two are a mess o' trouble, I can see that," muttered Charlie.

"Yeah, why are you guys here?" Wyatt said in a much sterner manner.

"None o' yer business," barked Charlie.

"Well, we're going to make it our business," Bates said in such a way that both Charlie and Daryl squirmed in their seats.

They knew this guy could be trouble—and they did not want to get on his bad side.

"OK," said Charlie. "We'll let you in on our little secret."

"No!" screamed Daryl.

"It's all right, Daryl. It won't be a secret long anyways, and we might need some help."

"Not this kind of help."

"You better shut your mouth there, sheriff. You might find yourself wishing you had a set of balls otherwise," said Wyatt.

Charlie made an effort to calm everyone down. "OK, OK, let's stop the jibber-jabbin. Set yerselfs down here."

Wyatt and Bates took a seat, both still a little wobbly. Wyatt turned his chair around and sat in it backwards. Bates just slumped into the nearest chair and burped a big loud one, followed by a disgusting fart.

Repulsed, Daryl braved a comment, "You guys are pigs. You know that."

"Just shut up and tell us what you're doing," shouted Wyatt.

"All right, well, we got a problem. There's this guy who's been nosin' 'round here. We can't let him find the bunker and the communications center, so we're thinking of a way to get him outta here."

"Nobody's going to care about this place. They couldn't even find it. That's why you guys were chosen to hide everything. You always said people around here mind their own business," said Bates.

"Yeah, but this is a problem. He's an outsider, and we have to fix it," insisted Daryl.

Then Bates quickly added, "You mean get rid of him? That's easy."

"If you mean kill, then no," breathed Charlie. "We can't do that 'cause we'd have the law after us."

"You have the law right here. What's the biggie?" laughed Bates.

"No, we gotta get him to leave or get him arrested for 74ome-thing', but we can't figure what."

"Can't figure. You guys must be simpletons," Bates jeered. "That's easy. Problem solved. Here's what you've got to do."

Wednesday, August 21, 2019

Everything had been quiet around Colewin for over a month. Not much happening except that Joe was getting ready to get back to teaching. The only situation he heard that was getting bad was this new guy Wyatt who's harassing George. Not sure how a guy as nice as George would end up in one situation after another with this guy, but then Joe knew very little about Wyatt.

He did talk a lot to young Tommy about what was going on, and it did not sound good. He could only hope that he and George stayed away from the guy.

Tommy said the word was that Wyatt was taking over the militia—and that it was turning into something nasty, and that he was afraid of what a nutcase like Wyatt might do with the backing of the entire group. He told Joe, "He and members of the group are always seen these days with assault rifles. Who needs a damn assault rifle all the time, or for that matter, anytime? We have a lot of guns at our house for hunting and collecting, but we don't have any of those."

Frank had also let Joe know that the Wi-Fi at school had been really good; however, then it was nonexistent off and on. He said it was like someone was jamming the whole area, although most times it was bad anyway. The funny thing was that over near Naubinway, everything was great because they had discovered some buried fiber optic cable, and the school had an interactive TV system and good Wi-Fi from an assist by NMU.

Joe had been preoccupied a lot lately at school preparing his new course, which had been approved after Joe aligned it with the standards. Joette was also spending a lot of time preparing for the new year. Ron was still with his ailing mother and also getting ready for school. His mom actually was getting a bit better, but she had a real scare for a while; she was 95, no 96, since she had a birthday this month.

Today, Joe was just sitting at home resting up for the long haul of a new school year. He was hoping for a game on TV and was musing aloud, "This is the life. I'm caught up and no work to do around the house. Guess this'll be the last time I'm caught up 'til school is out next June."

There was a special on TV about police and the killing of African American men. "It seems to be an epidemic," Joe heard the reporter saying. He had discussed this very thing with Ron a while back, and they both thought it was a tragedy—that something had to change. That got Joe to thinking about how he and Ron had not been able to move forward with their plan. He finally sat up and said, "Since I have only a few days left, maybe I'll try something myself. I just need to be more careful."

Friday, August 30, 2019

September 10 was the beginning of bear season in the Upper Peninsula, and George and Tommy had been working hard to get everything ready. Along with the baiting and constant checking, keeping the bait barrels intact and hanging properly was all important, and George and Tommy had been working on a cabin to house and feed the Fudgies—non-U.P. guests. That way they'd be able to collect around $1,200–$2,500 for about a five-day hunt. Much of that would be profit. Sherry would do all the cooking, and George and Tommy would take care of all the other essentials of the hunt.

Needless to say, they were excited. Before, George had charged around $150 per day for the hunt because his people would stay at the motel. Now, he'd charge a lot less than the motels—and give the Fudgies more privacy and hot meals on top of that. Today they were putting some of the finishing touches on the cabin so it would look presentable for the hunters. They kept with a rustic feel, but they knew it had to be somewhat comfortable too. George's season would start on, eerily, September 11, so there wasn't much time left to prepare.

"I already got several people checking in. Your idea about 76omethi' it on the internet was a good one. I'd a never thought to do that." George was both amused and excited.

"Well, that's what people do these days. Our computer teacher at the high school gave me the idea. He's always doing stuff like that, but he says we have a very ineffective signal around here. Sometimes it's good, but most times it's really bad. He's hoping that changes soon."

"Lucky for me that you know this stuff, Tommy. I believe we'll have more people calling than we have in the past."

"I really only play around with it. Wendy has taught me some things though because she spends time when we have Wi-Fi playing with this stuff. I really don't have a lot of time for that since we've been working on the cabin, getting ready for the season."

"Remember to thank her then, will ya?"

"Sure, sure," said Tommy as he finished painting the last bit of the kitchen soffit. "I hope to see her tonight."

"Good. By the way I run into that Wyatt guy yesterday. He was as ornery as ever. Threatened me again to stay out of his bait piles. Honestly, I don't know what the heck he is talking about. He just thinks he owns the whole country out there."

"You be careful, Uncle George. That guy's not right, and from what I've seen, he could do something terrible."

"Don't worry yerself none. He's just a big spoiled baby. We can take care of him."

"I hope so, Unk. I don't know what I'd do if you weren't around."

Monday, September 9, 2019

Charlie wasn't sure how to handle all that Bates suggested would work to get rid of the school teacher. Lately, not much had happened, and he was less worried about the situation—but he knew that Daryl wanted this done and done fast. Who could he get to handle that part of it? Sam? He has a daughter and they might set it up so that no one really knew what was happening, but it was better not to get his daughter involved.

"Sam, you want in on a little mischief, maybe get some attention around here?"

"Attention? What you 77omethi' at Charlie?"

"Ya know that we got a problem with someone snoopin' around our perimeter, right?"

"Heard sumpin' about it. None of you guys really say anything, and you keep us troops in the dark."

"Well, here's 78omething' you might like. That guy who's been snoopin' around is the school teacher. One that lives over between Poplar and Colewin."

"Shoulda knowed it. Can't stand that guy. He's got my daughter wrapped around his finger and a lot of other kids too. Talks to them like they know sumpin' that we don't. Got her doing stuff with this here climate change and sayin' that oil is bad, and specially that guns ain't good for us. What the…"

"I hear you."

"Problem is a lot of people 'round here like the guy, and I can't say I know why."

"True. It'd be best if we get rid of him somehow. Make him move, I mean."

"Yes, can we do that?"

"I'm guessin' it'd be tough, but I got an idea."

"What kinda idea? Any way I can help and be part of that?"

"Sure is! But you can't say a word to anyone, got it?"

"Well, yes, and I'm in, Charlie!"

September 11, 2019

Bear season was in full swing and George had several people lined up for hunts, and he was excited. Three people had already sent their checks or paid on the internet, and he couldn't have been happier. All three opted for the full amount, staying in his cabin and three squares. Right now, George and Tommy were waiting for the person to emerge from the cabin. It was about an hour before daylight, and they could start in thirty minutes. They were ready, and hopefully their man was too.

"Whoopie, Tommy, it's gonna be a good year. Today is the first hunt. We got five days to get this guy a bear, and the way we been seein' 'em, we may be able to bag one right away today."

"I sure hope so. Will we take the truck to the bait pile near the old dump first?"

"Yep, that's the idea."

"Make sure you're ready and loaded too in case he misses and we have a problem."

Since many hunters used bows, some even crossbows, early in the season, George had a few situations that went awry, so he was always cautious and had a gun ready just in case a mad bear came after them. Since they hunted from the ground, he knew they could not outrun a wounded bear.

"I've got my rifle cleaned and ready to go."

"Here he comes now. Right on time."

September 19, 2019

School was in session, and everyone connected to the school was very busy. In a K-12 building, teachers had many responsibilities as did the administrators and paras. School was a dynamic place and getting back together with colleagues and friends for faculty, staff, and students was especially fun in this very rural area where students, teachers, and friends sometimes lived miles from each other.

The first few days were enjoyable, but now Joe had gotten into the routine of day-to-day school. He was very busy with schoolwork, but he was still focused on what had been happening with Charlie and his troops. He hadn't been able to come up with a plan regarding what was going on with the militia. He was beginning to wonder if he was going off the deep end with this, and now with school in full swing, he had less time to be spending on the situation. Besides, Ron was still home taking care of his mother, and he was a little doubtful that alone he could find out what was up. He did believe that something illegal was going on, and that it involved a lot of people, but why the militia? What would they do with all this training, and why so secretive?

Besides, Joe thought, Joette was not into his sneaking around anymore. Isn't that why they came here to get away from it all and get some peace and quiet? When the kids visit, they're supposed to be settled into a comfortable quiet life. Not really working out that way with all the school business, but that was the plan. Time to take the grandkids fishing and hiking and looking for bugs and other fun adventures.

October 1, 2019

Charlie still wasn't really sure how the plan would unfold, but he knew that Daryl and Bates had talked long into the night, and they had a plan.

"All right, what exactly is it?" asked Charlie.

Daryl just sat there quietly wondering why he got involved with this guy who might botch the plan on his own. Yet, he knew he had to trust him because he needed some of his people.

"It's a good plan, but like I said, we need to be very secretive and not involve anyone else."

Charlie was confused. "What do you mean by no one else?"

"I mean, nobody. Don't say anything to anyone but the people we get involved."

"But…I told some of the troops that we were going to do something big about people snoopin' around."

"What, who did you tell?"

"Only Sam."

"Of all the people, why in holy hell did you tell him? He can't ever do anything right. You said it yourself."

"I know, but you said we need to involve some of my troops."

"When the time is right, yes. How is Sam going to help?"

"'Cause he got a daughter."

"Ah, you took my advice about that. So, you think you found someone that we can use to get this going."

"For sure, and Betty. I think Betty will help."

"Well, maybe that's a start. We've got to get this going soon, and I can't be any part of it, so that I can come in and do the arresting."

"Right. Should we start with Betty? She's a tough one, and she'll do anything I ask," said Charlie confidently.

"You need to meet soon and get her on board so this can happen before the snow flies. I hate driving all around in that weather."

"What should I have Betty do?"

"Well, the plan is to first get her on board, then we need her to go to the teacher's place someday when we know that he's alone. She has to do a few things. One, make sure she has a good reason to go there. Two, be alone with him and somehow scratch him. We need his skin under her nails. Three, she's got to do it without his thinking anything is out of the ordinary, like a mosquito or bug on him and she wiped it off. Four, you have to slap her a good one across the face so she has something to show me that it was a result of her fighting him off. Finally, she has to head to town and call me and report a rape or attempted rape. It'd help if we could get some pictures of them together too. Not so much there, but anywhere. Make sense?"

"Yep. I think we can do that."

"OK, get ahold of her and get started, but make sure you leave me out of it."

"Will do. I'll head over to her place now."

Charlie went right to Betty's place and found her outside working on a tractor. He was a little nervous, but excited to know that the plan was ready to unfold.

"Hey, Betty."

"Hallo, Charlie."

"How ya doin'?"

"Great, but it's gotta be somethin' awful important for you to come all the way over here. You've never been here before."

"Yep, it's important. We got a serious situation, and we gotta take care of it."

"You know I'm always in for that. We been playin' around for too long, and we need some action so's to keep the troops on their toes."

"You up fer it? I mean you ready to do anything it takes?"

"Yes, yes, just give it to me."

"OK, well we need to set up that teacher who's been snoopin' around. Found him out near the road to the bunker."

"How we gonna do that?"

"Well, we gonna get him caught in some kinda sex situation."

"What?"

"Yeah, and it's gonna work. But we need your help."

"Give it to me."

"Well, we're hopin' you could lure him in—and then we could say he raped you."

At that, Betty shot out a raucous laugh. She laughed and laughed until Charlie finally said, "What's so funny?"

"You want me to lure him. I couldn't do that in a million years. Look at me. I ain't purty and I ain't likable. I got calluses on my hands the size o' my farm. I'm downright stinky and ugly. How's that gonna work?"

"I don't know. I just thought you'd do it, and it would work."

"It won't! You gotta come up with a different plan."

"No, that's the plan."

"Who come up with that?"

"I can't say, some guys, but it'll work."

"Then you need somebody else. I'll help you in any way I can to get that nosy SOB out of the way, but it won't work with me doin' it."

"Well, now I'm lost for what to do."

"I can't help you there. You need a better plan."

"Can't, like I said, this is the plan."

"Wait a second, I got an idea. What about Lane? She's purty and got all kinds of feminine things to make her right for a job like this."

"OK," said Charlie.

"And, Charlie, if I'm in, you and your idiots are not going to use your plan. It's plain stupid. Men are so stupid sometimes, and they ain't got a lick o' brains when it comes to things like this. Oh, yeah, they can rape and humiliate women, but they still ain't got no brains."

"Now you watch it, Betty. You know who yer talkin' to here."

"Oh, I know, and for all the smarts you and your buds think you have, you know nothing. So, here's the plan. These days, all you got to do is say you been raped or someone tried to rape you. You don't need no proof. It'll get that teacher in a whole lotta trouble. He may even go to jail, especially if we can get one of those young girls he teaches to agree with us."

"That doesn't sound very good to me."

"Do some readin' or watch the news. You'll soon agree."

"I can't agree. This plan comes from the top of our militia leadership."

"What? You and a couple of goonies who think they know sumpin'. You ever hear of the "Me Too" thing going 'round the country?"

"I heard somethin' bout it. Bunch of cry-babies whining about men touching them or somethin'."

"That's what you heard, huh? You got that bully mentality when it comes to those things, especially rape."

"What you mean, bully? I'm no bully."

"Pay attention to how you treat your troops and your women, especially your wife."

"Now you gone too far. What the heck do you know about any of it anyway?"

"Well, 'cause I see your wife regular and she talks. I know you hit her, and worse—when I was a young girl, I was *raped* by a bully just like you!" Betty screamed this at Charlie who took two steps back and just stared at her.

"You're crazy, lady!" Charlie yelled back.

"Maybe I am. Maybe I'm jus' a little pissed that no one helps your wife 'cept me, and no one believed me a long time ago, and it still eats at me. That's why I don't trust any men, none, never will!" Again Betty was screaming at Charlie, and this time her face was bright red and her fists were clenched.

Charlie knew he had lost the battle. He could not understand all this looney crap that she was spoutin', but he wanted to take the teacher down. "All right then. I'll tell them, but they ain't gonna be happy."

"Make sure you tell 'um that down the road we'll need proof or this will not work."

"We got that part covered with the law. Don't you worry none."

They talked, or rather yelled, for a while about the plan and how they would approach Lane to see if she would do it. Betty was sure she would since she was ready for some action that had been promised for such a long time. She knew it wasn't the type she wanted, but they could get involved in this to help make the rest of their militia training stay on track.

October 2, 2019

Wyatt was not satisfied with his season so far. He wondered how he had three hunters and only one bear to show for three weeks of work. Old George was baggin' them one after the other this year. Wyatt thought, lucky he hasn't been around my stuff this year, but there must be a reason why he's getting so many—and I haven't had much luck. Wyatt yelled, "Did George and that kid do something to my bait piles or do they have some trick that they're doing to make all the bears go someplace else? I've got to find out."

"But, today is going to be fun," he blurted out. "Today, Bates, semper fi, is going to be my hunter."

Bates and Wyatt had become fast friends since that night at the bunker. They drank together, caroused together, and now hunted together. They understood each other, and came from the same mindset when it pertained to people in general—*they didn't like any of them.*

Bates was a hard-headed ex-Marine who loved doing anything that was on the wild side. His life most days was sitting behind a computer passing along information or searching for those who wished to be compatriots with their group.

Bates never had a serious relationship in his life, and probably never knew how to begin one. Oh, he had his share of hookers and one-night stands along the way, but he just wasn't that person to settle with anyone or, for that matter, love anyone but himself. He knew about rape too, having been accused a few times and caught once, but he was able to intimidate the victim even though his DNA was found under the victim's fingernails—sadly, this is where he got his plan for Daryl to get rid of the teacher. He had few family members left that he knew. His father left his mother when he was young, and his mother died while Bates was in Afghanistan. He had a chance to go home for the funeral, but he didn't really rank it as very important. He never went home even after his commander gave him a ten-day pass. He left, and instead of going to the states, he spent it partying in Europe. Yet, he became friends with Wyatt. Even he could not explain it; they were just two of a kind.

"Hey, dude. What's up?" Wyatt asked with a huge grin.

"Nothing going on. Just left the post to come hunt and brought a few pieces of equipment. How's this one? An old AK-47 with a banana clip."

"You won't need that kind of fireworks for this job. One bullet well placed will do the job."

"Yeah, but we're going to have some fun too."

Even Wyatt wasn't convinced about this kind of fun, but he'd never had a friend before and he was happy to oblige…. "Well, have a beer anyway before we get started while I get all set."

"How about you?"

"Already got one. Filled a whole cooler for us to take to the blind. We'll have to be careful because this blind is way up in a tree. I built it this summer just for observing my prey, but it'll work out well because there's enough room for the two of us."

"Sounds great."

"We can take the truck to the crossroads just below the ridge; then we can walk to the blind. Don't want to put any scent out there we don't need, or make any noise we don't have to."

"Hey, got another? I'm really dry."

"Got plenty. Here you go."

They drove to the spot that Wyatt had mentioned, and then walked quite a distance to the blind. They were both a little winded when they got there.

"How we going to get up there?"

"Got a ladder." Wyatt pointed to a thick pile of brush just behind the tree. "It's not the best, but it'll hold us."

They were both on the heavy side, especially Bates who sat at a computer for hours. He had a fairly good belly. He ran about 235. Wyatt was a thick-muscled 220 himself, so, yes, they needed a good ladder. Once in the blind, Wyatt pointed out several places that they might see their prey. Bates really wasn't interested in the hunt. He just wanted to have a little fun. After about six beers, they both started getting loud to the point that any animal would avoid the area, and after a few hours of boredom, Bates yelled, "Let's have some fun!" *Rat-tat-tat-tat-tat-tat* filled the air, as he unloaded thirty rounds into the tall red pine across the small clearing where the bait pile was placed.

Startled, Wyatt screamed, "What the hell!"

But after Bates laughed a good one, Wyatt started laughing too, unloading his rifle into the same tree. They reloaded and shot again. It was *bang, crash, boom*—fireworks and beer for a while until they ran out of both.

At the same time, not far away, George and Tommy had their client on a hunt across the river from where Wyatt and Bates were situated. When they heard all the racket, they knew that it must be Wyatt, and after that noise, their hunt was over for now. Too much shooting and hollering for them. They told the hunter that they would come back later in the day. George was getting angry and blurted out, "Why that feller even tries to do this type of work is beyond me. I know he sets up close to us just to use our skill in drawing bears to our spots. The damn fool."

After somehow climbing down the ladder, Bates and Wyatt loaded the gear into the truck and headed back. They bounced over the road that seemed much worse going back than heading there. They were both a little drunk, but not so much that they didn't make sense.

"So, what's next, Bates?"

"What do you mean?"

"Are you staying at the bunker this winter?"

Bates thought a bit and then said, "You know I think I will. I'm not so sure I can stand those guys I work for, but hey, they pay me well and I can do what I really enjoy—and that's hunt the web. Nothing better in a day's work."

"What exactly they got you doing?"

"Well, what they think I'm doing—and what I'm really doing—are different. They think I'm just a communications idiot relaying information from one cell to the other and making websites for them, but I do a lot of my own stuff. I'm doing a lot with bitcoin and making a small fortune on their time, and they have no idea. When I get enough, I'm outta here."

"Not me. I found a home. I really enjoy this guide stuff. Just need to get the business going. That George guy has me all messed up, so unless I can put him out of business, this spot won't work for me." Wyatt liked hanging with Bates, so he didn't tell the real reason he had been sent to Colewin.

"I can help you there. I can put him out of business and out of his misery real quick like."

"I guess we could, but I'm going to work on him this year and see what I can do."

"Well, as I heard from the commander in downstate Michigan, this area is going to get a lot more interesting. They're planning to triple the size of the stash up here and bring in some big equipment at night, so they'll have to improve and widen the roads a bit. Some real shit is going to hit the fan if the election doesn't go right."

"Hmph," Wyatt blurted.

Monday, October 14, 2019
Daryl asked, "Have you got everything set?"

Charlie answered, "I think we got 'er. But Betty and Lane will only go along with their plan, plus they got a young girl they're gonna have her say she was kidnapped and raped, or 89nything89' like that, by that teacher Joe, and I got Wyatt and Bates to help out if need be."

"What, you got two psychos to help you do this? This will not end well. We already have Bates involved with this, why that Wyatt guy? And what's this new plan?"

"I'm just doin' what yer said to do, and I didn't want to get no scaredy cats involved. These two guys will do anything."

Daryl repeated, "OK, so what's the plan? This has got to happen soon."

Charlie explained the plan that Betty had come up with, and the two of them discussed it for some time. Finally, even as frustrated and uncertain as he was, Daryl thought the plan had potential.

"If we can get the teacher out of here real soon, we can start bringing in the heavy stuff to the bunker. I have word that our base is going to be a key one for storage of all kinds of equipment in the near future. Seems we might get some action this winter, and we got just the right guy in charge so this could happen."

Charlie was excited. "Well, whatever, we just want to protect our property here and stay somewhat secret until 89nything89' good comes along to change this country."

Tuesday, October 15, 2019

George was extremely happy since this season was going so well, and now he had a police officer from downstate Cadillac coming up to hunt for a week. He'd paid $2,500 to stay at his cabin and hunt until he got a bear, and George was going to make it the best hunt of the year.

"Tommy, next week you got to come over here to get us ready early and make this the best hunt ever. That cop is depending on us to give him a good hunt next week."

"OK, Unk, I'll see you right at six-thirty a.m. next Monday. Do I need anything special for that hunt?"

"No, but we'll have to be careful. We'll have to go past that crazy guy's land because we'll be using the bait pile on the other side of the ridge."

"But, Unk, he keeps saying that it's his land, and he's been so ornery."

"Yeah, I know, but he's all talk and no action. We'll be fine, but we'll also be prepared."

Tommy was not convinced, but he agreed because his uncle was usually always right. He was able to get along with anyone, and everyone in Colewin liked him, even the DNR guys. Tommy did consider one other thing that he said forcefully, "I'm going to take my Winchester .30-30 this time—and it's going to be loaded."

CHAPTER 7: THE ACCUSATION

Colewin High School, Thursday, October 17, 2019, 1 p.m.

"What!" Joe exclaimed. "I've done what?"

The principal continued, "You heard me. Two women, well, one woman and a high school girl have both accused you of raping them. I don't know what to tell you. The woman is on her way to find Daryl. They want you arrested."

"Elizabeth, you know me. That's not like me at all."

"Well, you have been here for only three years, so I don't know your past history, and the board knows you even less than I do. Some of the board members said they really liked you until this report. I've met with them—and they want you dismissed right now."

"What, I haven't even had a chance to see who accused me and what exactly I did. Innocent until proven guilty, and no one will be able to find me guilty because I have not done anything."

"Sorry, Joe, you have to leave school right now. Pack your things until further notice. I've lived here my whole life and this type of behavior is the kind that gets people in real trouble, so get yourself a good lawyer and make sure you can cover for all your time here—you'll have to, very soon."

"You're really serious, aren't you? I have rights, and you know what you're doing is wrong."

"Maybe, maybe not, I'll let you know if anything changes. I'm sure you'll be hearing from Daryl."

"I'll get the union lawyer to back me as soon as I can. They'll show that you need proof to make accusations like this. You can't just send people home and assume they're guilty."

"Good-bye, Joe. You have thirty minutes to get out of the building or I'll have security walk you out, and that won't look good."

"Right, right, I'll check in with Joette and be gone as soon as I can. Keep me posted."

Joe packed his things and went right down to speak with Joette who was teaching reading in the elementary. She was stunned as was Joe. She decided to take the day off and head home with her husband, but first she had to get her lessons ready for a sub. Joe headed to his Chevy Equinox and put his things in the back seat. He was pissed, and he knew just why this was happening and who was probably behind it—but he had no idea how deep this group of people was and no idea of the kind of problem it was.

The bunker, Saturday, October 19, 2019

The troops stood at attention as Charlie barked orders and presented the new information. This was an important day because their base was going to be used as a strategic site in the insurgent activity that was being planned, but the plan itself was vague and distant for the troops who were hoping for something more.

"So this base will be improved and a lot of equipment and personnel will be coming here. We need to be sharp and well-drilled and we got a lot o' work to do on this here road. Most of the equipment will come at night in large semis and will be dropped near U.S.-2. It'll be up to us to get it the rest of the way. We got several pieces of big equipment ourselves to get the road in shape, so you all will have to volunteer sometime after work on weekdays."

"Aw, come on Charlie, we got enough to do," whimpered Sam.

"If'n you want to be part o' this, you work. Otherwise, get out."

"Good point, Charlie, we don't want any softies here. We got to be tough and hardened, otherwise we'll lose," barked Wyatt. Wyatt had become one of the important cogs in the machine now that he had befriended Bates, and also been a part of the plan to take down the teacher. He and Bates were a formidable duo in the group now, although Bates didn't do anything new, same old communication stuff, but he was the brains behind most of it. Wyatt was the spirit and kept everyone on track while Charlie was the glue that kept it all together because he knew everyone and had started the group, but as for being the leader—that had shifted to Wyatt.

"Today, we're going to brush out a section of the road leading to the bunker road. It needs widenin' and fillin', so we got to start there. We have all kinds of logging equipment that we borrowed, and we can move a lot of the trees and brush with that. Betty, can you drive the big truck? Take the deuce and a half and dump everythin' in the woods out by the clearing on the back road."

"Sure can, Charlie," Betty replied. "Been driving those things my whole life."

"Some o' you grab the chain saws and shovels. I'll take the stump remover, not sure it'll do any good out here, but the backhoe isn't workin'. Some o' you can take the big logging truck with the log loader. We gotta get as much done as we can afore the heavy snow flies. If we can get that backhoe working agin, it'll save a lot o' time. Bill, you stay and work on it, and get someone to help you. Let's move."

Wyatt was in agreement that all the work had to be accomplished quickly, and he decided to take the lead in the effort. "As soon as bear season is over, I'll take the reins of this operation and make sure it's done right. Anyone object?"

Not a word was said, not any affirmation or disapproval. No one objected to Wyatt because they were all, including Charlie, afraid of Wyatt and what he might do. He was a wild one and teamed with Bates, no one trusted either of them, and the two had become a force in the operation. Even though most people never saw Bates, they feared him because of what Charlie had explained about him. Wyatt's leadership was not something they wanted, but it had been planned for some time by others who had also hired Bates.

"OK, then, let's get at it!" Charlie said and moved off with his head hanging and muttering a word or two that no one heard. He had the stump remover loaded onto his truck and stormed off for the section of road they were going to clean up. Wyatt moseyed into the bunker to touch base with Bates, and after a brief conversation, took the back road to his cabin to continue a hunt that had been interrupted.

As he drove off, Charlie could see the dust from Wyatt's four-wheeler in the rearview mirror of his truck. He did not like Wyatt, but he could not think of a way to get rid of him. Charlie was the boss, and Wyatt was in the way. He wondered, how did this madman take over so quickly, and what the heck is he going to do next? He could hurt somebody.

Same day, Saturday, October 19, 2019

Daryl knew he had to come up with a warrant to arrest the teacher, so he was headed to get statements from Lane and the girl from the school who also said she had been touched by the teacher. Daryl drove out to Lane's house to get as much of her story as he could. He had arranged to have the girl there too, and her mother.

Her mother was pissed at Joe for not making her daughter the lead in the school play last fall, and he gave her a bad grade on her last two assignments. The mother was up in arms about the outsider who had the guts to treat her daughter this way. She had never liked him because he also made his room a safe-haven for all those pedophile homos and queers. What next?

"Tell me what happened to you, one at a time. I'll start with Lane. Fine if I tape this?"

"Sure," moaned Lane.

"By the way, how did you get that bruise on your face?" queried Daryl. He knew the real story, but he had to play along like he knew nothing, lest someone figured out he was in on this.

"He hit me to shut me up. I was screaming a lot, so he stuffed something in my mouth and hit me hard in the face."

"OK, when was this? When did it happen?"

"Last week, Monday, no Saturday. I was off running some errands, and when I finished, I headed home. He was waiting for me in the road, and he must have known that no one else was home. He had his car in the road and I couldn't get by; then he got out and talked to me through the window. Then, all of a sudden, he opened the door and pulled me out. He was strong and even though I tried to fight back, I could not. He dragged me to his car and threw me in the back and did the deed. That son of a no good brute. You know the rest of the story."

"All right. Keep going. What happened next?"

"When he threw me out of the car, I screamed and he said, 'You tell anyone and you're dead.'" She was sobbing by this point, and Daryl thought *what a good act*. He got this all on tape too.

"I was scared and ran to my car, and he was gone."

"All right, then, I got your story." Daryl smiled, but hid it quickly. He added, "Oh, yes, what time did this happen?"

"I can't remember. It was after the errands I ran, so it was sometime in late afternoon."

"Did you go to a doctor to get checked out?"

"No, why would I do that? I was already embarrassed, and they wouldn't believe me anyway."

"Yes, but they could have tested and gotten some DNA or something," Daryl choked out.

"Sure, sure, that's what they say, and then they blame the woman for being seductive or something, and I don't need that. Is that what you're going to do? Blame it on me?" she belted out.

"No, I'm not. I'm going to get you help."

Daryl finished with Lane and directed his attention to the young girl. He was excited now because he thought they might have a good case against the man. Even if they just get him to move, it'll be a success.

"What about the girl?" Daryl said to no one in particular, but her mother tore into him right away.

"Paige will tell you what he did. That no-good bastard of a man. Go ahead Paige, give him the details, and don't leave anything out." Paige's mom was agitated to the point of almost fainting because she got so worked up.

Now Paige was actually a very nice girl who was also a good student, but she liked the limelight—and she enjoyed being the center of attention. She could have any boy she wanted; all she had to do was flirt a bit and it was a slam dunk—a new boyfriend. She was very pretty and affectionate when she wanted to be. It didn't take much for Lane and her mother to convince her to do what they asked. She always felt so much more superior to the teachers at the school, and this was her day.

Daryl reiterated, "What happened, Paige? It is Paige, right? It's all right to call you Paige?" When he turned to look at her, his eyes did not meet hers. He was looking at Paige's chest and body, and she could see that she had him too.

"Sure, I'm Paige. Where should I begin? Do you want the whole story back to the end of last year?"

"If it involves his advances, then yes. Tell me what you can remember."

"Don't leave anything out that we talked about, Paige. I mean that you talked about," added her mother.

"OK, it started a long time ago when he would put his arm on my back. I didn't think much of it, but then during play practice he put it down lower and lower. One day he had me in the prop room and …oh, I don't know if I can tell you. It's so horrible."

"You need to tell us if this is going to work. I mean if we are going to catch this guy," Daryl said quickly.

"So, like he touched me down low on my butt in that room the first day. Then the next day…"

"Do you remember the exact day?" asked Daryl who was still recording everything.

"Well, it was during play practice, so it must have been in late April or early May. I'd guess the first week of May."

"All right, then what?"

"Then, one day when we were in that prop room and no one else was around, he touched my top."

Paige's mother was quick to add, "She means her breasts!"

"Is that what you mean?" Daryl asked.

"Yes, and then his hand went down to my bottom parts inside my pants."

"I told you he was an old fart son of a bitch, mother fu##er!" yelled Paige's mom.

"OK, OK, what did you do then?" added Daryl.

"I tried to scream, but he put his hand over my mouth and then he stopped. I was scared and ran home and told my mom."

"Why didn't you say something to the principal?"

Paige's mother jumped in, "We knew nothing would have happened, and we didn't want Paige to get a bad name like the other girl a few years ago who said she was abused by a boy in school, so we just kept it to ourselves, but when Lane come to me and told me everything that happened to her, then we knew we had to say something."

Daryl videotaped the rest of the inquiry, and then said he had enough to maybe get him arrested. He would let them know if it happened, and then he asked, "Would you be willing to say this in court to the judge?"

All three looked at each other with sudden fear and Lane said, "You got the tape—that should be enough."

"It could be, but I'll let you know. Thank you for your time." Daryl walked out the door with the biggest grin on his face and a skip in his step.

Although all seemed fine, one element would later be tough to get around—that Paige had become a pathological liar and everyone knew it, not her mom so much, but every kid in the school.

CHAPTER 8: WYATT AND GEORGE

Monday, October 21, 2019, 6:30 a.m.

It was the last week of hunting season, and George had never had such a good year. All was coming together, and this final hunt would be a good one financially. It was still dark but George and Tommy knew their way around everything, especially on this starry fall morning.

"Tommy, I'm so excited for this year. The cabin worked out great, and Sherry's food was fit for a king, least I thought it was."

"It's been a fun year, that's for sure. When does the cop get here?"

George was as giddy as he'd ever been, announcing, "He's here already. I told him to come to the house before sunrise, so he should be here soon."

"What should I do right now?"

"Just get all the equipment ready for the blind. I'll go in and get some fuel in case it gets cold out there today. Shouldn't be bad though, but you don' know if the Fudgie will get cold."

"All right," replied Tommy. He placed his gear, backpack, rifle, and gloves in the back of the truck. Then he filled the rest with tarps, bait, a small heater, sleeping bags, bug spray, toilet paper, a small tent, mosquito nets, and, of course, lots of beer.

When all was completed, George came out of the house and placed a small can of fuel in the back. "Here comes the cop! Let's get this hunt started."

A stocky middle-aged man came walking slowly from the direction of the cabin carrying a backpack. He looked tired and unshaven, a typical middle linebacker would be a good description for this guy who was dressed in full camo with a boonie hat, just like Tommy had, and mosquito net tucked up on top of his hat to boot.

"Here I am, bright and early. Man, it's dark out here in the morning. Never have I seen so many stars in the sky. It is really nice out here. Hope this is a sign of good luck."

"For sure," George chimed in with a big smile. His morning look was not much better. Seldom did he shave early, and it looked like he had slept in his clothes, something that he often had to do on hunts, but last night he slept in a bed.

"Anything else we need, Unk?"

George looked over everything. "Got bug spray?"

"Yep, right under the tarp."

"Ah, by the way, Lester, this here is my nephew, Tommy. He goes on all the hunts with me 'cause he's learning the trade. Knows about as much as I do now since he's been with me for years since he was a little tyke."

Lester looked Tommy over and seemed to approve and shook his hand, clenching it until it hurt. Tommy's mouth opened a bit and he breathed deeply. Tommy was no slouch, but this guy was strong and tough. Not as tall as Tommy, but he was probably twice as wide.

"Let's go then," George said, and he jumped into the truck. Lester got in the passenger side as Tommy finished loading the man's backpack.

Then Tommy got into the cab and Lester had to squeeze next to George. It was a tight fit for all three in the cab, but they didn't mind. It was all knees, shoulders, and elbows, which made all three burst out in a laugh that seemed to bond them to the task at hand.

Off they moved in the direction of the bait pile that they were going to observe for the next few hours until a decent-sized bear came to eat. George kept them occupied with stories of hunts he'd had in the past. He had a million of them, and soon Lester realized that this was a very friendly and fun guy to be around.

"We'll have to take the road past the ridge and then over by the river. It's not much of a river 'cause it's purty shallow this time o' year, but there's enough water to still attract animals, and that's what we want."

As they drove, the darkness gave way to light, and they could see the outlines of the trees, sticks now that most of the leaves had fallen, but eerie shadows just the same. It wouldn't be long before full light so they had to hurry. As they neared the ridge, Lester asked, "What's that up ahead? Looks like a person in the road."

"That'll be Wyatt," said George.

"What's he doing there at this time?"

"Same as us, he's a bear hunter guide too."

Tommy groaned, "I don't like or trust that guy."

As they drove closer, Lester said, "Hey, let's not go any closer, that guy has an assault rifle!"

"Yeah, he always has one with him, but he's all bark and no bite. I know him and I'll handle this. He's probably going to ask why we're going to our blind this way. Thinks he owns all the land."

Lester was nervous. He had never hunted in such a wild place and he wanted out, right now. "Yes, but he has a banana clip on that thing. Probably has, at least, thirty rounds."

As they approached, Wyatt stood right in the middle of the road with the rifle held up high and his left-hand motioning to stop. "What the hell you doing on this road again? I told you to stay away from my bait pile."

"We're not going to your bait pile; we're going to ours. The one we been using all year and for the past many years. You need to know that you don't own all of this, and we can put bait wherever we are allowed to."

"Just not here," Wyatt hollered.

"You need to get out of the way 'cause it will be full light purty soon. We need to get to our spot."

"You aren't going past me," shouted Wyatt.

"Then we'll go around you, won't we," laughed George.

Lester then said, "Let's just go back for now, George."

"Do as the man said! You'd better turn around now!" yelled Wyatt.

"No way." At that George started to slowly move his truck forward.

As the truck moved forward, Lester begged George, "Man, he's got an assault rifle, let's turn back."

George laughed, "No way."

Just as the truck made it first movement, Wyatt went berserk, aiming his rifle at the truck and unloading thirty rounds into the cab.

October 21, 2019, 7:30 a.m.

Daryl was happy that he was able to get so much information from the girls, plus he now had a videotape which he could use to take down the teacher. He was sure that everything could go as planned, so he took it upon himself to arrest Joe on suspicion of rape and abuse of a minor. He went directly to Mr. Joe's house to get him and take him to jail, but in case there would be any problems, he had called Deputy Jason to come and help. He used his cell phone because they had an excellent signal in several areas since fall.

Northern Michigan University had helped the school district get their system up and running. The whole area was now served, and the young people were especially happy.

Two cars pulled up to Joe's house around seven-thirty a.m. Daryl and Jason parked back-to-back. Daryl headed for the front door, and Jason went around to the back just in case.

Daryl knocked. "Hello, anyone home?" he yelled. He was very excited. He knocked again and again. Finally, he heard footsteps.

"Yes," Joette said quietly. "We're home. Come in, Daryl." Joette looked like she had just gotten out of bed. She was dressed with slippers, T-shirt, and shorts, but she looked like she hadn't slept a wink.

"You must know why I'm here," he said, not even apologizing for the early hour.

"No, not really. But I can guess. You know this is all crazy." Joette looked frazzled and out of sorts. Her hair was not combed and her eyes had dark circles around them.

"Rape is a serious matter, and this is not crazy. Is the teacher home?"

"You mean my husband, Joe."

"Yeah, yeah, that's who I mean."

"Just a moment. Joe, Joe, we have company."

Joe emerged from the back room in a T-shirt and jeans. He looked muscular and ready for a fight. He had not slept in two days, and he knew the seriousness of the claims against him. He wondered if he could get the individual to tell the truth about whatever it was that she was insinuating. "Yes, what do you want, Daryl?"

"I'm here to bring you in, sir," he said with a smug look as he pulled out his handcuffs. "You'll have to be cuffed, so put your hands behind your back."

"Hey, this isn't right. You don't have any proof of anything—and you're going to arrest me. What gives you the right to be the judge and jury?"

"Well, just keep quiet and turn around."

"I'm not turning around. You have no right. I just got off the phone with my lawyer, and he said there is no proof of anything yet."

"Doesn't matter. You're coming with me either quietly or I can use force."

"You and whose army, my friend. You're not taking me anywhere. I'm going to fight this, and the truth will come out."

At that, Daryl pulled out his Glock 22 and aimed it right at Joe.

Joette screamed when she saw the weapon. "Put that away, Daryl, no one is going to do anything stupid."

Daryl just said, "I have fifteen rounds that say that's the truth, and if you'll turn around, you'll see Jason in the back door just waiting for my signal."

At that, Joe knew he had to go along with him so no one would get hurt. "OK, just wait, and I'll get my jacket and put on a pair of shoes."

"Hold it right there. Don't move or I'll shoot. Your wife can get those for you while I cuff you."

Joette yelled at Daryl, "You're being ridiculous, Daryl." While saying this she retrieved a jacket and shoes for Joe. "Here you go, Joe."

Daryl was on him in a second with cuffs, clamping them as tightly as he could until Joe said, "Hey, that really hurts."

"Too bad, Lover Boy, you're with the law now."

"You know, Daryl, I'd have never said this before, but you are one kind of jerk."

"Yeah, too bad. Get your butt outside and into that squad car. This'll be a joy taking you in."

"Where are you taking him?" yelled Joette.

"For starters, we'll head to the St. Ignace lock up. From there I'll just let the system take care of that. Let's go."

At the car, Daryl shoved Joe inside and slammed the door hard. He was so pumped to have this man out of his and the group's hair. Now, he thought, they could really make some progress without anyone poking around. Daryl knew his real boss, not Charlie, not anyone around here, would be very happy. He would have to contact him to let him know. Maybe there will be a reward!

Joette wasn't about to let this take its course without a fight. Joe had told her the story about how he was getting close to an answer when Charlie had interfered. She decided to take a leave of absence and do some inspecting of her own. She'd let Cathy know so someone was aware of what she was doing—and how she was going to investigate this to get Joe back home. "HOME," she said aloud, "is this really going to be home anymore? What in the world am I going to do?"

October 21, 2019, 7:35 a.m.

Wyatt looked at George's truck cab. It was riddled with bullet holes and blood was everywhere. He didn't care. "That's what you get, you old son of a bitch. Thought you were better than me, did you? Well, here you go. Have another round." He put in another clip and let ten more rounds fly directly at George. The body jumped a lot as round after round hit and split him almost in two. "There you go!"

Wyatt thought for a minute and then realized he had to get the bodies out of the truck and up the hill where he could bury them. He'd have to bury the truck too. He could dump that in the hole in the ground down the road from his place, but even though it was about fifteen feet deep, he'd have to cover it with a lot of dirt.

"I guess I'll take the old man out first. I can drag him a lot easier than those other two," he said calmly.

Tommy was still breathing and heard everything.

Wyatt pulled George out and dropped him on the ground. Lester's body slid to the driver's side and his head flopped over like it might fall off. Wyatt jumped a bit thinking he was still alive, but he only laughed when he saw the blood flowing out of him onto the seat. Wyatt noticed some rope in the back of George's truck, so he decided to tie a rope around George so he could drag him up the hill. He could put the rope over his shoulder and dig his feet into the ground. He tied him up and tried to move him, but it didn't work. He'd have to drag him a little at a time.

Tommy squinted a bit so he could see what was happening, but his eyes were cloudy with tears. He realized that Wyatt was going to take his uncle to the top of the ridge, but he had his rifle over his shoulder and Tommy thought he might have about twenty rounds, so he tried not to move while he made a mental check to make sure he wasn't hurt.

Wyatt got very close to the top of the ridge with George and looked back at the truck. All was quiet, very quiet. Sometimes when alone in the woods a person can hear himself thinking. This was one of those times for Wyatt. Man, the boss is not going to like what I've done. Wyatt took a deep breath and heaved the body the last few feet up the hill. It was exhausting work.

Tommy saw his chance. He had to quietly open the door and get out. The ridge was on one side of him, the river on the other. If he could make it to the river, he could run in it because it was so shallow that it was almost dry, and he knew it had a firm bottom. Slowly, centimeter by centimeter, his hand moved for the door handle. It took a long time because he did not want any movement to be enough for Wyatt to notice. His hand grabbed the handle.

Just then he heard Wyatt grunt real loud. He looked up and Wyatt had thrown the body near the ridge and was headed back to the truck. Tommy knew he could not wait for him to take the next body out. It was too risky, and what if he decides to riddle Lester and him with bullets too? Now was the only chance he had. He cranked on the handle and sprang out of the door. His 6'2" frame was too large for his exit, and as he hurried, he smashed his head against the top of the door frame. The noise of the door and the bang of his head alerted Wyatt, and when he looked at the truck, he saw that Tommy was on his feet and running for the river. He knew this was child's play: him, the AK-47, and Tommy—no chance.

October 21, 2019, 7:50 a.m.

Paige was very excited about everything that had transpired this week. She was once again the center of attention. She could hardly wait to tell everyone—and get the sympathy she deserved.

She had been overlooked too long. Because she had Wi-Fi available now, and her cell worked better than ever, she had been texting her girlfriends from home, since her mother made her take several days off. She was excited about telling her friends exactly what was going on. She probably should have kept to herself until the word got out that Mr. Joe was arrested, but she didn't care. One of her texts went to Wendy, Tommy's girlfriend, who idolized Mr. Joe in a good way. He was her hero and represented what every teacher and parent should be.

Wendy was at school early when she received the message, and she was upset at Paige's text and wanted to know exactly what had happened, but she could not find Paige—maybe she wasn't at school yet, so she texted:

> Hey, Paige, I just got your text and was wondering exactly what is going on. Could you clue me in?

Paige did not like Wendy that much, but she was popular and she wanted to get in on that too, so she decided to get back to her.

> I just told the truth about our teacher. That's all. Like how he took advantage of me during the play last year.

Wendy was really interested now:

> Took advantage of u? How? Do u mean in school during play practice?

Paige wasn't ready for questions, because she was worried that she might say something wrong, so she tried to keep it short and to the point and end the conversation.

> Yes, it was in the prop room when we were alone. Like he put his hands all over me. I tried to scream, but he covered my mouth. He's so strong! That's all I can say right now. Good talking to you.

Wendy responded:

> OK. See u soon. I hope u r feeling better.

Wendy was furious now. Paige was a liar, always had been, and she loved the spotlight. This was just like her to say something like this, but Mr. Joe would never do anything like that. He would apologize if he bumped into anyone. He was the best thing that had happened to this community in a long time.

She wanted to talk to Tommy, but she knew that since he graduated last year, he spent all of his time with his uncle guiding clients on bear hunts. Maybe she could call him. No, they might be in the middle of a hunt, and she didn't want to bother him.

Of course, it wouldn't have mattered since Tommy's phone was still in his backpack in the bed of his uncle's truck.

Wendy thought she would go to Mr. Joe's room, hoping he would be there today. He had been absent the last part of last week and no one knew why, but now she knew what the reason probably was. She suddenly gasped out loud, "I bet that liar Paige got Mr. Joe in trouble—and he had to leave school."

Now she was on a mission. She thought, I wonder if his wife is here today, and so she swiftly turned around in the hall and headed to the elementary wing. When she got to the classroom, a sub was sitting at the desk. "Well, that makes sense," she said to no one. "I bet they are trying to figure out what happened." She then realized that she had to speak to Mr. Joe and his wife today after school.

October 21, 2019, 7:55 a.m.

Tommy was fast, but who can outrun a bullet, so he thought he better run zig-zag to the river. Once there he could turn right and run in the middle and Wyatt would lose his line of sight. Wyatt raised his rifle; it was like old times in the Marines, but he was moving and breathing heavily and too excited to shoot and his bullets carried above Tommy, so he lowered his aim and shot the rest of the clip. He missed.

Tommy was running as fast as he could as bullets were flying over his head. He felt his boonie hat move forward. Had he been hit? He kept running. Wyatt put in a new box clip and fired away. Wyatt had run out of banana clips and so had fewer bullets, and he expended them in a second. They flew around Tommy like mosquitoes attacking, and he kept running out of sheer terror.

Tommy was taking deep breaths now. His lungs burned and he could hardly think or breathe. He kept running as fast as he could. If only he could get to the bend in the river, then he could outmaneuver Wyatt. Wyatt was running down the hill to the river now. He wasn't too fast, but he didn't need to be. He just had to get there before Tommy turned the corner at the bend.

For Tommy, the bend in the river seemed to be a mile away, but it was really only about 100 yards. His legs were feeling heavy and his breath was fast and furious. He couldn't keep this pace up much longer.

Wyatt reached the river and put in his last box clip. He had ten rounds to make this count. You'd think that Wyatt could have easily hit Tommy, but his movement and Tommy's made it that much more difficult. He saw Tommy near the bend in the river and he started shooting. It was over 200 yards to Tommy, but close enough for him—except that he was breathing heavily. He fired quickly, but Tommy had reached the bend and dove for the river's edge just before he fired. The bullets went over his body. Wyatt started to chase him down the river, but he had no more clips. His Glock hung at his side so he tried that, but he didn't have any good shots, so he kept chasing.

Tommy realized that Wyatt had stopped shooting and when he looked back, he could see him running after him. He bolted to his feet and ran as fast as he could. He knew these woods well having spent many years with his uncle hunting all parts of this country, so he cut into the woods at a spot he recognized and headed for town.

Once Wyatt got to the bend in the river, he thought he would have a shot, but he had lost him. His next thoughts were either to pursue Tommy—or get back to his cabin, get his truck, and get the hell out of the area.

Tommy kept running through the woods. It was difficult since this was a very dense woods, which meant that he was making a lot of noise brushing aside and stepping on branches. He knew if Wyatt caught up to him that it would be the end, so he did not stop to rest even though he was almost puking up a lung, and his legs were like jelly. He needed to find anybody who could help.

Tommy figured he was about two miles from town, but if he could find some loggers, he could get a ride in right away, but no luck. He was now walking, hoping he was ahead of Wyatt. His feet and clothes were wet and torn, and he was full of blood from head to knees. He wanted to cry for his uncle and the guy who got shot, but his heart was pounding so hard that it hurt, and no tears would come. He took off his boonie hat for a minute to cool down a bit when he noticed a bullet hole, and he almost fainted; he had to hold himself up on a tree, and then he vomited, all his breakfast coming up in spasms of puking and shaking.

He finally stopped and looked up and noticed that the sun was almost all the way up now. Sunrise in the U.P. in late October is around eight-fifteen, so he figured he hadn't been running that long—and that made him nervous. Where was Wyatt?

October 21, 2019, 8:05 a.m.

Wyatt decided to follow Tommy through the woods. He knew it would get lighter, but he wasn't sure he could find his tracks since there was so much thick brush and marsh land. After a few minutes in the brush, he gave up and decided to return to his cabin. He turned around and wasn't quite sure how to get out of this spot because it was so dense, but he moved forward and finally saw an opening leading to the almost dry riverbed. He turned and ran back to the cabin.

Once he reached the truck, he screamed, "F##K," as loud as he could. He realized he had to get the other body to the ridge and then bury both, and he had to ditch the truck. Wyatt muttered, "If that kid reaches town before I can do that, I'm screwed." He hastily grabbed the body from the truck and pulled the man out, but by this time he was fatigued. This guy was very heavy, and Wyatt knew it would take a while, so he suddenly just dropped the man and sprinted to the cabin. He took George's body and rolled it to the cesspool that had been installed weeks earlier, lifted the cover and threw him in.

Then he headed back to the other man. He thought of digging a grave next to where the man was, but that would be too easy to spot and would take time, and time was important right now, so he decided to take his four-wheeler and load the man on and then drive his body to the cesspool and drop him in. He ran back to the cabin and fired up his machine. It did not take long to load the body on it and walk the machine and the body to the cesspool.

Next, he jumped into the truck and drove it to the ravine. He stopped just before, got out, and let George's truck roll down. He was satisfied when it buried itself in the foliage below. Then he went back and covered the trail and the mess around the truck. He got his Ford Ranger loaded with all his things and decided to hit the road, but not before he torched the inside of his cabin. He burned as much as he could of anything of his, but left the cabin a skeleton still standing. Then he thought, *the big boss is not going to be happy*. Could be he'll blame it on my old man, and that'd be sweet! This all took time, but he felt it necessary. By nine a.m. he was headed for U.S.-2 going west.

October 21, 9:15 a.m.

It took Tommy until after nine to reach a house on the outskirts of Colewin. He didn't see anyone around, so he immediately went to the door and began pounding and yelling. "Help, help me!"

He heard footsteps in the cabin and when the door opened, he faced a double-barrel shotgun about head level. The woman said, "What the hell you want?" Then she recognized Tommy who looked like hell himself with blood all over and soaked to the bone.

She put down the shotgun and said, "Tommy, what's wrong?"

But Tommy could not speak. He kept choking on his words and spitting out phlegm.

She took him by the arm and led him to a chair where she was able to calm him a bit and he was able to speak. "That guy on the ridge killed Uncle George and his hunter."

Shocked, she asked, "What, are you sure he killed them?"

"Yes. Call the sheriff. The hunter he killed was a cop from downstate." And then Tommy passed out, knocking his head on a cup and pushing it across the table.

She made sure Tommy was all right before she went to the phone. She decided to call the Michigan State Police first. "Hello, this is Sheila Hanson out in Colewin. I got a kid here who says his uncle and a cop were killed by a guy living over here. You need to get here quick and find out everything, and call the sheriff so I don't have to."

The startled officer asked, "Ma'am, who is this again and what happened?"

"That's all I know, get over here. My fire number is 21943. We're just a quarter mile outside of Colewin. Get here quick."

The officer never got his answer because she hung up, but he had a car on the way immediately, and he notified all law enforcement that a police officer had been shot and possibly killed. He notified all officers in St. Ignace, Manistique, and his own post in Newberry. He also realized that if the man ran, he would have to exit on U.S.-2 or M-28 and so he called for road blocks trying to pin him in even though they weren't sure what the guy looked like, but they would get that soon. He didn't think he would try Lake Michigan as an escape, but he had to get some people on that too. He also said over the airwaves, "Troopers, be on the lookout for anything suspicious, especially anyone speeding or looking out of place."

October 21, 2019, 9:35 a.m.
Wyatt had driven as fast as he could through the two-track trail and then the wider dirt road as he turned west. He had to drive slower as he moved through Colewin. He didn't want to draw any attention, and most people did not know his truck so he thought he was good going through town.

"Wow, nice truck," shouted a young boy who was skateboarding on the sidewalk on his way to school.

"Just what I don't need, someone noticing my truck," Wyatt said angrily. "I need to get through town quickly." He picked up a bit more speed, but not too much. As he passed through Colewin, he was doing about fifty, the most this road would allow, but as he reached U. S.-2 and Lake Michigan at nine forty-five a.m., he put the pedal down hard and was cruising at seventy-five before he knew it. The speed limit was sixty-five here, so he thought he might be all right as long as he slowed through some of the small towns.

By ten a.m. Wyatt was past M-117 and the iconic town of Engadine that Sonny Elliott had made famous, and headed west toward Manistique. He had slowed to sixty-eight, feeling that he could get by at that speed. Near Gould City, he passed a blue state police car that was heading east at a high speed. "Are they after me already? I need to find someplace to hole up for a while until this cools off." He remembered a small resort north of Manistique near Highway 94, and as he recalled Fifth Street, a place he had scoped out for bear hunting and fishing. He thought he could get there by about eleven a.m. "I won't get a room. I'll just lay low a bit north of the cabins where I know there's a nice, abandoned campground."

By ten-forty he was taking a right turn in Manistique headed for the campground that he knew would be a good place for him to hide for a while. He had plenty of food, sleeping bags, tent, bug dope, a small heater, and ammunition if it came to that. He would pitch his tent in the brush where no one would look.

By ten fifty-five he was near the cabins he had remembered, and it was just as he had thought. He said aloud, "I gotta take a left at L, it started with an L, I know, LaD." Then he saw it, LaDuc Street. He took a left and he kept driving for another fifteen minutes past the Bear Trap Resort and found the campsite, but to his horror, it was filled with campers. It looked like someone had fixed it up and put in outdoor toilets and running water. "Now what?" he exclaimed.

Several campers had seen his truck pull a U-turn and head back down the only road. Where would he go now?

October 21, earlier that morning around 9:45

Just after Wyatt had left Colewin at nine forty-five a.m., a blue state police car came racing down U.S.-2 from Newberry. It blew down the dirt road and into Colewin where it turned right and headed straight for the fire number that had been identified at the office and relayed to Mark, one of the finest troopers around. He was talking to himself as he drove, "I have got to hurry and find this place. The dispatcher said he killed a cop or thought he killed a cop and a civilian. We gotta find this guy quickly or he'll find a way out."

The officer pulled into the home at fire number 21943, stopped the car, bolted out the door, and ran up to the house. He pounded on the door, and it swung open. Sitting at the table were Tommy and the woman whose house Tommy had found, and she was holding a double-barrel shotgun aimed at the door. Tommy was still a mess and afraid that Wyatt might have followed him.

"Come on in. We've been waiting for you. Here's the kid, name's Tommy, who gave me the information."

"Ma'am could you put down the weapon?" Trooper Mark strode to the table and took a look at Tommy whose head was hanging and whose whole demeanor was terror-stricken. The woman lowered the shotgun.

"You all right, young man? Could you give me some details, and the quicker we get them, the sooner we can get after this person. There was a killing right?"

Tommy looked up. "He could still be following me. I ran from his place through the creek and down the river. He was right behind me, and he had an assault rifle and likely the Glock that he carries."

"Don't worry about him right now. We have men in the woods already and people on their way here. Soon there will be a lot of law out here, so can you give me some details?"

"He was the guy who lives on the ridge. Everyone calls him Wyatt, and he has a lot of firepower at his cabin."

"What exactly did he do, son?"

"We were up near the ridge, headed to our blind. We were in the truck, the three of us in the cab. My Uncle George was driving, and I was in the passenger seat and a cop, his name was Lester, was in the middle. Wyatt unloaded his rifle into the cab and killed them instantly. He thought he had killed me too and he began dragging the bodies out of the truck, and I, well, I just ran. Somehow, I made it here. Look, look at my hat. There's a bullet hole right through it. I almost died. He killed my uncle and that guy." Then Tommy began to sob, huge heaving sobs so loud that the trooper almost teared up.

"OK, I'll get this message to headquarters so they can be searching the right area. Thanks for that, and I won't leave until you have more protection. If you want, we can take you home, Tommy. And ma'am, we can keep someone here to protect you too."

"Oh, I got protection right here in my hands, and when my husband comes home, he'll have more protection in his, but thanks anyway."

"I think I'll assign a couple of guys here for the night just in case." As he said that, he heard sirens closing in on the place. "This must be them now. Come on, son, we'll take you home."

October 21, 2019, 10:15 a.m.

Joette paced around the living room wondering if she should take a ride out to the area where Joe had been to see what she could find out, but she knew that she needed help. "Ron! I've got to call Ron and Shanice. They'll know what to do." Joette raced to the landline in the kitchen and called the number. She was so nervous that she had to try three times before she got it right. "Hello, Ron?"

"No, this is Shanice. Is this Joette?"

"Yes, Shanice, I am at my wit's end. Joe has been arrested, and I need help. He has the union rep on standby and the guy is finding out what he can, but I need to do something."

"What the heck? Joe, the model citizen arrested. He wouldn't hurt a flea."

"I know, but two women, or one woman and a young girl have accused him of rape or something like that."

"What! No way, not Joe. Here, let me get Ron on the other phone." Ron was at school, so Shanice set up three-way calling. "Ron, it's me. Joette is on the line."

"Hey, what's up? How is everything in Colewin?"

"Just terrible, Ron, I need your help. It's about Joe. He has been arrested!"

"What! Joe? Why, what's going on?"

"I think it has something to do with what he was investigating." Joette informed Ron of all that had transpired since he had left, as well as all she knew of the accusations.

Ron was mystified. "If you need help, I'm there. You can count on me as soon as I can get out of here, but, please, don't go investigating by yourself. Joe and I got a real bad feeling when we did, and we didn't even get close, but I have some ideas and I'll let you know when I get there."

"We'll pack as soon as we get home," yelled Shanice into the phone.

"Joette, don't do anything until we get there, promise."

"OK, Ron, I promise."

October 21, 2019, 10:20 a.m.

Just as Joette hung up the phone, she heard a knock on the door. "Now, who is that?" Immediately, she thought Cathy or Wayne, but it was neither. Standing in her doorway was Wendy.

"Wendy, what are you doing here at this time of day? You should be in school."

"You should too, Mrs. Joe." Funny how kids are about nicknames and calling Joette by her husband's first name, but that's how it is in schools where both spouses teach in the same building.

"Seriously, what are you doing out of school?"

"I couldn't take it. I heard about Mr. Joe—and I just like have to do something. At first, I thought I would come here after school, but then I realized that this is a real mess, and I need to do something."

"Really, what can anyone do right now? I'm not even sure what to do."

"Well, a bunch of us girls were talking at school, and we are sure that Paige is like probably lying. She is a constant liar, and when she did not get picked for the play, she kept swearing and said she would get even one day. And if she is lying, so is that other lady. Paige said that Mr. Joe abused her in the prop room. She was seldom there, and when she was, most of the other stage crew were there too, so how could that happen? Once she didn't get the lead, we never saw her again."

"We need to let the authorities know all this. I think a lawyer for Mr. Joe will be at the school this coming week, and my friend Shanice is a lawyer too, and you have to make sure you and any other girls tell the lawyers what you know."

Joette and Wendy proceeded to brainstorm for a plan to get the truth out of Paige and Lane—truth that would free Joe.

October 21, 2019, 11:27 a.m.

At eleven-twenty Wyatt was back on Highway 94 wondering which way to go. His instincts told him to turn left and head farther north. He kept driving until he reached a little mission church and passed it until he saw a less-traveled road. Then he took a very fast right, spitting dirt, and he drove until he could find a good hiding place in the woods. He felt safe and alone deep in the forest—or so he thought.

But a few church members and the pastor of the church noticed the truck taking a crazy wild right turn. The pastor commented saying to the others, "Did you see that truck moving down the road so fast? It took that old road up ahead on two wheels. Wow, some people are crazy."

The police had raided Wyatt's cabin in the woods. They did not find the bodies and were a little wary until they uncovered blood on the road near the cabin, and tire tracks that seemed to have torn up the dirt and left in a hurry. They had ten officers searching the woods and checking everything out. Four stayed to search further, and the rest followed the tracks as best they could, all the way to Colewin.

In Colewin, officers talked to a lot of people, and a few knew of Wyatt.

"I've seen him around. He didn't come into town much, but one night we saw him and another guy at the Sportsman's Pizza place. They were very drunk, but that's about the only time I saw him."

"Any idea what he drove?" the officer asked.

"Not sure. All I know is that it was a truck, but I couldn't tell you what kind it was."

After checking with several people around town, the officer checked with Mayor Don, and sure enough, he said, "I thought he drove a Ford Ranger, black."

"Thank you. If you have any other information, let us know."

"Sure will."

"Thank you."

Don was worried. "Do you have any idea where he is?"

"Not yet, but we have officers with road blocks all the way to Escanaba, Munising, St. Ignace, even Marquette, Sault Ste. Marie, and the Mackinac Bridge, and that's only a few of the places, so he's not going to get away, especially now that we have a lead on his truck."

The Manistique police, once they had the make and color, put out information on the radio, television, and the internet, and began asking the public whether they had any information. Soon they received several hits about a black Ford Ranger, especially one that was very interesting from a pastor of a church way up on 94.

October 21, 2019, 11:00 a.m.

Back in Colewin, people were just finding out about George. George was one of the beloved people of the town, and everyone knew him. It was a loss for Colewin, his positive attitude and upbeat personality would be missed at the Sportsman's Pizzeria and Bar.

But not everyone shared the same remorse. Charlie was feeling sadness for the loss of a friend, but more so, he was feeling that he had made a big mistake letting Wyatt in on the intricate workings of the militia. Holding his phone, he talked to it like he was talking to someone, "Hell, I gotta call Daryl and 121nythi' this out. We might have some real trouble if that guy is caught."

"Hello, Daryl here."

"Are you in on all this stuff about Wyatt?"

"Yes, it's a police matter, and I'm stationed at a roadblock near St. Ignace. You shouldn't be calling me so hang up. I'll talk to you when I'm not on duty. That might be a while until Wyatt is caught, but keep your mouth shut and stay off the phone."

"You," is all Charlie got out before Daryl hung up on him. "That guy pisses me off." He threw his phone on the passenger seat of his truck. He thought he had better see if he could find out any details, and then head out to the bunker to figure out what they would have to do if the investigation led there.

October 21, 2019, 11:00 a.m.

Joette and Wendy sat down and talked for a bit, and then as Joette offered Wendy some homemade chocolate chip cookies, her cell phone rang. She knew it must be Cathy since few others ever call her on her cell, but Cathy was at school. Joette answered, sure enough, "Hello, Cathy. What's up?" All of a sudden Joette's face turned red and her eyes seemed to bulge out of her face. "What! When did it happen?" Something was horribly wrong. She looked at Wendy as big tears formed in the corner of her eyes.

Wendy saw all this and cried, "What's wrong?"

"It's George. Somebody said he's been hurt badly, maybe even…" And she stopped there, not wanting to alarm Wendy.

Terrified, Wendy asked, "What's going on? Was Tommy with him?"

"OK, thanks for calling and letting us know." Joette let the phone drop on the table after the call. "I don't have any other information. Cathy said that she had just heard about it. It sounds like there was a shooting."

"I have to get to Tommy's house and find out if he's all right."

"Yes, I'll take you there."

"No, I drove out. I have my mother's car here."

"Well then, I'll follow you. You shouldn't be alone right now. I'll just grab a jacket and my purse and we can leave."

Seconds later they were on the way to Tommy's house, tearing up the road as their tires spun down the dirt road.

October 21, 2019, 12:45 p.m.

After setting up camp Wyatt created a perimeter to the front, so if a vehicle came down the road, he would easily see it. He was all set for now, but he was very thirsty, and he realized he had only one bottle of water and no beer. He then mumbled, "I need to get water if I'm going to make it for any length of time." He had his truck buried in the woods and he had camouflaged the area, and he felt he had bought himself some time, so he decided to make a quick run to get water and some beer. He had passed a general store not too far away, so he could be there and back in no time, but just in case, he packed a lot of firepower.

Nervous and jittery, Wyatt kept talking to himself, "I can be there and back in no time, and then I should be good for a long time. I just have to be careful." He drove the speed limit, and it took only a few minutes to get to the store. He bought three cases of water and two cases of beer and was out of the store in no time. The young girl at the register didn't even bat an eye, just rang him up, and he made a few trips to the truck from the store, and he was on the way.

Just as Wyatt spun out to 94 again, he saw three police cars heading north. That made him nervous. He thought he might go south a bit and wait out the police. "If I can find a good hiding place for a while, I should be OK," he murmured. He headed south, and just as he did, he saw two more state police cars heading north. Now he was really agitated. He grabbed his rifle off the passenger's seat just in case; then he saw in his rearview mirror the two state police cars make a U-turn. "Shit, why didn't I just stay put? Now I've got to lose them. I'll head for Manistique and try to get back to the Hiawatha National Forest. I can lose them on the back trails where I'll be able to hide."

Wyatt was doing eighty-five, with both squad cars hot on his tail. Then he saw three more police cars with lights flashing heading from the south. He passed them, and he saw them do what the other police cars had done: stop and turn around. He was now doing ninety-five and his truck was bouncing up and down on the road. He feared he might tip over because the road was so rough in spots.

The officers in the cars behind him were in constant communication. They knew they had him now. There were roadblocks on both sides of Manistique, and if he tried to go either way, he'd be in trouble.

Wyatt knew he had to turn right to get to the forest, and he also knew he could not go to U.S.-2. It would be swarming with cops on the main artery. In no time he was in Manistique, and now had to slow some. He saw a chance to go right on Deer Street and 442. He took a wicked right on two wheels and lost control, his truck slid across the street and into a field where his truck stuck in the dirt. It tipped sideways, throwing him against the window hard, his air bags blew open, trapping him.

The cops saw what had happened and headed right for the truck, setting up in strategic positions and pulling out their weapons, ready for a showdown if he did not surrender.

Wyatt was stunned, but he was awake. He unhitched his seatbelt and stuck a knife in the airbag. His nose was bleeding and his right eye had a gash above it. He tried to get the truck moving, but it was stuck deep in a hole. He grabbed his rifle and turned toward the cops.

The officers had three rifles pointed at the truck as they announced, "Come out with your hands up and lie on the ground. Do it now!"

Wyatt heard, but he wasn't about to give in. He opened the door and crouched near the front wheel of his truck. It was tipped enough that it gave him some protection—and yet a line of sight to the cops. It was Afghanistan all over again, but this time there were no buds to back him up.

One of the officers said to the others, "Let's just let 'em have it. He's a cop killer. No one will ask questions."

"Can't do that, Len," one of the men yelled. "By the book."

Just then a volley of shots rang out, hitting the troopers' cars and smashing the window of the first one.

"There's your answer man," Len yelled. "Now we got just cause."

"OK, let 'im have it." Then a barrage of shots rang out, hitting the truck and filling it with holes. Just then two more police cars pulled up; then three more. The men jumped out and began shooting. The truck was just riddled, but Wyatt did not give up. He kept firing, just like he did in Afghanistan, and since he had several clips available, it was going to be a while unless someone got him.

Just then, the telltale *womp, womp, womp* of a helicopter roared in from the West. It looked like a UH-60 to Wyatt and he thought it might have an M134 minigun mounted on it. "Shit," was all Wyatt could say.

The police were surprised. They had no knowledge of a helicopter, and they wondered where this had come from.

"What the hell! I hope they're here to help," yelled Len.

"Must be the boss. He's ex-military and has a lot of friends."

Just then the radio buzzed and a trooper from the Manistique post yelled into the mic. "Hey, this is me, Pete, got this chopper to give me a lift. What's the plan?"

The chopper swooped around, and then Pete's voice broke in again, speaking to the leader on the ground. They strategized, and the plan was to get behind Wyatt, and if he did not give in to take him out. The pilot just needed to get a good angle and avoid the electrical wires and trees on that side of the road. Wyatt had good cover from both his truck and the trees, so the chopper would have to get either real high or go down the road and get real low, away from the tree line.

"Yeah, just take him out if he resists at all. He killed a cop, remember," the lead officer blared into his mic.

"Roger that." Flying low, the pilot sent out a warning from the chopper, but all Wyatt did was fire about twenty rounds at the chopper that was not very far off. He put a few holes in the fuselage, which pissed off the pilot and the guy manning the gun, so as soon as the chopper gunner had a shot, he opened up and let Wyatt have it. The shots tore into Wyatt and threw him against the fender of the truck, and it literally tore the sheet metal and plastic right off the truck.

There was a cheer from the police as they all settled down a bit and looked on. It was quiet.

The pilot of the helicopter reported, "Well, that guy won't be making any more trouble. He's on the ground and not moving. Lots of blood. You can slowly move in and check him out."

"Roger," said the lead officer on the hunt. With weapons ready, the cops moved slowly in to check out the body. When they got close, they knew it was over. He was mostly in one piece, but it did not look good.

"Good job, up there, gunner. You got him!"

"Just doin' my job, but thanks man," and the chopper swung right, swooping higher into the sky and was gone.

October 21, 2019

Charlie did some asking around and found out as much as he could about what must have gone on near the ridge today. There wasn't much, other than most people had heard that George and some law officer had been killed. Most people in Colewin knew that Tommy hung close to his uncle—and they were worried about him too. The word was that Tommy was all right, but nobody had seen him yet. Charlie really wanted to know what happened out there and how involved Wyatt was. Most said he was the one who pulled the trigger, and that a manhunt was on for him. He decided to find Mayor Don, to see what he knew.

As Charlie headed to the town hall, Don came out of the building, half running and half walking to his car. "Hey, Don," Charlie yelled.

"Hey, Charlie."

"Have you heard anything' about what happened out on the ridge?"

"Yeah, think I got most of the story. Just spoke with Daryl. They got him."

"Got who?"

"Wyatt. Somewhere in Manistique. I guess he tried to hole up out there. Musta thought he could outrun the law. Bad decision."

"Why the hell he go that way? Although I can see he'd have some good hiding in the National Forest if he could get there."

"Yep, not sure. I gotta run, Charlie. See you later."

"Sure. Take care. This whole thing puts a bad mark on our little town. Wish'd that guy had never come here."

"I'm thinking the same thing. See ya."

Charlie now knew that Wyatt's actions might get more people coming to the area, and he had to do something to make sure no one found the bunker. But how? He crossed the street and headed for his truck, and then he figured he had better head out there. "Wonder what that other psycho is gonna do next?" He started his truck, and roared down the street heading right for the road to the bunker.

Bates was in the bunker and was in constant communication with Escanaba and the Lower Peninsula. He was also watching what was going on with Wyatt. They had become friends, but not in the sense that others become friends, but only for drinking and carousing. Other than that, he didn't care what Wyatt did.

Then he came across the news. "Holy shit! They killed Wyatt. That stupid shit. I told him he was in for trouble if he kept harassing that bear guide, and now he's gone and done it to himself. Well, good riddance, you stupid jerk," but he felt a pang in his gut like something you feel when you're really excited. Then the door opened and was slammed shut.

"Bates, you hear about that guy Wyatt, your buddy?"

"He ain't my buddy. We just hang out."

"Well, that SOB is dead. They got him. He was trying to go somewhere, and they found him in Manistique."

Bates showed no emotion. "Huh, he was a crazy dude. You know anything about him?"

"Nothing, 'cept he messed up our town and our militia. I'm glad he didn't try to hide out here."

Bates continued, "Sure, you would be. You don't know anything about the guy. He was actually a spoiled rich kid, you know. His parents live in Chicago and are loaded. They disowned him after he came back home from Afghanistan. They thought he went off the deep end, and maybe he did, but they didn't want to deal with it. Gave him a bunch of money and said, get the hell out. Thought it would do him some good if they sent him to the U.P. Guy actually liked the U.P. because of Hemingway. Wyatt had read some book about his fishing and hunting up here, and so he decided to come here. You know the tough-life, tough-guy stuff."

Charlie was confused. "Who the hell is this Heming' guy? Not sure I know 128nything' bout that. How the hell you know this?"

"We used to do a lot of talking when we went out. He once said something about working for the boss. Like he knew the boss! His parents got him involved to get him out of Chicago. He was supposed to take over here, and he pretty much did. I listened as much as I could, but that man needed something more than that. People call me a psycho, but really, he was the psycho. I just don't care about other people. Don't care what happens to them, just leave me alone."

"No shit! Yeah, you're sane all right."

"Listen, I keep to myself and work for these loonies because they pay me well, but I can take it or leave it. I just keep to myself."

Charlie said, "Well, this time I think the bunker might be in trouble if the law starts snoopin' around because of what happened. They'll know he was part of our group."

"Too bad. They had big plans for your place. Probably going to change now. They want the bunker to be increased by three or four times its size, and they want to bring in helicopters. Did you know we already got a delivery of small rockets the other night?"

"What? Why didn't they tell me?"

Bates said, "You weren't around. You've been too busy with the teacher thing. They came in late at night in a small covered truck. It looked just like something you'd see any day on the road."

"We're going to have to close things down a spell, so the cops and feds don't find what we have—and how we are connected to everyone. I'm going to get the troops out here to take all the road widening equipment outta here. Then we'll stop all meetings for several months. Maybe block the old road that we haven't worked on yet."

"Well, I'm going to be here."

"No, I think we'll have to shut 'er down completely. You can work out of the downstate location. Bates, you need to get the word out to everyone at the communications center as soon as you kin."

"You're not my boss, and you don't get to stop anything. I really don't care what you all do, but I want to get paid. It's my ticket out of this mess. Although, it'd be nice not to have to come up here in no man's land for a while. So, yeah, I'll let them know what you think."

"All right, I'm heading back to town to let everyone know. Let me know if you hear anything."

"Will do."

Charlie knew that they would have to shut down for three or four months, but it would be better than anyone catching on to the plan. He left, jumped into his truck, and headed back to Colewin as small flakes of snow hit the ground and fell on his windshield. He turned on his wipers and moaned, "Well, here she comes. We better get going on that equipment as soon as we can or we won't get it out until next spring."

Earlier that day, October 21, 2019, 11:15 a.m.
Joette and Wendy made it to Tommy's house in record time. When they pulled in, they noticed a few other cars in the driveway. One of them was a state trooper's. Wendy jumped out of her car and bolted to the front door calling, "Tommy, Tommy, oh my God, Tommy, be all right. You've got to be all right."

Joette was right behind her with the same thoughts. They had no idea Tommy was in the house lying on the couch. He was in perfect physical health, but healing his mental health at this point would take some time.

Wendy knocked and then just threw open the door and ran in. Joette was right behind her. "Is he all right? Please, tell me he's all right." She was met by Tommy's mom who threw her arms around Wendy and said, "Yes, he's here, but he's not in a good state." They cried and held each other for a long time. Joette just gave a huge sigh of relief. "It'll help to have you here. Go. Talk to him and listen if he talks."

In the corner of the kitchen leaning up against the counter, an officer was talking to Tommy's dad, George's brother, who was angry and ready to take someone out—Wyatt, if he hadn't been already. The word was that the police had killed him in a shoot-out in Manistique.

Wendy broke from the embrace and silently moved toward the living room. And there she was, holding his hand—Paige.

"What the hell are you doing here you lying, sneaky witch," shouted Wendy. Paige immediately knew who it was and looked up, and she quickly dropped Tommy's hand. Tommy looked like he was sleeping. His eyes were shut and his head was sunk into a pillow.

"I, I'm just here to show my support for this family. I liked George, too."

Joette was standing in the archway staring at Paige. She did not want to get into anything with her in front of these people who were mourning, so she quietly turned and left, giving her best to Tommy's parents.

Paige stood up and said, "Well, I guess I better be going."

"Yeah, I guess you better," Wendy said in a cold and distant voice.

Paige walked quickly past Wendy and out the door without another word. Wendy sat in the chair by Tommy and just looked at him as tears of rage ran down her face.

CHAPTER 9: *ME-TOO* WORKS

Thursday, October 31, 2019, 5:45 p.m.

When Ron and Shanice pulled into the driveway, Joette was on the porch waiting. They had been delayed on their end, working to be able to take time off. Ron had an easier time of it since he had many personal days he could use. Shanice had to finish work on a case she was involved in before the firm would let her take a week, but here they were.

Out of the car and stiff from the long drive, they grabbed their luggage and went straight to Joette. "How is it going? Has anything changed?"

"Not much. They still have Joe, but he is able to call occasionally. I spoke with him last night."

Shanice gave her a big hug and said, "Today we get him out of there on bail. What is it with this place anyway? How can you keep someone like that without any real proof?"

Joette replied, "I think that this whole thing is rigged—and that someone in the sheriff's office is in on it. That's all I can say."

"OK, honey, we'll get to the bottom of this."

The weather was getting colder, and snow flurries were in the forecast, so they decided to just take the rest of the day to talk over what was happening—and see if they could come up with something. Shanice also wanted to talk to some of the main people involved. "Have you talked to anyone about what went on at school so that the girl was able to come up with a story about abuse? Can you think of anything that might be off?"

"Well, the kids at school, specifically a girl named Wendy, told me that Paige, the girl who accused Joe, is a habitual liar, and she likes the spotlight. Joe didn't cast her in the school play, so she was very upset."

"Is there any way we could talk to the girl? The one who told you."

"Sure. I could call her. I haven't seen her lately because I've taken a leave of absence until this is over."

"OK, let's see what we can do."

November 1, 2019

Wendy was on a mission to get Mr. Joe out of the mess that Paige had helped cause. She had the students up in arms over it. Well, at least some who felt Mr. Joe was innocent. She cornered Paige in school and asked her why she did it.

"Why I did what?" Paige blurted.

"You know what I mean. Why did you lie about Mr. Joe?"

Paige looked around and didn't say much. No one was around, so she felt powerful. Then she twisted her face into an ugly snarl and said, "I hate him. The man is a moron who doesn't recognize talent when he sees it—he will live to regret that. Yes, we got him good, didn't we? He'll realize the mistakes he's made, and I don't even care."

"Then you did lie, didn't you? I knew it."

"Yeah, well, who cares what you think, and like I said, he'll rot." Then Paige laughed a loud, sinister laugh and walked away.

Wendy checked her phone. It had worked and she had a recording of Paige. It wasn't much, but maybe it would help in some way, but she realized if she were going to get anything better out of Paige, she'd have to befriend her. Hating her felt good because she had never really liked her, and now she knew that the girl was lying. "I'll just have to get on her good side, I guess," she whispered as she walked down the hall to her next class.

November 5, 2019

Joe was a bit despondent. He could not understand how they could be holding him on no evidence, but he had a hunch that Sheriff Daryl was behind a lot of it, and he knew it must have something to do with what he had been investigating. He knew that Lane had to be in on it too. She was an open member of the militia, as was Betty. How Paige fit into the whole scheme, he was not sure, but he could guess.

Ron, Shanice, and Joette headed for St. Ignace to see if they could talk to Joe. It took them about forty-five minutes until they parked in front of the station where Joe was being held.

They all walked up the steps to the door while brushing snow from their jackets. They had fought a small snowstorm all the way from Colewin. It was getting colder each day, with warnings of snow in the forecast, and Joette felt they had to hurry, or they might not be able to get to St. Ignace for several days.

They were greeted at the desk. "Hello, may I help you?"

Shanice was going to do all the talking since she had the most experience in this area. "Yes, we would like to see Joe DeLuca."

"Sorry, ma'am, he isn't allowed any visitors."

"Um, what about his lawyer?"

"Ah, lawyer, let me check."

The officer was gone a while, as they waited on a bench near the door. When he returned, he looked nervous and mumbled to them.

"Sorry, no can do. He's not able to have any visitors."

"Well, sonny, that's against the law. I am his lawyer and I will file for wrongful imprisonment."

"I'm sorry ma'am but that's the rule. You can call in a few days and he should be able to see you."

"Has bail been set yet?" Shanice asked.

"The judge said that in this case this guy should be held until further notice. No bail has been set."

"That is also illegal. Bail must be set in most cases. I can't imagine Joe would be considered a risk."

"Who's to say?"

"I want to speak to your superior, please."

"He won't see anyone right now. He has too much on his plate these days."

"Could you, at least, give me his name?"

"Sure, name's Daryl."

Joette jumped up and spoke when she heard the name, "I know him. He is in Colewin a lot, and I am sure he'll see me."

"Nope. You might as well go home. We'll contact you."

They all felt defeated, but they knew there was no way they were going to see Joe tonight. So, Shanice asked, "May we talk to him then, call him?"

"Too late for that now. See you. Have a good day."

When they left the building, they thought they should do more investigating, but the snow had picked up and it was coming from the south, so Joette said they had better get back home before U.S.-2 became impassable. If the wind kicked up over Lake Michigan, it could be a blinding storm, too dangerous to be on the road, and so they left St. Ignace.

Wednesday, November 6, 2019

Shanice was on the phone the first thing in the morning. She was able to get ahold of the judge, and sure enough bail had been set. She asked, "When might we be able to get Joe?"

The judge answered, "I think anytime. Check with the sheriff. However, you'll have to be careful. I guess there's a three-day blow kicking up, and you don't want to be on the road in that."

"Thank you. We'll make sure to check the weather first before we leave."

Joette had just watched the weather, and when Shanice told her what the judge had said, Joette agreed that they should stay put until the storm was over.

Ron was wondering if they could maybe check out the area that he and Joe tried to investigate in October.

"I wouldn't do anything like that in this storm. You could get messed up in the woods and not find your way out. We'll just have to sit quietly. Hopefully, we will be able to talk to him later today."

Thursday, November 7

School was cancelled for a few days in Colewin due to the storm, and so all was quiet. Wendy kept trying to text Paige, but she would not answer.

9 a.m.

> Hey, Paige. How r u doing? This storm is crazy.

10:15 a.m.

> Paige, have u heard anything from Sheila? She was wondering if we could get together if the storm lets up.

10:30 a.m.

Hello, are u all right? Haven't heard
anything from u in a while.

Paige did not like snow days when she had to stay home alone,
nearly alone. Her mom and dad were there, but they weren't the
type of company she needed. She kept getting texts from Wendy,
but she really wasn't sure what her intentions were. Paige also still
had a crush on Tommy whom Wendy had wrapped around her
little finger! Then Paige thought maybe she could get on Wendy's
good side, or she could do to Wendy what she had done to Mr.
Joe, at least in some way. She could spread rumors about Wendy
and make her life miserable—and maybe she could win Tommy
over. What could she do? She had a few days to think about it, or
she could go to Tommy's right now. She could take the snowmobile since it was only a short jaunt through the woods.

Friday, November 8, 2019, noon

The storm was over, but the roads were a mess around Colewin,
so Joette and Shanice spent the afternoon watching television and
playing card games. Ron spent the better part of the day searching
information about the militia, but after several hours, he didn't
know much more than he already knew.

Joe was waiting to head home, but the snowstorm prevented
any traffic in or out of Colewin or St. Ignace, so he had to just wait
his time.

Across town in Colewin, Paige was once again sitting at
Tommy's house under the pretense of wanting to make sure he
was all right. Tommy wasn't sure what to think of her, but she had
always been nice to him. Wendy did not like her and he knew that,
especially after what she said about Mr. Joe. Tommy thought he

might be able to use the situation to find out something. Wendy had been talking to him while she was stuck in her house, and he knew that she was trying to get on Paige's good side. Maybe he could save her the trouble.

Finally, a plow blew through Colewin and opened the main roads. Ron had used Joe's four-wheeler and plow to clear the driveway, so now they could get out—and maybe Joe would be home for the weekend.

Ron decided that he would be the one to pick up Joe, and he left a little after noon. The trip was difficult, and sometimes he had to drive just twenty-five miles an hour, but he got there safely. By one-thirty p.m., Joe and he were on their way to Colewin.

Friday, November 8, 2:30 p.m.

Charlie was happy he had gotten all of the heavy equipment out of the woods before the storm hit. He hadn't spoken to Daryl in days, but he had informed his troops that they would stand down for the duration, or until he gave the word. They were to say nothing to anyone, and they needed to operate just as if the militia did not exist.

Charlie jumped on his snowmobile and headed for the woods. He hoped to get to the bunker as soon as he could so that he could get back home in the light. He knew he had until about five-thirty p.m. After that it would be too dark in the woods, and with all the snow, he would never find his way out.

When he arrived, he realized that he would have to move some snow once the gate was unlocked. It took him a while to get the gate to open a little so he could squeeze through. He got Bates to help him move some snow to open the gate wider to get the sled in.

Charlie was inside the bunker at three-thirty. Bates had been stranded there during the entire storm and he was running low on supplies. Charlie brought some things to keep him happy, but Bates wasn't sure he wanted to spend another winter in the U.P. It is long, boring, and cold, and he did not see anyone for days.

"So, what you doin'? Are you gonna be here for the winter?"

Bates looked at Charlie and said, "I'm not sure. You've got the entire place shut down—and people *are not happy with you.* They're still planning on your troops increasing the size of the bunker and being there for the delivery of all the munitions."

"I don't give no darn nothing about them. We're closed for the next few months. Gonna be spring afore any of these roads are usable anyway."

"They don't care what you think. I keep getting info that says you could be thrown out if you don't comply."

Charlie was shocked. "This is my group. This is our bunker. They ain't got nothin' to do with it if'n I say so."

"Charlie," Bates yelled, "you have no idea who you are dealing with. They'd just as soon get rid of you and take over."

"They'd have to come and find me first. I gotta lot o' people who are part o' this deal—they'll stick together and we'll be fine."

"Charlie, they have millions of dollars—billions! Money talks. What do you have?"

"Money ain't everything."

"Yeah, but they want to change this country and take over. Not violently, that's what they say, but the way they are going it looks like that."

"That's what we all want. Get rid of these politicians and liberals who think they own the place. So yeah, I'm with 'em."

"Then you'll have to do what they say," Bates said.

"I'll do what we want to do, and that's that!"

"OK, OK, you just don't get it, I guess." Bates backed off because he could see that Charlie really wasn't like the people who hired him. They are ruthless and will do anything to get their way: lie, cheat, kill, whatever.

"So, are you stayin'?"

"Probably will, but I'll need some form of transportation besides what I had last year. I was stuck out here for weeks, unable to even get fresh supplies. It gets really cold and the snow gets so deep that I can't even get out of the bunker sometimes. Now that Wyatt's gone, so is the snowmobile he loaned me. There will be no one to shoot the breeze with or bring me things I need."

"I'll see to it that you have a top-notch snowmobile. You'll be able to drive it in and out to the vehicle that you have just outside of Colewin."

"That sounds good. Bring some extra fuel for it. The supply here is low, and I know you won't be able to deliver any for a while."

"Sure, I'll have Sam help me, and we can deliver the machine and gas at the same time. I gotta get goin' now 'cause it's gonna get dark soon. Stay put 'til we deliver that stuff. It's a mess out there. I had all I could do to get here. It's tricky in all this snow, but we'll get the supplies out to you tomorra, then we're shuttin' the place down. When we're back, the three of us will have to move more of the snow around the gate so we can get in and out easily."

"Ok, see you next time."

"Yep," and Charlie was out the door. On his screen, Bates saw Charlie fire up the snowmobile and drive carefully through the gate and out to the trail.

Saturday, November 9, 2019

Joe was finally home and happy to be there, but he was concerned about the way that the police were controlling his life—it was as if *he had no rights*. He was determined to find out something soon. His union lawyer was coming to town tomorrow and would be doing some checking around. Hopefully, they might be able to figure out this situation.

"Ron, what do you say we make another run at that spot out in the woods? There shouldn't be anyone out there at this time of year."

"Sure, we could do it today, since we have time. Shanice has to head back on Sunday, but I took a leave of absence."

"Hopefully the roads are better by tomorrow," Joe added.

"I was thinking the same thing. Have they opened the Mackinac Bridge? I know it was closed during the worst of the storm and has been closed on occasions just like this in the past."

Joette spoke up, "I heard that it opened last night when the winds died down."

"Yes, I heard that too," Shanice said.

"What about the two girls who are accusing you?" Joette was more concerned about that than what Joe and Ron could find in the woods.

"That's a good point. Maybe Joette and I could find out something about the girls. We already know that the young girl has a history of lies. Maybe we could get something out of her."

"I doubt that, Shanice, her parents wouldn't let us within a mile of her. They're very protective, and they really don't like us."

"OK, but maybe we could get Wendy involved—the one who told you that Paige has always been a liar and a problem."

"All right, let's try that."

CHAPTER 10: SEARCH FOR AN ANSWER

Joe and Ron got ready to drive out and see what they could find. They were in a hurry so they could complete the trip all in daylight. Joe knew what it was like in the woods when it's cold and the snow gets deep. He had one snowmobile, so they had to borrow one from Wayne. He had a big Arctic Cat M8000 and Joe had a Polaris 600. Both machines would be reliable and could handle the current snow situation. They bundled up and packed as much gear as they could on a utility trailer: food, water, blankets, hand-and-foot warmers, survival kit, knives, and guns. It was a load, but they would split the supplies between two trailers when they got to Wayne's.

They would have to ride together to get the other machine. It was still morning when they left for Wayne's place. They had his snowmobile and large trailer before eleven-thirty, so they figured they had five or six hours of light. They kept away from the main trails and headed out of Colewin on back roads where they knew no one would follow them.

It wasn't long before they were on the same trail where they had met Charlie when they first tried to investigate. It was quiet and cold out here. The snow hung on the trees like huge pillows, and the trees reached for the ground, their branches weighted down. Someone had been here on a snowmobile because there was a trail down the center of the road, and it looked like it must have been recent, but it was snowing lightly again, and the snow was beginning to fill in some of the trail made earlier. Joe also noticed that some trees had been felled, plus it looked like someone was widening the road. Could be loggers, but why widen this road?

Once they left the old logging road, they turned on a road that seemed much wider, but they were in deep snow now, causing it to be a lot harder to make good time. Even with a trail to follow, the machines kept sinking quite deep. It took over an hour, but soon they saw the gate, and it was open. Joe wasn't surprised. "I think we found what we've been looking for." Somebody had cleared the snow so the gate opened and closed, but that was the only sign that looked like someone might be there.

They stopped their machines right by the gate; then they checked the area for signs of life. As they slowly moved toward the bunker, they saw the door, no more than twenty to twenty-five yards from the gate.

Ron noticed first. "Joe, by the shed. The trail of footprints leads right to the door." Two snowmobiles with gear sleds were sitting off to the side of the door.

"I see. We better be quiet."

"I wonder what's up? Those footprints have fresh snow on them, so someone was here before the snow started today. By the look of those machines, someone is probably inside."

"I agree. I think we better be careful. Who knows what's going on?"

From inside, Bates saw the approach. "Who is that? Who the hell would come out here?" He grabbed the nearest weapon he could, an AR-15 with a full clip.

Charlie and Sam had brought some supplies and were putting the last of the gear in the storage area. When they came out, they saw that Bates had a weapon ready.

"What's goin' on? You goin' huntin' or somethin'?" Charlie chuckled.

"I think you've been followed out here. Two guys. Take a look at the monitor."

Charlie and Sam both took a look. "I know who that is. That's the teacher and the guy I shooed away from here a while back. This is not good."

"I think we gotta do sumpin'," moaned Sam.

"No shit!" Bates sounded aggravated.

Ron and Joe searched the area near the machines and then looked at the door. It was huge and solid. It looked like they would never be able to open it, and maybe they didn't want to do that. Joe spoke first, "Let's get our rifles so we have some protection before we pound on the door. We need to find out what this is."

"Gotcha," replied Ron.

As they turned, the door opened and Bates stood there with his AR aimed right at them. "Who the hell are you, and what do you want?"

Joe spoke up, "No need for the weapon. We're just looking around." Both Ron and Joe decided to hide behind the trees near the machines inside the fence.

"Just looking around in the middle of a winter storm. Well, find your way out of here. This is private property."

"What exactly is this?" Joe questioned.

"None of your business; now get out!"

Both men had seen the AR-15—and knew they were no match.

Joe thought he would be up front and tell this guy who he was. "Sir, I'm Joe DeLuca, a school teacher, just trying to get some answers."

Then he heard another voice, "We know who you are." Charlie came out with another weapon aimed right at them, and then Sam came out too, laughing and smiling.

"We got 'em now, Charlie. No need for those women…"

Charlie yelled, "Shut the f##k up, you idiot!"

Sam said, "Geez, quit yellin'."

Bates was pissed. He lifted his rifle and let a salvo of shots ring around the two men.

"Crap!" Ron yelled as he dove in the snow. The trees had protected them this time, but who knows? This guy means business.

"Get the hell out or you'll be sorry." Another round of shots flew past Ron and Joe.

Joe turned to see if Ron was hurt. Ron looked up and gave the thumbs-up sign that he was fine.

Then Bates yelled, "All right, stand up and move toward us and no funny business or you're dead."

Joe knew if they were going to get out of here, they had to do it now, but looking down the barrels of three assault rifles didn't give him much choice, and in this deep snow, no chance to run.

Ron seemed to think the same thing as he said, "Let's just do what they say and try to figure this thing out."

Bates took charge and decided that they needed to get these two inside and then talk to headquarters for what to do. He did not want something to go wrong, and if they killed these two, it might lead to more of a mess. "Sam, go in the big door inside and get as much rope as you need off the pile in the right corner. You'll see it. Don't get that real thin stuff. Find the good rope. I think it's nylon."

"OK," replied Sam.

"Charlie, when he comes out with the rope, you and I will keep these two in line as Sam ties them up. OK, you two, I want you to separate about ten feet apart and do it now!"

Joe and Ron moved as he indicated. Joe thought a minute and wondered if they would really kill him, and by hesitating, he got Bates' ire. Shots flew over his head and he knew enough not to hesitate, but on the sly he did drop something in the snow, and then he moved quickly.

"Take it easy, guy. We're moving," Ron barked.

"Yeah, yeah. Just do it quickly."

When Sam returned, Bates directed him first to Joe. He tied his hands behind his back, and then Bates told him to also shackle his feet, but then he realized he wouldn't be able to move in the snow, so he told Joe to go inside, and then they would bind his feet. He did the same with Ron. Soon both were seated in the kitchen area, surprised at the size of the interior.

They were against the wall looking out at the enclosure. On their right was a huge garage door which wasn't visible from the outside. They obviously drive huge equipment in here. To their left was another huge door, something which also resembled a very large garage door. It was at least ten feet high. Straight ahead was a room that looked like a bedroom with an unmade bed, and next to that room was a series of computers and television sets. One TV showed the outside, so that's how they knew they were there. To their left was what looked like a bathroom, but they couldn't be sure.

Once they were seated against the wall, Sam tied their feet together and put some kind of bag over their heads. They smelled ammunition or something like that.

Then Bates ordered Charlie and Sam to stay and watch them, saying, "I'll take care of it from here."

"What you gonna do with 'em?" Charlie asked.

"I'm going to call headquarters and see what the long-range plan is. They'll know what to do with people like this. The boss is smart and has a lot of personnel, equipment, and money. I've informed him about everything that goes on around here, so he'll want to know about this, and we'll just let him decide. I know he doesn't like putting people out of their misery if he doesn't have to."

Meanwhile, Joe knew that if they did not return, Shanice and Joette would find someone to help. Hopefully, the police. About six feet from each other, Joe was trying to think of a way to communicate with Ron.

"What do you want us to do?" Charlie spoke up.

"Wait until I get a response from headquarters, and then we'll see."

"We'd like to get back before dark, you know."

"Sure, well, this shouldn't take long. I'll send an encrypted message, and they'll know it is important. They usually get right back."

Bates worked on a message and tried to include everything he could. He sent it at two-fifty p.m. and received a quick encrypted response. Bates informed Charlie and Sam that it would be around three p.m. before he'd know anything, so Charlie and Sam pulled up chairs at the table and got a couple of beers out of the fridge. Bates asked, "Where's mine?"

"Gotcha, here you go." Sam retrieved another from the fridge and took it to Bates in the communications room.

It was only about five minutes later when Bates received a long, encrypted message straight from the head man.

> Bates, do exactly as I say and do it immediately.
> First, separate the two men and put them inside the storage area. Don't let them see or hear anything. Do that now before you read any more of this. These two guys are trouble and have a history of working for the military.

Bates did as the message said and did not read the rest, but took care of Joe and Ron. He turned to Charlie and Sam. "Get those two guys on their feet and move them to the storage area. Put them in separate areas. One in the motor vehicle side and the other as far down the center as you can, near that fan that runs. We don't want them to hear or see anything."

Charlie jumped up and grabbed Joe. "Get to your feet!"

Joe tried to stand, but his feet were bound and he had trouble, but he managed to finally stand.

"OK, I'm going to move you to your left." At that point Sam hit a button and the large door opened with a screeching sound. "Yeah, now waddle in that direction until I tell you to stop."

Joe moved slowly forward. When he had gotten about forty feet, Charlie pushed him to the left and he bumped into something like a fender. Charlie opened a door and said, "Git in."

Joe slid onto a seat of a vehicle. He was then tied in the seat and could not move much, and then Charlie slammed the door shut. It must have been a jeep or a small truck, Joe thought. At least it's more comfortable than the floor.

Next, they took Ron who had the same trouble moving his feet while trying to walk down a long concrete floor. It took several minutes when Sam said, "All right, sit on that thing there."

Ron said, "What thing?"

"The box right in front o' you."

Ron felt around and found a wooden crate that he sat on. Charlie and Sam tied him to a post and left, shutting the lights and the large door. Both Joe and Ron heard the screech. Once it was down, Joe yelled for Ron, but Ron could not hear or see a thing, nor could Joe.

Bates went back to the message.

Second, tell any people who are there not to say a word or anything that has happened under penalty of ... well, I don't like to say that.

Third, we will not have any eliminations done on the property. Do not harm them in any way, or leave any blood, clothing, or even a fingernail behind. We need to take those guys out of there. I will have a van go to the drop off point on U.S.-2 where we have sent most of the big equipment. You will move them there, and we will take over from that point. You will forget ever having seen them.

Fourth, make sure they have no phones or tech on them. Strip them and have them wear some of the military gear we have stockpiled. Pack all of their belongings in a military duffle bag, and don't leave anything of theirs behind, not even so much as a hair. We'll make sure someone is there in one hour. He will transport the men to a designated drop off.

Fifth, take their snowmobiles to the highway and abandon them about five miles east on the shore of Lake Michigan. It'll look suspicious since the one guy is out on bail as you noted. Make sure you cover any tracks they might have made in the area and have your men run over the tracks that were made by the snowmachines so no one can identify anything.

I hear you had a lot of snow up there, so get going right away. Bates, as I've said before, do this right and there will be a nice reward for you. Screw up and you'll be the next man in the van.

Bates was not happy. He did not like the boss. He only liked his money. He told Charlie and Sam what to do, and they were on it. It wasn't long before both Ron and Joe were standing in army fatigues in the kitchen, both about to have their mouths taped and eyes blindfolded again.

Joe spoke before they got that far. "What the heck is going on? Who do you guys work for? Are you *alt-right* or something?"

Bates didn't answer. Instead, he told Sam and Charlie to ready the two snowmobiles and trailers that Joe and Ron had brought. "We need to bundle all their supplies and clothes and take them along to get rid of them."

Once they were gone, Joe asked Bates again, "Really, who are you working for?"

Ron also pitched in, "Yeah, you're not going to get away with this. You don't know who you're dealing with this time."

Bates laughed, "Sure, Sure. I bet you guys are tough and you work for the CIA or something."

Joe shook his head, "No, but you won't beat this. Your people aren't that strong."

"That's what you think. You might wish this organization were *alt-right or far-left* like you said, but they are neither. They want the two groups to keep fighting each other and the worse it gets, the better for them. Charlie and Sam have no idea who this group is or how powerful they are. They have cops, judges, generals, politicians, and probably even supreme court justices, all kinds of people on their team, and they are very, very, rich, like billionaires. That's why Wyatt was here, poor SOB. He was from one of the wealthy families and they wanted him to make sure everything was ready, but he was so wild that he messed up big. They have power and money. They're just waiting for when things get really bad to swoop in and take over. They lie, cheat, steal, and do whatever to make their ends meet. So, good luck to you."

Joe had a feeling like he had never had before. Current events started to make sense to him. He also feared for his life. While waiting for Bates to move them outside, Joe said quietly to Ron, "Sorry I got you into this. We've got to come up with something."

Ron whispered, "We will."

Bates said, "Shut up and move."

At that point, Charlie and Sam taped their mouths and covered their heads with cloth bags once again. They took a duffle bag of their belongings so they could get rid of any evidence that they were there.

Joe thought of all the survival equipment he had on the sled and could not come up with anything. He had already planted his iPhone in about a foot of snow when he knew they were taking him inside. Hopefully, that will be a signal for someone.

At any rate, what could he do since his hands and feet were bound?

Saturday, November 9, 4:30 p.m.

"It's getting dark and the boys are not back yet," Joette noted.

Shanice was worried too. "Yes, I thought they were going to be back before dark."

"We'll give them until six and then I'm calling Wayne just in case."

Time moves slowly when you are waiting for someone, especially if you think they are in trouble. They waited until six-thirty p.m. It was very dark and very quiet outside. Joette decided to call Wayne. Cathy answered, "Hello, Joette. How's it going? Did Joe find out anything?"

"Cathy, we are really afraid. They are not back yet. We're worried something might have happened."

"Let me get Wayne. Wayne, can you come here?"

"Just a minute. It's the end of the fourth quarter and the game is close."

"Wayne, this is an emergency."

"What? What's wrong?"

"It's Joette. Joe and Ron aren't back yet."

After listening to the discussion, Cathy and Wayne knew they had to help Joette. Wayne knew the area very well, but if he had to look for Joe and Ron, he would need help. He seldom traveled trails alone on nights like this. He thought about whom he might call who would be able to assist them, and who would know the area well. "Tommy!" He shouted to Cathy, "Tommy! If we need to look for them tonight, I'll need help—and Tommy would be the best one. He's in on the whole situation with Joe and he wants to help him. He also has a snowmobile, and I know his family has a few more." Wayne and Cathy decided they too would take a snowmobile to Joette's because of the weather.

Joette and Shanice were stressed. They feared for their husbands, not really knowing why this was happening. When Wayne and Cathy arrived, Joette and Shanice explained as much as they could to them about what their husbands knew and were planning to do. Wayne said he would need help and that the best person was Tommy. Joette was a bit hesitant. "Isn't he a bit young, and he's had such a horrible experience."

Wayne answered, "Yes, he is, but he's the most knowledgeable about the area since George was killed, plus we need vehicles, and he has several snowmobiles at his folks' place. Also, since we will be traveling in the dark and deep snow, Tommy will be able to keep us on track. We'll need to pack survival gear, blankets, food, and water since we don't know how long this will take, but the sooner we get going the better. I better get Tommy right now."

Wayne called Tommy and he answered right away. "Tommy, are you in for an adventure? I know you mentioned that you felt that Wyatt was in the militia, and you wanted to see them pay for what happened to George. Well, here's a chance to maybe do that."

Tommy did not hesitate. "I'm game. When do you need me and what can I do?"

Before long, Tommy and Wendy arrived with two snowmobiles and a sled full of supplies. They went inside where Wayne and Tommy made their plan of action.

"We'll need to follow their tracks in the dark as much as we can. Do you think we can do that?"

Tommy was confident. "For sure. I've pretty much lived in the woods with my uncle for years. We can follow them if we know which road they took. It was your Arctic Cat and Mr. Joe's Polaris, right?"

"Correct," replied Wayne.

"Well, let's go. I'll be glad to get some revenge on these people."

"Tommy, we're not out for revenge although I can see where you're coming from. We really need to be focused on finding Joe and Ron."

"We will, but maybe there'll be a chance to take care of some other business."

"OK, let's get going."

"Be careful, guys. If you can keep us informed, that would be helpful," Joette said with a bit of fear in her voice.

"Just a damn minute," added Shanice who also was feeling the same way. "We are not going to just sit here and wonder what's going on. These are our husbands. We're going too. Right, Joette?"

"That would make me feel better, and we would have four people instead of two."

"Can you guys both drive a sled, and do you know how to shoot a gun?" asked Wayne.

Joette laughed, "You know that I do, and Shanice has been here many times with me during winter months driving the trails. You know I can shoot, and Shanice and Ron are both ex-Army, so, yes, we can handle ourselves around guns."

"I have no objections. We'll have to get two more machines."

Wendy spoke up at this point, "No, you only need one more. You can take mine, and Tommy and I can run quickly to his house and get another."

Tommy spoke up, "I have another Ski-doo and a sled we can take with extra gear. We'll go right now and be back in fifteen minutes."

"All right. Wendy, could you stay here since Cathy has to leave, so we have someone else who knows where we are and someone we can contact if we need anything? Check with your parents and let them know what you are doing. Let's all make sure we have our cell phones at one hundred percent, and make sure to keep them close to our bodies so they stay warm and charged. We can use them to communicate since we have good service anywhere now."

"Shouldn't we call the police?" Joette added.

Wayne did not hesitate. "I have a friend at the State Police Post, and I'll call him if things get out of hand. I'm not sure exactly who else to call since we think some of the local ones are involved in the militia. Joe and I have discussed this before, and it makes us uncertain of everyone and everything."

"OK, let's get ready," Shanice ordered.

"You'll have to dress in the warmest clothes you have. Do you have snowmobile suits?"

"Yes, we have all kinds of winter gear."

"Do you have helmets?"

Joette answered, "I have my own. Not sure what we can do for Shanice."

"She can use mine if it fits," Wendy blurted quickly. "Here try it on."

Shanice did, and it fit nicely. "There, we're all set," she said proudly. Shanice then also scolded them a bit, "And don't you boys worry about us. We're tough and resourceful, so we'll be an asset."

Tommy and Wendy left and returned quickly, even before the girls were completely ready. "I checked with my parents, and they are all right with me staying here," Wendy told Joette.

While they were gone, Wayne had taken Cathy back home since they had left in such a hurry. She wanted to stay, but she knew she had to get home and make sure everything was all right there. "I'll come back as soon as I can when the weather is better, and I'll keep checking in with Wendy."

"OK, good," Joette said.

When everyone had returned and all the equipment was packed, they were ready to go.

Saturday, November 9, evening

It took a while for Bates, Charlie, and Sam to get all the gear together, plus get the sleds ready. They retrieved Joe and Ron's sleds with the utility trailers and brought them near the door where they could load them. It was getting late.

"We just need to get this done," Bates said. "Just tie them on the utility sleds and pile the gear on top of them."

Joe fit nicely on the utility sled. He was bound legs and hands, and they tied him to the sled. Ron was another story. He was big and they could not get him situated right. They finally got him seated in the trailer. He was half sitting, half lying down, but he fit, and then they tied him to the sled. Joe and Ron were still blindfolded and, at this point, very cold. The fatigues they had on were not as warm as the clothes they had worn, and Charlie and Sam did not put jackets on them, so they were already shivering. They put all of Joe and Ron's supplies in a duffle bag and tied it on top of Joe, and they put all of their clothes in another bag and tied that on top of Ron. They were going to take the Arctic Cat and the

Polaris and leave them near the lake as Bates told them. Bates would have someone pick up Charlie and Sam later—and they could retrieve their sleds the next day.

"How the hell is this gonna work?" moaned Charlie.

"Not sure it will," said Sam.

"Well, it better, or you guys will be in a lot of trouble with the boss man."

"Who the heck is this guy anyway?" Charlie asked.

"You don't need to know, just do what you're told," Bates ordered.

"I'm not liking any of this. I'm glad we put a hold on the bunker. We might stay away until spring," said Charlie, as mad as ever he had been. "OK, Sam, we'll need to take it slow. Everythin' is ready I guess, so start the machines. Go slow because this is going to be rough."

All Joe could think about was how he could pull away from these guys when they start, but he knew it was dark and he was blindfolded. Was escape an option right now? How would he do it? The same thing was going through Ron's mind. What could he do? He was bound so tight, he thought that if anything happened to this sled, he was toast. He felt unstable and being blindfolded gave him an eerie feeling—and he was cold, very cold. The temperature had fallen to twenty-eight degrees, and Joe and Ron had no gloves.

Then the two machines roared to life, and they took off down the hill toward the lake. It was a bumpy, sickening ride for both captives as Charlie and Sam swerved and gunned it over the rough trail, if it could be called a trail. Their speed went from slow to fast to zigzag, but they never stopped. Soon they were at the split in the road where they had come in. They, however, were not turning right, they would go straight through what looked like forest, but was a hidden road to the highway. As they passed the road, a light flickered on the right in the distance, but neither Charlie nor Sam noticed anything.

Tommy saw it first. Two lights moving down the trail. They were between a quarter and a half mile from it, but in the woods on such a dark night, the light was not mistakable. In the distance it was a flash and then another flash, each followed by red lights. Tommy stopped his sled, turned to Wayne and said, "Did you see the light?"

"I caught just a flash, possibly two flashes. It happened fast."

"Those were sleds. Let's move to the bend in the road and take a look." Tommy motioned with his hand.

"Right," added Wayne.

Joette and Shanice heard what was going on. Shanice had pulled her sled as close as she could to Wayne, with Joette right behind. They moved forward as fast as they could, and when they came to the bend, the obvious move would be to go up the hill, but as they looked south, they knew they had to follow. All they could think was it must be Joe and Ron. They huddled up for a minute and decided to split up. Wayne and Joette would go up the hill, and Tommy, who had a very fast Yamaha, would head south. Shanice would try to stay with him as best she could.

"I'll try to keep up, but just in case we get separated, keep going until you see who that was. If I get lost or can't find you, I'll just stay put with the gear." Shanice was trying to make a plan that would keep her safe, but also give Tommy a chance to get to figure out who was on the other sleds.

Tommy took off like a frightened jackrabbit with Shanice on his tail. She was able to stay with him for a long time, but she eventually lost sight of him, but she could see the trail just fine. Shanice was not used to riding snowmobiles long distances in the dark, and every tree looked sinister as it reached its branches out to snag her as she drove by. She couldn't hear anything except the whine of the machine and her own cold breath going in and out, but through all of this, her one thought was on keeping up and not getting lost.

Since the road was very straight in spots, Tommy just let it rip as he knew how—and made great time heading south. When he was close to U.S.-2, he slowed and held back, shutting off his lights, then he saw an opening with a van and two snowmobiles. He stopped and shut down his machine. He was sure they hadn't heard or seen him yet. He saw three men loading something into a big box in the van. He could barely make out anything else because it was so dark, but he did see that one man had what looked like an assault rifle. Tommy moved closer on foot, but it was slow going because the snow was deep. He saw one of the men put a lid on one box and put several nails in it to seal it shut. Two boxes were in the van. One of the men fired up his snowmobile and the light showed into the van, and Tommy saw Sam and the license plate. He could make out a Michigan plate. It was a standard blue plate, but 102 F was all he could see. Snow blocked the last two letters, but he was sure of the numbers and the F.

"Holy crap, that's Sam, and that's Wayne's Arctic Cat that Joe borrowed. I'm sure of it!" said Tommy.

Just then a snowmobile appeared behind him. He leaped and hit the snow, but it was Shanice, thankfully, who saw his sled, shut the light, and stopped.

Sam jumped down from the van, shut the doors, and cranked his machine as Charlie roared south across U.S.-2, and Sam followed. The man with the rifle moved to the van, got in, started it up and fled south with the cargo inside.

Tommy jumped up and waved to Shanice. "What was that?" she yelled.

"Not sure, but that was Wayne's machine that Joe borrowed, and I saw Sam in the van as clear as could be. We should see if we can follow the snowmobiles. I saw a trailer on the one that just left.

It makes me wonder what they were transporting." Tommy retrieved his machine and they were off.

Wayne and Joette had just made the crest of the hill when they saw a gate up ahead. They moved slowly, and they were cautious because of all that Joe had told them about the area. They stopped about fifty feet from the locked gate. They saw all of the snowmobile tracks. They also saw two snowmobiles parked on the side of the gate. It was very dark, but Wayne was close and could see quite clearly. "I know that machine," he said. "That's an old Yamaha that Sam drives. He's got to be here. I'm going to try to call Tommy." He dug deep into his clothes and pulled out his cell and called Tommy. It rang several times, but then he heard a voice.

"Yeah?"

"Yo, Tommy, you there?"

"It's me."

Wayne was a bit rattled. "Hey, we found an old Yamaha that looks like Sam's. You know Sam. Any idea why he is out here?"

"He's in the militia, but we also saw him here. We were just going to follow him and someone else on sleds. We gotta hurry. I'd say get yourselves out of there. One of these guys had an assault rifle, and I've seen enough of those to last for the rest of my life."

Wayne thought otherwise and decided to spend some time looking around. Joette was in complete agreement, feeling that Joe might be there. Suddenly, she realized she might be able to locate where Joe was. Wayne, I think I can find Joe. She had the app "Find my Friends" on her iPhone, so she whipped it out and turned it on. She punched in her access code and hit the app. There it was. "Wayne, it says that Joe is right here."

"What? Then we have to do some looking and find him."

Meanwhile, Bates was inside watching all the outside activity. The mics they had were not the greatest, but he could hear them talking, yet he could not make out what they were saying. He saw that they began to mess with the lock on the gate. He wasn't too worried whether they got in or not because he had locked both the large security door and the regular door. There was no getting in unless they had some explosives, and he doubted that. He would just sit quietly and watch the fun until they gave up.

Joette was now determined to get inside. "Wayne, let's look to see if we can get around the fence somewhere. We probably can't get too far in this deep snow, especially at night, but let's give it a try."

Wayne was leery and thought it was time to get the police involved. "Shouldn't we call the cops?"

"Who would we call? You know Daryl is in on this whole militia stuff."

"We could try the state police. Remember the guy I told you about earlier tonight? He seems like he is on the level, and I could call him."

"Sure. But first let's do a little investigating."

"All right. Might as well."

They searched for the better part of forty-five minutes, but the snow was too deep, and it was dark, and it was cold.

Tommy and Shanice tore after the machines Tommy had seen, crossed U.S.-2 and followed a trail, but it led nowhere. They could not find anyone or hear anything. They searched for an hour and then saw some lights on the shore near Lake Michigan. They were definitely snowmobiles, so they headed there. Lake Michigan had not frozen yet, and the snowmobiles were on the shore running back and forth. Tommy knew it wasn't safe, not knowing who these snowmobilers were, but they had to give it a try. When Tommy and Shanice got close, Tommy said, "That's just some of the high school kids racing in the dark. They do it all the time. I can see if they saw anything."

Tommy moved toward the light and when the machines stopped, he drove over to them. "Hey, you guys, anyone see any other machines out here tonight? We're looking for someone."

"What's it to you? Who are you anyway?"

"It's me, Tommy."

"That you, man. What up?"

"Out looking for someone. Have you seen any other machines around?"

"No, it's been a quiet night. Just a few of us here, but you know that this area is traveled a lot by snowmobilers so you're not gonna be able to track anyone at night, especially here."

"That's what I figured too. Well, thanks for the help. If you see anyone, give me a call, would you? You got my number?"

"Not really. Give it to me."

Tommy gave the number to the kid and off they drove trying to see if they could pick up a trail. When they reached U.S.-2 again, they knew they had to go back to meet up with Wayne and Joette. It was just not feasible tonight to keep looking. Trails were all over the place, and it was so dark and cold that it made it quite impossible. They called Wayne and told him they were headed back up the trail. "We'll meet you in about fifteen minutes. We're already across U.S.-2. Have you guys found anything?"

After Tommy told Wayne what was happening, Wayne gave the phone to Joette, and she updated Tommy. "I think I found where Joe is, but the gate is locked and we can't get in through the fence anywhere. The snow is too deep to do too much, but I've located his phone, and it's showing that he's inside the gate, but we are not sure where."

"We'll come up the hill then. It'll take us a bit longer if we go all the way, so it should be less than thirty minutes. We'll see you there."

After Tommy told Shanice what the plan was, they began their trip back north toward the hill.

Bates was half asleep now. It was getting late, but the two people were still outside the gate and had been snooping around. He could not identify them, but surmised that they must be related in some way to the two guys they had just gotten rid of. Should he just wait it out, or should he call for assistance? He chose the former. He knew he could listen in if they would talk a bit louder. His mic made it just barely audible, but he could make out a few words. He thought if only they would say names!

Tommy and Shanice's trip back was uneventful. The trail was better because all four vehicles had packed the snow and made the trail easier to follow. Their lights led the way to the logging road, and then they began the climb up the hill. It took almost the entire thirty minutes, but they made it and pulled up next to Wayne and Joette. They were both standing by their sleds eating power bars. It was a long night and they were all getting hungry.

Tommy spoke first, "Any luck finding a way in?"

"Nothing," Joette said as she sat on the seat of the Ski-doo. She looked tired and worried. "What if he's on that machine that went south? Did you notice if they might have been there?"

At that point, Tommy informed her of the story regarding the snowmobiles with trailers, the van, and the boxes. "If Joe and Ron were in the boxes, we needed to rescue them right then, but there were three men with assault rifles, so when the van left, we decided to follow the snowmobiles, but in the dark and in that area, we lost them."

Joette let out a stifled scream, "Oh, my God! What if they are?"

Shanice also gasped, "I'm really worried. Are we in above our heads? Who are these people?"

Bates was surprised—two women were out there. He was sure that what he heard confirmed this suspicion. He knew who one of them was because she had taken off her helmet to eat something. "I bet it's the two wives. It has to be. I don't know the other two, men or women, but that one is really tall and big. That's a guy, but I don't know who."

The four of them just stood there looking at each other. Wayne finally spoke, "I think we really have to go to the law, and I know just who to call, not Daryl. Let's go with the state police. I know two good guys up in Newberry who could help us."

"That sounds like it makes sense to me," said Joette, slumped on her snowmobile again. "I know Joe's phone is in there someplace. The police might be able to get in and find it."

Shanice agreed, "Can we call the police from here? I'd hate to leave and then have someone move them if they are here."

Wayne pulled out his phone. "I'll call right now."

"It'll take time for the police to get here, so why don't you and Shanice head back. It'll be a cold night and we have a tent and a heater, so Wayne and I will stay," Tommy said. "If that's all right with you, Wayne. We can hide our machines in the trees and set up a tent and keep watch until the police get here."

"Sounds good. Let's do it. Can you two find your way back?"

Joette thought they could. "I think we can follow the trail. Once we hit the old logging road, we'll be fine."

Bates was on it. He contacted headquarters about what he had seen. The response was that the two men they picked up were taken care of, and they would take care of the two women and the others. They just needed more information about where they could find both. "One lives in Colewin," Bates noted. "The other I don't know, but you could find out from the other woman if you can get to her. I think one is the teacher's wife."

"No problem," came the response. "We got it from here. Just stay out of sight and don't talk to anyone."

CHAPTER 11: WHERE ARE JOE AND RON?

Saturday, 10:30 p.m.

Joe was alert, but uncomfortable. His hands and feet were tied and he had tape over his mouth and a bag of some kind over his head. He could feel the jolt as the van hit every bump in the road, and as it swerved, he would get pounded against the top and side of the box. He tried to lean back and use his legs to kick the top off, but it was nailed tight, and he could not get enough force as the van kept bouncing and moving back and forth.

Then he felt the van slow and turn. It wasn't long and he began to hear a humming sound from the tires. He knew immediately what it was: He was on the Mackinac Bridge heading south to Lower Michigan. In about ten minutes, he knew he was on I-75. The van picked up speed, and he had a much smoother ride. It was still a bad ride in a box, but it was better and quieter.

Joe tried to yell to see if he could get a response from Ron, but the tape on his lips was too tight. However, he kept moving his lips and it slid down a bit. Joe was exhausted having fought for about an hour to try to kick off the top of the box, and he must have slept for a while. When he awoke, they were still moving, but going a lot slower, and no longer on the highway. The van kept up this slow pace for a while, and Joe could tell they had hit a rough road. They made what seemed like a big left turn, like they were going in a circle. The van slowed more and came to a stop. He heard what sounded like a motor running and a scraping like a garage door opening. After everything was quiet again, the van moved forward and came to a stop.

Ron was happy that the moving stopped again, and when it did, he thought he heard some muffled yelling. Suddenly the box started to move and he could tell it was being lifted out of the van. The box slid and then tipped back so far that Ron hit his head on the end of the wooden box as it was dropped slowly to the ground. He could hear some other noise and realized it must be the other box being moved out.

Both boxes lay on a concrete floor in a warehouse deep in the woods in Lower Michigan. "This is the end of the line for me," the driver said.

"OK. These boxes can just sit here until they come and get them," said the other man who looked like he might be in charge.

"This never happened, right?"

"You better believe it. Keep it to yourself and cover your butt if you know what's good for you. These guys do not play around."

"Thanks. I'm outta here." The man jumped into his van and drove away with the bags of Joe and Ron's clothes and supplies still in the back.

The man in charge walked to the open garage door, turned off the lights, pushed the button to shut the door, and then left as the door closed behind him.

All was dark and silent. Joe and Ron lay quietly. They could hear some of what had been said, so they both knew this could be the end of the line if they did not do something. Ron just fit in the box and could only push his feet against the end of it in the hopes of breaking out. Joe, on the other hand, was able to push his feet up against the edge of the crate and push hard. The nails creaked and the top of the box gave ever so slightly. He knew if he was going to get out, it was going to take some time.

Saturday, 11:00 p.m.

By the time Joette and Shanice arrived at Colewin, it was late. They could see the lights on in the house, and Wendy was standing in the window. They parked the snowmobiles and jumped off, hoping that Wayne had gotten through to his friend at the State Police office.

Wendy opened the door as they walked up the steps of the porch. "Hey, guys, did you find anything? Where are Tommy and Wayne? Are they all right?"

"Oh, they're just fine. They're staying out for a while until the police get here."

"The police?"

"Yep," Joette answered.

Then Shanice choked out, "We need help on this. We cannot find Joe or Ron, and this is getting serious because we saw a van drive away with something in two large wooden boxes. Not sure what they were, but they were large enough to put bodies inside."

Near the militia base

Wayne made the call to his buddy at the post in Newberry. He explained the situation and asked if he could help. The officer said, "You mean the guy who is being accused of some sexual stuff out in Colewin? He's missing?"

"That guy and another one who was helping him find out why he was being accused. He thinks it has to do with the militia," Wayne responded.

"The militia, I mean, this guy is out on bail. If he's missing, he might be in some really big trouble, and it won't look good for him. What do you want me to do?"

"Could you guys come out and investigate the place? It looks like some military base. Not sure what might be inside this thing, but we know we're getting a signal from Joe's phone inside the gate."

"Well, that might mean he is there on his own."

"I don't think so. He came out here looking for answers, but we can't find his Arctic Cat or the Polaris that the men were driving. I did see someone drive off with the Arctic Cat and I saw another guy, Sam, who works down here someplace, get on the other machine."

"It sounds to me like that teacher guy just took off and is covering his tracks. I think we could investigate him for sure right now as a bail breaker."

"No, he's not. He came out to find answers to the people who were accusing him."

"The best I can do is get someone out there in the morning. I'll have to clear it with the Lieutenant first."

"Aw, man, do you have to? We're trying to keep this to as few people as possible that we can trust."

"You can trust him, Wayne. He's a good man and he does the right thing. We'll get someone out there in the morning. Where exactly are you?"

"You can go to the teacher's house in Colewin." He gave the officer the pertinent information. Then he told him that Joe's wife would be home and she would know where they were. He continued, "Her name is Joette. She'll guide you out here. We're camped on the hill above the gate to keep out of sight. We'll be good here tonight since we brought plenty of equipment."

"Right. See you then."

Saturday, 11:30 p.m.
"Wendy, you should probably be getting home. It's almost midnight." Joette knew Wendy was afraid for Tommy.

"Not until I know Tommy is safe and sound."

"What are they doing anyway out there at this time?"

Just as Joette was going to answer, her cell phone rang. "Hello, Wayne?"

She and Wayne spoke for a while and he caught her up on the details. He mentioned that he and Tommy would be out until morning when the State Police would arrive to investigate. He also told her that the police would stop by her place to have someone lead the way out to the base. When she hung up, she had a somber look.

"The boys are staying out tonight, and we need to guide the police to them in the morning. They need to make sure no one leaves or goes in."

"Then I'm staying and going out with you in the morning," a determined Wendy said.

"Sure, just let your parents know you are safe and you're here," Shanice told her.

Saturday, 11:45 p.m.

Charlie and Sam had parked the snowmobiles where they were told they should go, then they walked out to the spot where they were supposed to be picked up, but no one was there. Sam wondered if they had the wrong spot, but Charlie did not.

"That damn Bates probably doesn't have anyone to pick us up. He's a bastard if there ever was one. We might as well start walking to the highway. It's uphill a long way, but we'll freeze if we don't move."

"Aw, crap, Charlie. Do we have to walk all that way?"

"Shut the f##k up, you nit! Sometimes I wonder why I take you along. If you weren't related to me, I don't know."

"You take me 'cause I don't never say a word to no one, and you know that."

Luckily, the road was plowed, and they had walked for about thirty minutes. Both men were getting very cold and tired when headlights appeared.

"Hey, you think that's our ride?" shouted Sam.

"How the hell do I know? Let's flag 'em down."

As the truck got closer, they saw that it was no one they knew—at least they did not recognize the truck. When it pulled up next to them, the person inside put the window down about two inches and said, "Get in the back and lie down."

Charlie argued, "I ain't sittin' in that snow and cold. You're nuts."

"Then you can walk. See ya." The truck began to back up down the road.

Both men looked at each other and ran after it and jumped in. The guy in the truck said, "All right. Get down. I'll take you as far as the Colewin road, and then you're on your own."

"That's a mile from town. We don't want to walk in this cold and snow."

"No choice, shut up and lie down." Off they went, backing down the road until the truck could turn around and move forward.

It was cold on the truck bed, and they were mad. "We still gotta get our snowmobiles from the bunker. Shit!" Charlie scowled. "I ain't leaving one of our snowmobiles for that Bates after this! That fool."

"How we gonna get up there? We can't walk."

"Not sure. We'll need more'n one machine or we can borrow one and both ride back and then get the other one. I don't wanna involve any more people in this." Charlie was uncertain and worried. "Maybe one of the troops has a couple sleds, then we only need to get one more involved."

"I know Lane's old man got about three. Betty got one. Old Bud's got a couple. What about Gunnar? He has some."

"Can't get some of those people involved. We'll have to see."

Sunday morning

Joe had been working for some time and had gotten the top of the box opened about an inch. Then he heard the sound of a vehicle outside. It must have been a snowmobile.

Joe's heart pounded and so did his feet as he began to push and kick as hard as he could. In no time he had a hole about three inches wide. It's surprising what adrenalin can do. He couldn't see the nails between the cover and the box because of the blindfold, but his foot felt the opening, and it gave him hope that he could get the top off. He kept kicking and kicking, hoping to beat anyone who might want to open the door and get them. It now felt like he had ten inches of open box. One more time and he might be able to climb out. When he decided to push on one side with all his strength, the box popped open enough to get out. He knew he would have to be careful because the nails would probably be sticking out, but he was able to exit just as the garage door began to open.

Light streamed in and a cool breeze hit Joe as he slid over the box and onto the cold concrete floor. The bag on his head caught on a nail, so Joe pulled as hard as he could, and the bag moved up to his chin. Carefully, he pushed back up into the nail that ripped through the cloth bag; he pulled hard, and it was off. As it came off, the tape on Joe's mouth tore just enough so he could talk. Joe moved away from the box, but his hands were tied behind him and his feet were bound too. As he tried to run, he tripped and fell. "Shit," Joe tried to exclaim through the tape. He lay quietly on the ground.

Then, he saw three or four guys outside of the open door. They looked ugly and mean. One of them pulled out a cooler and whipped out some beer. One guy sat on the cooler, and the others leaned on the vehicle they had driven. One guy sat on a snowmobile. None of them entered the building, but he could hear them talking and laughing.

Joe knew this was his chance to get Ron out, but search as he could, he could not find anything to open the crate. There was nothing that he could use to free himself or to pry the top off. He knew he did not have a lot of time, so he searched frantically. There was nothing. He decided to crawl back to the crates and talk to Ron.

"Ron, can you hear me? I was able to get out!"

Ron mumbled.

"I can't find anything to get you out. Can you kick the top off?"

Ron just mumbled. He really could not move, and he could not get the tape off his mouth since his hands were tied behind him.

"Three or four men, make that four for sure, are outside drinking beer. They opened the garage door, and I'm sure they will come in here next to get us."

Ron just mumbled again.

"I'm going to check to see if there is a way out of here besides the garage door. If I can get out, I might find something outside to free myself and get you out."

Joe crawled quietly around the perimeter of the room. It was a very large warehouse, and he could not see much, but he did find what looked like a door on the back wall. He was afraid to try to open it lest it alert the men on the other end by letting light in or making noise; yet, what choice did he have? He braced himself against the wall and pushed his legs hard against the floor until he was standing. He was able to turn the knob slightly. He opened the door quietly, just enough to slip through to the outside.

Joe knew he had to get his legs and arms free first, but there were about eight or nine inches of snow on the ground, but not so much next to the building where the air inside had warmed the metal and melted the snow. He looked, but there wasn't anything outside near the building, so he crawled in the snow along the north wall until he found where the metal siding had been turned up a bit near the bottom. He thought he could use the edge to cut the rope on his hands, so he moved toward it and sat backward and started moving his hands up and down. His fingers were very numb and his nose felt like it had frozen, but it didn't take long before he was able to cut through the rope and untie his feet. He tore off the tape that was left on his lips and squeezed back through the door and crawled back to the boxes which he reached very quickly this time.

At that same time, one of the men threw a beer bottle into the woods, got up and took a leak right there. Then he said, "Let's get this done. I don't have all day."

The snowmobile dude, who looked a lot neater and cleaner than the other three, glared at the man who threw the bottle and said, "I don't care when you get this finished, just complete it to-day. You were supposed to do this last night." Then he turned, got on his Arctic Cat, fired it up, and drove away.

Sunday morning, 10:03 a.m.

Bates had been checking the cameras for a long time. He did not see anyone anymore and felt confident that he was alone once again. He had been in touch with the command center, and it sounded like everything was under control. He considered the sit-uation and thought—*it's great when you have the cops on your side. We don't need many, but I'm glad they have enough to make this work. Money talks I guess, and I want some of that money.*

Wayne and Tommy were quite comfortable on the hill in a tent with a small heater. They were completely out of Bates' view in the bunker, and they were taking turns watching the gate to see if anyone came or went. Nothing so far.

Charlie and Sam were dropped off around twelve-fifty a.m., and then they walked the last mile into Colewin. Sam went one way and Charlie the other. They needed to get home and warm up some before they did anything else. Both had a short jaunt to get home, but they were cold and tired, and short didn't seem so short. The walk hadn't been too bad on the plowed road, but the wind was picking up and it was brutal. They planned to meet later and to somehow get their snowmobiles.

Sunday morning

Wendy stayed the night at the house and kept in constant contact with Cathy, but in the morning before breakfast, she decided to return home for a while. Prior to leaving, she spoke to Joette, "I have some things to do before we go to find Tommy. I'll head home and call you later. Let me know if you hear anything and when you are leaving."

Both Joette and Shanice gave her a hug and waved good-bye as she got on her snowmobile and drove away.

Shanice was worried about Ron and Joe, but she knew she had to be back at work on Monday, so she had a decision to make. When she had called her office, they indicated that she had to come back on time Monday or her job was in jeopardy.

Joette realized the quandary, and told her, "Go back and do what you have to do. I'll hold down the fort here and see what I can come up with. Let's keep in touch as much as possible."

Shanice was not sure what to do, but there was little she could do here, especially if Ron and Joe had been taken somewhere. "I guess I'll head back and see what I can do to facilitate this client's case. I'm the only one who knows what's going on, but I could get someone else up to speed, and then I could head back here as soon as I can."

"That sounds good. We can keep trying to investigate. Hopefully, Tommy and Wayne can find out something soon."

Just then a police car pulled into the driveway, with two snowmobiles on a trailer. Shanice and Joette were relieved that they had more help to find their husbands. Two officers in the car both got out and walked up the stairs to the front door and knocked.

Joette immediately opened the door. "Thank God you're here. We need to find our husbands."

"Hello, I'm Lieutenant Smith and this is my partner, Officer Lopez from the State Police. May we come in?"

"Yes, we've been waiting for you. Please, have a seat over here." Joette led them into the living room where they both sat on the couch.

"Let's get right to it. Tell us what you know, and then you need to take us to this spot that we've been told is somewhere near here in the woods past Colewin."

"Yes, we can tell you everything," both Joette and Shanice replied at the same time. They told the officers the story—then waited for a response.

"Sounds to me like a guy on the run, trying to get away from a bad situation. This guy who's helping," he turned to Shanice, "he's your husband?"

"Yes, but they are not on the run," she said matter-of-factly.

"Sure, sure, what are you doing up here?" the officer asked rather rudely.

"We're old friends with the DeLucas. Both our families were in the military together. Ron and Joe both served in Vietnam years ago. They spent eighteen months there in '70 and '71," Shanice responded.

"Is that true, ma'am?" He turned to Joette for verification like he didn't believe Shanice.

"You don't believe me, do you, officer?" Shanice said in an icy voice.

"It's true, officer. We're best friends and have been for years and, yes, our husbands spent time together in Vietnam."

"Sorry, I didn't mean…"

"Sure you didn't. I get that all the time." Shanice had that look on her face, and Joette knew that she was upset.

"Well, I think you have to take me to this place, wherever it is. I can't believe that anyone would build something that important out here, but who knows."

Joette then spoke up, "I think, Shanice, that you should stay here. You need to get ready to go back to work tomorrow, and I think I could take them to that spot."

"Whoa, no one is going anywhere," the officer interjected. "You're both staying here until we know more about the whereabouts of your husbands."

"I am required to be back by tomorrow. I have a huge court case, and I'm the lead attorney. You'll have to contact the courts if you want to keep me here. I'd like nothing more than to stay and help, but I can't."

"We'll see. Just don't go anywhere 'til we get back, you hear?"

"Oh, I hear you, but I'm leaving in the morning and you can't stop me."

"Now don't get testy or I'll have to take you in, lady."

"I'm not getting testy, but you are."

"Hold on. Are you getting belligerent here? I'll have my partner put you in the squad car."

Joette bristled, "She's not getting angry. You're putting her in a spot right now. Can't you see what you've said and done? This is how it all starts. I can't believe it is happening here. Let's just stop and take the machines out to the spot where I think my husband is."

"All right, we'll deal with this later. Let's go right now. Hopefully it's not a wild goose chase."

They all stood up, and Joette donned her snowmobile suit, boots, helmet, gloves, and walked to the door. Shanice whispered to Joette, "Be careful and stay safe." They hugged and Joette turned to leave.

The officers were already unloading the machines from the trailer. The lieutenant said, "You'll ride on the back of my machine. Just tell me which way to go and then tap me on a shoulder in the direction that you want me to turn. Make sure you do it before we pass a road."

"OK, but I could take my machine," Joette said.

"No, it'll be better this way. Just make sure you lead me directly to the spot."

It took longer than usual to get to the bunker. Joette knew the way, but in the daylight, everything looked different than the night before. The shining sun cast long shadows across the snow and some of the spots looked very familiar to her, but she wasn't quite sure. She did get them to the right roads, however.

Colewin, that same day, Sunday, about 10:10 a.m.

Charlie and Sam rested until about ten a.m. and then Charlie called Sam and said he had gotten one of the troops to give them a ride out. They were going to try taking a big Cat and a large utility trailer, which Sam, a lightweight, could easily fit in. Charlie would ride on the back of the Cat. It'd be slow going, but as long as the snow was packed tight enough, they could do it since they had the time, and luckily this would only involve one other person.

They arrived at the bunker after noon and immediately sent the other guy back before they even opened the gate.

Bates watched from inside and recognized Charlie and Sam. He opened the door so he could talk to them a bit.

Charlie opened the gate and he and Sam waltzed in like they owned the place.

Later that same day

When Joette left, Shanice called Wayne and Tommy as she and Joette had planned. She told them that the police were on the way with Joette. Wayne and Tommy were still in place on the hill and Tommy was on watch. He heard a snowmobile approaching and wondered if it was the police. When he saw the sled heading up the hill, he immediately got Wayne to watch with him. It wasn't the police, but they recognized Charlie and Sam as the machine approached the gate, and Tommy was certain that Charlie and Sam had to be the two who loaded the boxes the night before. Tommy and Wayne could only wonder why those two were involved in this. What in the world was going on?

"Do you see them, Wayne?"

"I do. What the hell? Why are they here, and why did the other guy leave? Are they planning to stay?"

"Not sure. Let's get a closer look. We can move down the hill a bit."

Bates yelled from the door, "You guys get everything done all right?"

Charlie looked at him with disdain. "Yep, we did. All taken care of."

"I spoke to headquarters, and they want to make sure you don't come around here anymore for the next couple of months to keep the heat off."

"We already closed her down for longer than that. It'll be spring 'afore we come back here. Hope you have fun by yerself. Besides, this here's our bunker. It don't belong to nobody but us."

"It might have at one time, but you're part of something bigger than your group here now. The guys in charge are super rich and super sure of what they want to accomplish. You're just a little cog in the wheel, but that's why they need to shut you down for now. Can't have anyone snooping into this movement."

"Movement, what the hell. There's no movement yet. We'll tell ya when there's a movement."

Bates said, "Mark my word. You'll see next year during the election. They'll control everything. Power and money. That's what they have. You don't have either of those, so see you around next year."

"We'll see. We got militia power. You'll see." With that, both Charlie and Sam jumped on their sleds and drove off toward town.

Bates laughed, saying out loud, "They have no idea. They are just cogs keeping the rich, rich. As long as they keep the division going, the super-rich can run the show."

Wayne and Tommy were close enough that they heard everything, even Bates muttering at the end. They just looked at each other and wondered what was going on, but they were sure of one thing, Joe and Ron were not here.

As they moved down the logging tail, the officers and Joette could see someone coming toward them. "Who the heck is that out here?" the Lieutenant asked.

"Could be anyone," Joette yelled into his ear, "but it could also be someone involved in this whole thing with our husbands."

They stopped and let the person or persons come to them. The Lieutenant had his hand on his Glock 9mm, not sure what they would run into here.

Charlie looked ahead, slowed to almost a crawl, and said, "Damn, is that the law out here?" He turned to Sam and said, "Don't you say a word. I got this."

They both stopped about three feet from each other. "Hello, officer, how doin'?" Charlie said with a lump in his throat.

"Good. What you boys doing out here?"

"Just out for a joy ride. We work out here logging most of the year, and we're just casin' out the joint looking for spots we can log next year."

"Hmmm, in this snow? Who are you anyway?"

"I'm Charlie and this here is Sam. We're related."

"Uh, huh. You see anyone out here today?"

"Nope, not a soul."

"Where have you been today?"

"Just took a ride down the trail and back. That's all."

"Have you been with anyone else? Wonder if you were with the person that we saw a while back. He was moving fast with a utility sled, just moved past us on a different trail."

"Haven't seen anyone."

"OK, we're going to move ahead here. I'd like to talk to you later. Where do you guys live?"

Joette spoke up right away, "I know who they are and where they live. I'll show you when we're back."

"Sounds good. See you boys later today."

Charlie and Sam sped up and moved slowly around them leaving the packed track, and then they were off. Charlie was grunting and cursing as they sped away.

The officers and Joette left the logging trail and came to the better road. It wasn't long before they were climbing the hill to the bunker. As soon as they came close to the gate, Bates saw them and noticed the insignia on the sleds: State Police. "Oh, man," he blurted out loud. "Where did these guys come from?" He quickly jumped up and made sure the doors were secure—then he sat and watched.

When the officers reached the gate, the first thing the Lieutenant said was, "What is this? Who put a gate and fence up like this way out here?"

Just then Tommy and Wayne came out from behind the trees. The officers were startled at first and reached for their weapons, but they soon realized that they were no threat as they waved hello to them. Their helmets were off, and they could see the two were not a problem—at least, not right now.

"Hello," Wayne said, as he moved toward the sleds. "Did you guys see the two men who left here?"

"Yes, we did," the Lieutenant answered.

"I'm not sure what they were doing, but they were the ones I think who took Joe and Ron."

Then Joette spoke up, "This is where I noticed that Joe's phone was. He must be inside the gate somewhere. I'm really worried that he and Ron might be hurt."

"Let's see your phone."

When Joette gave the phone to the officer, he saw the same thing. Joe's phone was there and he guessed, so was Joe. "This shows that his phone is nearby. I think we'll have to get into the gate."

"We tried that, but it has a heavy-duty chain and lock. We'd need some type of bolt cutters."

"No problem, we have 24-inch bolt cutters in our supplies on my partner's trailer. Lopez, grab the cutters and get those gates open."

"Yes, sir." Lopez searched in his utility sled and found what he was looking for. He walked to the gate and tried to cut the lock. It was tough. He tried again and again, and finally it gave way. "Whew, that was a tough one."

Once the lock was off, they were able to get the gate opened enough to get in. They all entered and Joette walked along with her phone out. They were close to the bunker door when she said, "I think the phone is right here someplace." She was standing to the side of the door near the trees. They all walked over and then Joette said, "I think we need to look around here. Let's get organized and see if we can find it. It might lead us to Joe."

They spread into a circle around where the phone should have been and began digging. Suddenly, Tommy yelled, "I found it!"

Joette said, "That looks like his phone all right!"

It was deep in the snow and lucky for Joe, it probably stayed warm enough down near the ground. It had very little juice left, but they had found it.

"This means he must have been here!" Joette screamed.

The officers became suspicious now. They saw the door and decided to see if they could get in, but they could see that was impossible. They pounded on it to see if someone was inside, but it was so thick with reinforced steel and concrete all around that they knew no one would hear them.

"We'll need another team out here to get into this thing. We don't have the right tools for that."

"Oh, one other important thing I forgot," Tommy said. "We got some of the license plate on the van that we saw last night. We think Ron and Joe might be in it."

"You should have told me that right away," Lopez explained.

"Yeah, sorry, it was a long night," Tommy apologized. "What I got was 102F. I couldn't get the rest because there was snow on it, but it was a regular blue Michigan plate."

"Thanks, good work, that will help."

Bates was watching all of this transpire, and he knew enough not to open the door. He thought his best bet was to tell headquarters that the place had been compromised—and then find out what they wanted him to do next.

Lower Michigan, that same day

When Joe noticed the men were still drinking outside, he snuck out the back door again, knowing he had little time. It was cold and he was not dressed for the temperatures, but it was a sunny November day. His eyes were so used to the dark that he had to squint to see clearly. The snow here wasn't as deep as it had been in the U.P., but there was enough to make looking for an implement almost impossible. He saw pallets and fifty-five-gallon drums against the building. It looked like some kind of acid. He scoured the area and searched the woods. He found a pile of junk covered in snow, probably some scraps from the original building of the warehouse, and he dug until his hands were freezing and he was shivering. He scrounged around, but all he could find was a six-inch piece of rebar and some pieces of concrete, which he thought he could use as a hammer to pry off the top of the box, but that would make a lot of noise; unfortunately, he knew it would take some time to get the top off even with the rebar and a rock.

As he walked toward the door trying to stay low, he spotted a small broken screwdriver. "That could work, if I use these together." He hurried inside, going right to the box. The men were still drinking and yelling at each other. He put the screwdriver in the end of the box between the top and the side and pried. Nothing. He tried again, and the little screwdriver broke. He grabbed the rebar, put it near the top of the wood and slammed it hard with the piece of concrete. It didn't make as much noise as he thought, and the guys were talking and yelling, so they may not have heard, so he kept pounding and then the top popped a bit.

When he was able to get it up about an inch, he used the rebar as a prying tool and the top lifted a few inches. He started going around the top, lifting at one spot after another until he had most of the nails exposed. He reached in and tapped Ron who realized Joe must have the top lifted. He sat up a little and bumped his head on the wooden top. Then Ron put some body into it and Joe lifted at the same time, and all the nails popped at once. Ron was free. Joe pulled off Ron's blindfold and tape.

Joe motioned to get out of the box, and so Ron kind of rolled out. Joe untied his feet and he directed him to the back door. They ran and were soon outside where Joe unfastened the hand ropes. His first gesture was a big hug before they both sprinted to the woods.

Outside, in front of the warehouse, the three men were still drinking and laughing. They thought they had a lot of time and so were in no hurry, and it was a sunny, but cold November day. What the hell! They were an unlikely crew. One had a full red beard, one guy looked quite young, and the third guy had an ungroomed gray beard and ratty clothes.

Joe and Ron were already shivering and did not know which way to run. The tracks in the snow would give their escape away to anyone looking for them. They moved to the edge of the woods to hide while they devised a plan.

Sunday afternoon
Charlie and Sam reached Colewin and decided to meet with a few of the troops. They knew now that their bunker was no longer safe, and they wanted to get the word out. Charlie was also upset about what Bates had said. "You're just a cog in the wheel." He was nervous and kept thinking about Bates and the bunker: What

the heck is going on? We have a plan with Escanaba, not some super-rich assholes who don't understand what life is like for many of us.

Charlie was very concerned about the cops and what they might discover. He called a meeting at his place. He didn't have a large room for a meeting, but if everyone squeezed in between the kitchen and living room, his place could fit most of them.

By now the militia had grown to over thirty people, and most of them showed up for the meeting. "We got a problem at the bunker," noted Charlie. "Ya got to stay away for several months 'til this mess is over."

"What mess are we talkin' 'bout?" Betty nervously chipped in.

"Too many people know the bunker is there, and they ain't the ones we want around there."

"Like who's there?" someone spoke up from the back of the room.

"Can't 'xactly say, but we got trouble. You already know that we cut training for a while, and now we're cuttin' it longer. Looks like we got some idiots that think they are running us. We ain't run by no one but ourselves."

"That's right," added Sam.

"Does this have anything to do with that teacher we been hearing about?" the same person from the back asked.

"Could be. He brung a lot of out o'towners here and they be getting involved too. The law is gonna stop a lot of it, I think, but our bunker is no longer secure."

"Where is that teacher now?" he asked.

"Don't know," replied Charlie. "That's all I really got. Any more questions?"

People mumbled and talked among themselves, but no one asked any more questions, and some began to leave.

"Yep, that's it. Ya can leave if you want. No talking about any o' this."

Several OKs and yeps came back as most of the people filed out.

A few people did not move. Among them Betty and Lane who were concerned about what Charlie said, "The law is gonna stop a lot of it." When most had left, Betty walked up to Charlie and said, "There's been a lot of people asking questions about that teacher—and Lane's been at the center of it. She's gettin' nervous."

"Why she gettin' nervous?" Charlie asked.

"Well, they been askin' a lot of questions—making her nervous."

"What kind o' questions?" Charlie asked quickly.

Betty saw his reaction and now she was nervous. "People who say they are representing the teacher in court. They been all over town asking stuff, and they were at the school the other day. They haven't talked to Paige yet, but I think they might. Lane keeps changin' the story a bit, which scares me. She's the nervous type, ya know."

Charlie was upset now. "I don't know why we got ourselves in this mess in the first place. What the hell were we thinking?"

"We had to get rid of that guy if we were going to stay safe and out of the long arm o' the law," Betty reminded Charlie.

"Yeah, but we ain't bad people. All we want is to make this country better and get rid of those lousy politicians and those teachers who make all o' us feel like we done somethin' wrong in this country. I ain't no racist like they say, and you talk to those teachers, and they make ya feel like we messed up the whole country."

"I hear ya and I agree, but we gotta do somethin'. That Wyatt guy give us a bad name, and even some people in Colewin don't trust none o' us anymore. They think we're nuts."

"Lane, what you been tellin' those people?" Charlie asked forcefully.

Lane looked like she had seen a ghost. She was sitting on the sofa, her legs pulled into her and her hands clenched. Her eyes were bloodshot and tears were streaming down her face. "I'm afraid. I don't remember what I tole 'um last time. I just can't remember."

"Did you stick to the same stuff we planned?" Charlie half-yelled which just made matters worse. Lane broke into a full sob and could not get a word out.

"Now calm down there, Lane," Charlie said in a way that did not make matters better.

Betty said, "Let's just stop right there. She's too upset to talk and you ain't helpin' at all. Let's go, Lane."

Betty turned and helped Lane off the sofa, and they headed to the door. Charlie pressed them a bit, "Don't you go saying any more stuff to those people, Lane. Just shut up for now."

Betty turned and looked at him with hate in her eyes and with fists raised. "You jest shut up now." And they left.

Sunday afternoon

After Bates explained the situation, he was patched through to a person he had spoken to only once before. He knew he had reached the top of the food chain with this one. "We heard what you said, and we will have to make some additional plans to keep the bunker safe. We cannot have anyone going there and finding out what we have. You hear?"

"I've kept the security door shut and locked, so they haven't been able to get in. They're just snooping around now. I think there are five of them. Not sure who they all are, except I know the woman and the two cops are State Police, not sure who the other two guys are. I've never seen them before that I can remember."

"We'll take care of all of these problems. Our resources reach far and wide, but you need to stay in the bunker and do not open it no matter what. Get that gate locked again when everyone is gone, lock the door, and eliminate anything that might give away anyone and anything. Keep one computer so you can contact us, and get rid of the rest somehow. And get rid of any written correspondence, plans for any attacks, and names of people. If worse comes to worst, we'll get you out of there. I can have a helicopter in and out in no time. We can fly low over Lake Michigan and swoop in to get you. This is the last correspondence you'll get, so wipe all your files, clean up everything online, and then get rid of what you can."

"Got it. I'll start right now. Hey, I think this might call for a bonus! It's getting a bit hairy."

"Don't push it. You get paid very well, but if this all goes without a hitch, there could be something for you. For sure there'll be something for you *if it does not.*"

Bates heard him loud and clear and knew he had work to do. "Got that. I'm on it."

Sunday afternoon

The only plan Joe and Ron could come up with was to circle around the building and try to steal the truck parked next to the building. They would have to make sure all three guys were not near the truck and that the keys were in it. They were freezing. Their hands, feet, and heads were very cold. Ron's ears felt like they might freeze and fall off. Joe thought his nose was frozen. Neither one had much use of his hands. It was bright and sunny, but it was a very cold day and getting colder. Ron and Joe talked as they snuck around the building, and Ron's voice shook as he asked, "How were those guys drinking beer and sitting outside?"

Joe wondered too. "I guess they're used to it, plus they have heavy jackets, gloves, and hats."

As they moved around the warehouse, they kept seeing pallets and fifty-five-gallon drums next to the building. Ron was inquisitive. "What are they doing with all this stuff? There is nothing else out here."

"Not sure," Joe said.

Right then they heard someone yell. "Hey, are there supposed to be two guys in those boxes?"

Ron and Joe were at the corner of the building now and saw two guys outside drinking beer. They both stood up when they heard the man yell. "What? Of course, there are two guys we need to take care of."

"Well, they're gone. Not in the boxes," yelled the younger guy.

Redbeard and old Graybeard were up in a second. "What? Where are they?" The two men threw their bottles and ran for the warehouse door.

Joe and Ron heard yelling and screaming, each man blaming the other. "We gotta find them. That's what we get for waiting."

"You're the one who pulled out the beer. Don't blame us," yelled Graybeard.

"You two go out back, I'll wait by the door in case they come running, and let's get our guns out of the truck so we have a chance if they are free."

The three of them bolted out of the warehouse, looking in all directions. They went right for the truck doors, two guys on the passenger side. They opened the door and pulled out two hunting rifles, Redbeard on the other side pulled out a large pistol. "I'll stay by the door and the truck, and you guys look in the building. Turn on all the lights. If they are not in there, be careful and you can go out the back and check for tracks. Don't be stupid."

Ron and Joe were on the side of the building in the woods, hidden enough among the trees, but they were sure the men would follow their footprints. "Ron, we've got to split up and make two trails. That'll mean they will have to split up also, and one man will be alone. Maybe we can even lose them."

Ron agreed, "I think we should split up just to make them work harder, but they do have guns, and we don't have anything including warm clothes, so we won't be able to run for long."

"Why don't we take two completely different paths and hope they do split up. I've got pretty good cardio right now. I ran all summer and I've been working out too. I can run through the snow better and keep them at bay. You take the road and see if you can find anything or anyone who can help."

Just then they saw two of the men come out from behind the warehouse following their tracks. "We better go now," Joe said quietly.

Ron agreed and said, "Good luck. Be careful. Hopefully, I'll be able to find someone to help."

"You be careful too." And they were off, heading in different directions—Joe going south into the woods, Ron headed west on the road.

Ron ran in the woods until he could see that the man by the truck could not see the road; then he dashed out of the woods and began running down the road. It was not as easy as he thought, even though the road was plowed. It was slippery, and he did not have the greatest traction. He knew this was not going to work.

Joe had run about one hundred yards in the woods and his lungs were already burning. Running in so much snow was not easy, and it was taking a toll. Joe was in good shape, but he was in his high sixties and old man time was catching up to him. He stopped to take a breath and wheezed, "This is tougher than I thought." He knew he had to keep moving, so he took only a few seconds rest and took off again.

Graybeard and the young man were not far behind. They were following his tracks and they noticed that the distance between footsteps picked up a bit. The young guy said, "He must be running."

"Yeah. He can't be too far ahead. Maybe he'll tire out and we'll catch him." Graybeard was already breathing heavily too.

"Hope so."

"No. Got to. It's him or us. We lose him, we're as good as dead. These guys don't play around."

"What! You mean they'll kill us?"

Old Graybeard slowed, "Yep, they will."

Ron kept trying to run, but it was no use. Although the road was quite wide and well-plowed, some of the ruts were deep, and the center was impossible to walk on and all of it was frozen. How they plowed this road he did not know. After he almost fell for the third time, he stopped. He'd never find anyone out here, especially at his pace, so he decided to do something that he thought might be dangerous. He turned around and started walking back. He was cold and shivering and talking to himself, "I'll get close and then duck into the woods. Maybe I can get the drop on these guys and get a gun. Wonder if one or two of them stayed behind. It's our only chance."

Redbeard was mad. He kept pacing back and forth looking in each direction as he stewed more and more. He was sure that he was a dead man if they did not find these guys. He liked the pay, but he had never worked for such vicious and secretive people. He had killed a few people right here at the warehouse on orders from them, but his partners were new to this.

Joe was trying to run in a straight line as far south as he could, and he thought he could come out somewhere if he did, but little did he know that if he ran straight, he'd have to run for ten miles in snow and frozen wetlands just to come to a small cabin in the woods. That was probably not going to happen. Joe kept running. He hit a little rise and the climb was extremely difficult. He stopped to breathe again. His heart was pounding, and he was sweating in spite of the cold weather. When he stopped, he felt the cold breeze—which woke him up to his situation, and he mouthed, "I've got to keep going." He reached the top of the hill and looked back. He saw both of them not far behind, and he gained renewed strength, turned and began running. *Fear will do that to you.*

Ron slipped into the woods and moved slowly and quietly in the direction of the warehouse and truck. He could not see anything yet, but he knew it was a matter of time. He'd have to be quiet and careful, lest anyone see him. A gun against bare hands is not much of a match.

The bunker, Sunday afternoon

Wayne and Tommy offered to stay behind with Lopez to make sure nothing else happened. Lopez drove his State Police snowmobile near the fence and sat on it. Tommy and Wayne went back to the tent to get some rest. They'd been up all night, and they told the officer to just yell if he needed them.

Lieutenant Smith jumped on his sled and told Joette to do the same. They'd head back and get more people involved so they could figure this thing out. "We can let the post know what we've found and exactly what we need. I'll have to file a formal report with the state too," Smith told Joette. He fired up the machine and they were gone.

Bates did not see them leave, but when he looked up, he noticed only one sled. "Have they all left but that guy? I'd better let the boss know." He sent a quick note that only one person was left, the cop. He was still a bit nervous and mumbling, "Well, what does it matter because it changes nothing for me. I've reported it and it's out of my hands." He continued to take things apart and destroy what he could of any incriminating evidence, especially any of his. Then he suddenly said, "I might have to go into hiding for a while if this blows up."

Wayne and Tommy were back in their tent and fast asleep after a night of watching and listening. They were both exhausted, and the tent supplied a very warm and quiet place to rest.

Lopez tried to lie back on his machine, but it wasn't very comfortable, so he sat on it and leaned back, pulled out his phone and tried to play some solitaire, but it was too cold, so he got up and walked back and forth to keep warm.

Sunday, late afternoon

Joette arrived home with Lieutenant Smith, and he told her, "I'll head back to the post and get help." He loaded his snowmobile on the trailer and left.

Joette was somewhat relieved knowing there would be help. She entered the house and was met by Shanice, who was getting ready to go.

Wendy came back to see Joette and Shanice, and to get an update on the situation. She had been gone longer than she wanted and was surprised that they did not call her about going out to the bunker, but she was happy Joette was back—and that the police had been there.

"I thought the police wouldn't be here for a while. When I didn't get a call, I assumed you had not gone yet. So, you didn't go then, Shanice?"

"No, I've been getting ready to go back home. I received an ultimatum from my firm that said I must return by tomorrow. I'd stay here, but I think that Joe and Ron aren't here anymore, and I am really worried. It sounds like they were taken somewhere. Tommy and Wayne stayed out with one of the officers. Tommy was able to get a license number and so the police are looking for a van with the numbers Tommy gave them."

"They'll find them, I'm sure. Did they say when Tommy would be coming back?" Wendy asked.

Joette replied, "No, they weren't sure. They're staying to make certain no one comes or goes."

"Good. I know there is something really bad going on out there. I hope they figure it out."

"It's time for me to leave. Please, Joette, keep me updated. I'll have my phone on all the time. I'm sure Ron and Joe will be all right. They've been in tight spots before."

"They have, and I will keep you updated."

At that point, they said their goodbyes with hugs all around; then Shanice was off. Wendy had to return to her parents' house, but she was going to come back and spend the day with Joette.

Lower Michigan, Sunday, late afternoon

Joe ran down the other side of the hill. He had gotten his second wind and felt like he could go for a while now. His thoughts were on Ron and where he was, hoping he had found something or someone to help. It was then that his foot hit something in the snow and he fell awkwardly sideways and felt a twinge of pain in his knee. He stood up full of snow and colder than ever. Thirty degrees isn't real bad, but when you hit the snow and you've been in it a while, it takes a toll. He stood up and tried to run, but his knee would not move well, and he had to drag his right leg as he plowed through the snow.

Not far behind him was the young guy with a rifle. Joe was now worried that he could not outrun the man. What could he do?

When he turned around to see where the men were, he saw the young man had just reached the crest of the hill, and he had a rifle pointed right at him. His buddy was not far behind.

Just then they all heard a sound like a car horn. It blared and blared and would not stop. Both men turned instinctively and Joe tried to run. A shot scared him into stopping.

The other man was there now. "Do it again and you're dead. Come this way and we'll walk back to the warehouse. Let's go. Put a hustle on and we'll see what the horn was about."

Joe hobbled up to the crest. "Can't you move faster than that?" the young man barked.

"Hurt my knee. I can't move very fast."

Graybeard said, "You take him to the warehouse. I'll run ahead and find out why the horn is honking like that. Keep him in your sights, and if he so much as tries to make any moves, shoot him in the head."

"But... you know that..." The young man did not get to finish his sentence. Graybeard gave him a look that made the young man freeze.

"Shut up. Just do as I say."

Sunday, dusk

Time was moving slowly for Joette. Wendy had gone home and Joette could not settle down. She was worried, and she thought that Tommy and Wayne would be back by now.

Tommy and Wayne were resting and waiting for any call for assistance from the officer when they heard a larger machine coming up the path. They both listened and wondered what it was. "Sounds like a groomer to me," Wayne said.

Tommy was confused, "Why out here at this time? It's going to be dark soon. Let's take a look from our cover."

"Yeah, too many strange things happening," Wayne agreed.

The groomer stopped right by Officer Lopez and two men got out, both with assault rifles. They moved quickly, just pointed their weapons at Lopez, and then told him to get down on the ground. He did. Before they were finished, they had him bound and inside the machine. One man got on and drove, and the other took the police vehicle and they drove away.

Bates watched the whole thing. He knew that powerful forces had taken over, but he did not think they would happen so fast. He was happy for what had transpired, and he went back to searching for material and sites he needed to eliminate.

Wayne and Tommy were shocked and startled. What just happened, and how did it happen so fast? They did not hesitate and broke camp, loaded everything into the sleds, and were gone in about thirty minutes.

CHAPTER 12: MISSING PEOPLE

Joette was about to call Cathy when she heard something in the driveway. That must be Wayne and Tommy. She walked to the door and opened it, but there were no snowmobiles, only the one she had ridden earlier, but there was a large truck and three men who were getting out. She stepped back and locked the door. One of the men walked to the door and knocked. Joette stood back, about to get a gun from the cabinet. In a very kind voice, someone asked, "Is this the DeLuca residence?"

"Who wants to know?" Joette asked.

"We were lost and someone said that you might help. It's about your husband."

"What? What about him?" But since she was focused on the door, she did not notice a man quietly entering a window in the bedroom. Before she knew it, she was grabbed from behind and the rifle was pulled from her grip.

"All clear," the man yelled as he held Joette and opened the door. Before long they had her tied up and carried to the truck. They completely emptied the house of as much as they could, making it look like someone left in a hurry. It only took a little over an hour. They loaded Joe's vehicles on to a car carrier, covered their tracks, and left.

On Monday, the school received two letters. Both were the teachers' resignations from the school district. The superintendent was shocked, but at the same time understood that the couple wanted to get away from all of the scrutiny. He wondered why Joe had run. He heard from the sheriff that he was now a fugitive, and he mused, why did he do that? The way things are going, it looks like he might be off the hook soon, but then, that was just a hunch.

Wayne and Tommy went straight to Joe's house. When they arrived, they could see that something was wrong. It was dark by now, but the vehicles were not there, the curtains were off the windows, and there were no lights on. Wayne banged on the door, "Joette, are you in there?" No answer. They both yelled a few times, and then realized that no one was home. Wayne tried the door. It was unlocked. When he looked in, he could see that all of the furniture was gone. "What the hell has happened?"

"I'm calling Wendy to see if she knows." Tommy called Wendy and she picked up right away.

"Tommy?"

"Yep. Hey, do you know where Mrs. Joe is?"

"What do you mean?"

"We just got here and everything is gone. It looks like no one lives here anymore."

"What? I was supposed to meet her tonight. I was going to wait with her to see if there was any news about Mr. Joe and to wait for you guys to come back."

"Oh, my God! What has happened? This is the second strange thing we've seen today. The officer that was out there was carried away, and when we tried to call the post to tell them, they said that Lieutenant Smith was transferred this afternoon and is no longer working from that post."

At the same time Wayne had called Cathy. She said she knew nothing, and that she had spoken to Joette—and she had felt comfortable that the police would find something.

At the warehouse, sometime earlier

Ron knew as he got closer that he would have to keep to the woods. He saw only one man with a handgun, so he decided to move to the back of the warehouse and enter the door at the back of the building. He was freezing and knew he did not have much strength left. Before he entered, he found a pallet that had been destroyed and he pulled a four-foot piece of hardwood from one. Then he quietly opened the door and moved into the warehouse. His plan was simple, but he knew it could fail, which might mean his life and that of Joe's. He moved stealthily to the front. His plan was to turn on the lights and see what kind of reaction he would get. He would pretend to be one of them.

When the lights went on, Redbeard asked, "That you boys?"

Ron answered, "Yep. Got 'em."

Redbeard was relieved but cautious and walked slowly to the building, but as he entered the door, a 2x2x4 piece of wooden pallet racked his head and he went down with a thud—out for the duration. "That'll teach you," Ron told him as Redbeard lay out cold. Ron had to think on his feet and his plan was to put the man in the truck like everything was all right, and he made it look like Redbeard was going to drive away and was honking the horn to alert his friends. The keys were in the truck, so before he got Redbeard into the truck, he decided to drive the truck into the garage. He moved the two boxes that he and Joe had been delivered in, and he backed it into the garage leaving just the hood sticking out. He left just a little space on the right of the door and a lot on his left. He dragged the man to the truck, found some rags and bound his hands and legs, and put a gag in his mouth. Then he picked up the pistol and put it in his belt, bent down, and threw Redbeard in the front seat and proceeded to blow the horn.

It wasn't long before Graybeard came out of the woods. He saw the truck was moved to the garage, and he figured Redbeard had his man in the warehouse. Good work he thought. Then he yelled, "Hey, we got the other guy, and he'll be here in a minute." He got close to the door and turned to go inside when he saw Redbeard sitting inside the truck. "What the hell you doing in there? You…" and that's all he got to say. Ron was standing with the pistol and the 2x2x4 inside the garage, and when Graybeard turned to look at his friend, *Whack!* His skull was racked with a pain that would last for quite a while.

"There you go. Two down, one to go," muttered Ron. He had no plan for the last young guy, so he picked up Graybeard, checked his rifle, tied him up and threw him in the truck with his buddy. Then he waited.

Joe was having a rough time of it, and he was worried that the honking horn meant that Ron was caught. He wanted to try something, but he had little strength and with his knee the way it was, he didn't stand a chance of outrunning the guy even if he knocked him down. It took some time, but finally he could see the warehouse and the front of the truck. It was getting dark and he could only see from the light on the warehouse gable, but he thought he saw the two men in the truck.

As they walked closer, the young guy spoke first. "Ha, I see they must have your friend. They're ready to get rid of you guys."

"Ha, ha," Joe repeated.

"Just get yourself in the door and don't say or do anything."

Joe walked slowly, wondering how he could beat three men. He was going to try something. If Ron was hurt or worse, he would fight to the finish. Joe turned into the warehouse, and when he did, the young man saw his two friends and could see something was wrong. He was stunned when he ran to the window of the truck to check them out. Ron only had to lift the rifle he had taken from Graybeard and put it squarely on the temple of the young man.

"Put that gun down slowly and sit your ass on the ground right now."

Joe turned and saw Ron and the young man. As soon as Ron said drop your gun, Joe had it in his hands. Then Joe yelled, "Man, I thought we were finished. You saved my life. You saved our lives. Who-Hoo. Let's get the hell out of here." At which point Joe and Ron high-fived.

Ron was pumped, and he knew they had to get moving. He also wondered if these guys had a cell phone they could use. They searched both men, took their jackets, hats, and gloves. They found very little on them, and they let them keep their wallets, but Joe and Ron kept the two rifles and the pistol. They decided to load the two older guys in the boxes and placed the covers on them, but they did not nail them shut.

Then they put some pressure on the young man. "You have a cell phone?" Ron asked. The young man handed over a rather new iPhone.

Joe asked him, "Who do you guys work for?"

"I don't know, but there was a guy here earlier on a snowmobile who seemed important, but he isn't the boss. The people we work for do not live around here, and we have never met them, but we're all afraid of them—and when they find out we lost you guys, we'll be dead."

"Why is that? How do you know that?"

"My dad always tells me that if we mess up, then it's us who'll die. I've only worked for a short time. My dad got me involved. He's that guy in the box on the right. I hope he's all right."

Joe felt for the kid, but they could have died because of them. "Why would you work for them then?"

"Money. We were always broke—and half the time we were hungry until these guys came along. Now we eat every day and can keep our families happy. We've only worked for them for a few months, but our lives are changing because of it."

Joe and Ron decided they would take the vehicle and the young guy and drive out of this place at first light. They would release the young kid later and let him take the truck as soon as they could find another vehicle—and when they could warm up a bit.

Late Sunday night

Shanice had been on the road more than five hours and finally arrived at home. She was tired and wondered why she was still working at sixty-seven. She was so worried about Ron, but felt he and Joe were all right, and that he would be calling her and letting her know that. She pulled into the garage and decided to leave her luggage until the morning. She took her purse, shut the door, and headed into their home. She decided to eat something but realized they had cleaned out the fridge and most of the pantry before leaving for the U.P., so she just went to bed to sleep for a few hours before she had to be at work.

About 1,500 miles away, decisions were being made about people in the U.P. Some people thought that a *plutocracy*—government by the wealthy—was the answer to the country's problems. They decided to put a plan in action that would result in complete rule by the rich, as if they didn't have control now. The political influence of the rich is wide and deep, but this group, more of an *oligarchy*—with a small group in charge—had decided to go a lot further in their influence and had begun to control certain parts of the country so they could extend their influence to all parts of life.

"All the individuals are taken care of. Am I correct?" asked the boss.

"Yes, sir. We'll have the last of them soon, and then we should be able to continue our work in the north sector," the boss's assistant reported.

"Good, I want to get as many troops and military materiels there as we can. We'll do it slowly and carefully this time. Most of the other bases are almost ready. We've got to have control of all sectors as soon as possible. I thought that the Wyatt kid had messed things up good, but it looks like we survived that." When the phone rang, he dismissed the man who had reported to him. Then he spoke into the receiver in a language that was not English, French, or Spanish, but something that sounded strange.

Shanice was fast asleep in no time, so she did not notice the two men who had destroyed the alarm system, entered her home, and walked directly to her room. They went straight to Shanice and placed a cloth over her face. She immediately awoke and was terrified. She saw a man and began to fight. She swung her fist and hit one of the men right in the nose, spraying blood all over the bedspread. This pissed him off, and he tried to choke her, but she passed out before he could get his hands on her.

It took these people a little more time to clear out the apartment than it did the men at Joette's, but in a few hours the place was empty, and it looked like no one was living there. The four of them were efficient and quick.

On Tuesday, Shanice's firm received an apologetic letter that she was retiring and leaving the firm. That made the partners very upset because she was the lead in the case, so they tried to call her, but she did not answer her cell or her landline at home. In fact, the landline had a message that the phone had been disconnected. So much for finding Shanice.

And surprisingly, Ron's school would receive his resignation, effective immediately. His principal would be shocked since he was a close friend and colleague. Why hadn't Ron told him about this change? What was his plan? It's so sudden. No one could really understand, but the superintendent would say it was real—and that was that. They would ask his sub to stay on indefinitely until they could hire a full-time replacement.

Monday morning

Joe and Ron figured it would be good to let their wives know how they were. Neither had said anything to their children, because they felt they shouldn't get them involved. Ron called first, but he did not get a response on Shanice's cell phone. He thought she was probably still sleeping, so he called the land line. What he got was a surprise message stating: "That line has been disconnected." He was now in a panic. "I'm calling her office."

"What's wrong?"

"Not sure. There's no answer anywhere, and our home phone has been disconnected." Ron called the office, but he realized it was too early to get anyone there, so he gave the phone to Joe to call Joette to see if she knew anything.

Joe called. No answer on the cell. He called the land line and received the same message as Ron. "How the heck could the line be disconnected?" Ron and Joe looked at each other and dread filled their eyes. Joe decided to call Wayne and Cathy to see if they knew anything.

"Hello," Cathy answered. "Who is this?"

"It's Joe."

"Oh, my God! Where are you? Are you all right?"

"I'm good, but I can't get ahold of Joette. My home phone said disconnected, and so did Ron's home phone."

"I hate to tell you this, but all of your belongings, your car, and Joette are all gone. Missing. We have no idea what has happened."

"What? She's missing? How could this be happening? We'll keep in touch. If you see anything or hear anything let us know when we call. You won't be able to call here, so please don't call this number. Thanks. Gotta run."

Joe hung up and told Ron what he had found out. They both just stared at each other. Joe told Ron to try Shanice's office again to see if anyone was in, but he had no luck. "I'll try later, Joe."

The two men who had been knocked out and placed in the boxes had been awake for a while. They both had splitting headaches and were very unsteady. The kid was tied up and sitting on the floor. Joe and Ron decided to try to find out as much as they could, so they changed their plans and decided to interrogate the older guys.

First, they got Graybeard. Ron was in his face. "Who the hell do you work for?"

Pale as snow, Graybeard looked like he was going to throw up, but he was also willing to talk, even though he mostly mumbled at first. "We…we really don't know." He took a deep breath and exhaled hard. "This was our first job and the guy who hired us, paid us very well, by the way. He was out here on a snowmobile yesterday." Graybeard stopped and took another deep breath and rubbed the back of his head. Then he continued, "He's the only one we know, and he said that the people he works for are very powerful and very rich. We didn't ask any more questions because we just wanted to get this over with and get paid. My buddy there has worked for these people before." Of course, he meant Redbeard.

Joe butted in, "You mean that you have just started working for them and this is your first job?"

"Yep, guess we're just amateurs."

Ron added, "Well, the young guy said that when they find out we're not dead that you will be."

"Guess so. That's what the boss said anyway." Then he lay back and closed his eyes.

The U.P.

Lieutenant Smith had left some information for the officers at his old post. He was sent packing quickly, but he was able to finish his report and give it to his boss. The police found the two snowmobiles that had been hidden near Lake Michigan. They did not seem to really be in a place that they would not be found, so they thought that was interesting. They did not have any hits on the license plate that Smith had given them, but they were still searching.

To the officer assigned to the case, this seemed like an opportunity for a guilty man to get lost and not have to face his accusers. On the other hand, the accusers' stories were all over the place and no one was sure whether to believe them. The older woman of the two was really falling apart. Some said it was the result of what the teacher, Joe, had done to her—but others thought that her lies were catching up to her.

Tommy and Wayne did not know what to think since they saw the officer taken away. They reported what happened, but they did not want their names included for fear that they might be next. The Michigan State Police wondered where Lopez was, and they thought the story was difficult to believe. They did not believe a word that was being reported about the bunker, and Wayne and Tommy could not understand why. Wayne and Tommy decided to stay put for a while and not talk about what had happened for fear of retribution by whoever was creating this mess.

Wendy was upset. "How can you just sit here and not do any looking for Mr. Joe and his wife? You know that they were both kidnapped! Why?"

Tommy did not want to talk. He had stuck his neck out and now he feared for his life. All he could do was think of his uncle and wonder if this was all related. "I'm sorry, but I'm afraid that the people who caused this might be after us, so we have to be smart and back off for a while."

Wayne and Cathy were perplexed, wondering if this was all a setup to get Joe out of there, but they had known the couple for years, and this just did not follow. They also knew Ron and Shanice, and the same was true for them. None of this made any sense, but Wayne knew what happened in the woods, which led him to believe that a force more powerful than the militia was at work. This made him worry!

All Wayne could think was that *this was a mess*. Everyone was in freeze mode and could not do much but hope this all would make sense in the long run.

Monday

Joe and Ron continued to question the men and tried to find out what they could. They felt this might lead them to the whereabouts of their wives. They also knew that if they could fake their deaths that the three men here could survive, but they would have to trust each other, and they figured they could since it would mean their lives too.

"What do you know about this guy, the one who hired you? Do you think he is in charge around here?"

"I think he is," Redbeard lied. He knew the truth, but he was playing dumb. "But he's the only one we know, and he approached me a while back."

"Do you know what they use this warehouse for?" Ron inquired.

"Don't know for sure. We've only been here a few times, but we know they always bring people in that they need to silence or get rid of. One time they had a whole bunch of people, looked like immigrants, and a big truck. Not sure what they were doing then. That was the first time we were here. When we told the guys in charge who we were, they made us leave right away, so we did."

"Man, that sounds like maybe they were into human trafficking or developing some kind of workforce for sex or labor. Who knows? Taking advantage of and using immigrants in the country who have nothing is just intolerable," Joe fumed.

"Yes, human trafficking," Ron declared.

"Could be," Graybeard said. "I saw all kinds of people, but mostly people of color."

"Ron, you thinking what I'm thinking?" Joe's eyes lit up like he knew something.

"Not sure. Unless you mean this might be a key place for them to transport or get rid of people."

"I think we'll stay here a few days," added Joe. "What do you think?"

"It's worth a try. We have no other leads, but we'll have to make it look like nothing happened here."

"We need help too if they bring in a lot of people. You guys want to buy your freedom and help us? We'll cover for you and hide out. We'll have to hide for a while anyway because it seems that someone wants us dead. That way they'll think you got rid of us, and you should be safe too."

"Sounds like a plan if we figure out how to beat them at their game," Graybeard said.

Redbeard wasn't so sure. "How can we trust you? We have no idea who you are."

"Do you have another plan?" Joe offered. "If not, I think we're all better off if we cooperate."

"Yes, yes. We need to get out of this mess," Graybeard said angrily. "You got us into this Red, so you need to help get us out."

"All right, you win. I'm in."

"OK. First, we get rid of the two wooden boxes, next we're going to need more clothes and more guns. Assault rifles if you have any, or can get them, and lots of ammunition," Ron added.

Redbeard was reluctant to agree, but Graybeard and the young guy were ready to do anything. They agreed right away. Joe planned out loud, "OK, one of you will go into town and get everything. We'll give you our sizes. I think Ron and Redbeard are about the same size, and I think the young guy and I are close. That way you won't have to buy anything extra and give away that you're helping us. How about guns? Do you need to buy anything? We have the two rifles and the pistol. Do you have any other guns? It'd be better if we don't draw too much attention by buying more, maybe just ammunition? We'll need food, rope, knives, duct tape, sleeping bags, and clothes. Anything else anyone can think of?"

No one could think of anything else right then.

"Yeah, we got plenty of firepower at home, but we can't be a part of the take down or they'll know what we did," said Graybeard.

"Agreed, but we'll need your fire power and help if they have a lot of people with guns, so we'll all need some ski masks and you'll need some different clothes. Would help if we could get some type of communication system too."

Ron jumped in, "The young guy can go to town and get all the supplies we need. He'll have to be careful when he returns in case someone does drive in here. Then, he should take the truck somewhere while we wait for something to happen."

What Ron and Joe planned, depended on whether the power structure used this warehouse as a place where any hostages or expendable individuals would pass through. Are they outright killers, and will they do whatever they need to secure their power?

Joe understood the monetary part of this whole problem. He told Ron, "When less than one percent make more than the lower ninety-plus percent, then we have a problem. They can control everything: people, media, the internet, politics, businesses, voting, and a few churches. They even control the political field by selecting people they want to run, buying elections, and just spreading cash wherever needed to meet their needs. Plus, they keep all of us working to get ahead with very little time to devote to stopping them. Many people are living paycheck to paycheck."

Ron agreed, "That's a fact, and we can't spend the kind of money on things that they can, so they're able to control so many parts of the economy and the country."

"Hopefully, we can take a small bite out of the success they have been having, and later we can get involved to make a huge difference."

"Got that," Ron said with a nod of the head and a shake of his fist. Ron then decided to call Shanice's office again. It rang. "Sundin and Sundin, Attorneys," someone answered.

"Hi, this is Ron Johnson. Is my wife Shanice in?"

"I haven't seen her. She was supposed to be in early today, but she must have been delayed. Do you want me to give her a message?"

"Ah, no, I'll try back later. Thank you."

"No luck?" Joe asked.

"No, and that is not like Shanice. She's one of those people who is always fifteen minutes early, or she feels she is late. Lombardi time she always calls it."

Joe and Ron were both preoccupied with not being able to communicate with their wives, but they knew they had to plan if Joette and now possibly Shanice, had been taken. They decided to stay near the warehouse for a few days to see what might transpire.

Tuesday, November 12

Sheriff Daryl was on his secure phone. He had a call from the communications center. It was not Bates, but one of his bosses.

"Are there any other people we need to 'invite' to our place?"

Daryl listened and said, "I think we should be all right. All the other people are locals that I know, and I can take care of everything."

"Right. Make sure you do."

"I'm on my way now to prove that the teacher and his friends are on the run to get away from the accusations."

"It had better work," a very deep and serious tone came from the voice on the phone.

"It will." And the phone went dead without any other discussion.

Daryl was on his way to assure anyone who needed to hear it that Joe had run away. He had all kinds of proof including the snowmobiles that they had left at Lake Michigan, the fact that his wife moved all of their belongings, and that they both resigned from their positions. "All is well."

Later, Tuesday, 1 p.m.

Ron thought it best to try his wife's office again. He called around one o'clock. "Hello, this is Ron Johnson. I called about my wife yesterday. Has she been there today?"

"Hello, Mr. Johnson. No, your wife has not shown up, but in this morning's mail, we received her resignation, effective immediately."

"What? Are you sure?"

"Yes, they had to assign her case to someone else yesterday— and today she is no longer a part of this firm."

"That can't be. Shanice would never resign. She's a workaholic."

"I'm sorry, Mr. Johnson, that's what I was told, and they said that she signed her letter."

"OK, thank you." Ron hung up and turned to Joe. "Joe, just as we suspected, she has resigned too. Something bad is going on. I've got to find Shanice!"

"What? What is going on, and who is running this horror show anyway?"

"Not sure, but we have to hope that whatever happened to them, they come through here. With any luck, they're still OK."

Joe agreed, "We have to stay positive. Let's get to work."

The young guy was sent to find the supplies they needed. He was nervous for his father and for their lives, and he wanted to do the right thing to save both of them. He took the truck and was able to get most of what they needed. Once he delivered the supplies, he left the warehouse area.

They all worked on a plan together in the event that anyone showed up. Joe and Ron set up a perimeter that kept them both out of sight. They had assigned spots in the woods where they had good sight lines to the large garage door. They had also assigned the two men to the back door in case they needed them. They could come in from behind anyone who might be taking cover inside. Ron had one cell phone, and the two men had one so they could communicate. They also wore ski masks to hide their faces.

They all camped out in the building to keep warm and took turns watching the road for any vehicles. The plan was, if they spotted anything, they would take their places. The left side of the warehouse was close to the woods, so Joe would take that since his knee was still bothering him, and Ron would take the far side on the right as he faced the building. It was quite a bit farther from the door than Joe. The only problem was the lack of phones. They really should have had three to be able to communicate with each person when in the proper spots.

Ron was the first watch, and just as he was ready to head to his spot, he heard a vehicle heading down the road. He moved back and contacted the others inside. Ron did not have enough time to get to his spot, so he and Joe moved quickly to the left side. Redbeard and Graybeard stood in the woods behind the warehouse ready to do what Joe and Ron requested.

After the garage door suddenly opened, the van came into view and pulled into the warehouse. The door remained open, and Joe and Ron saw a man open the back doors on the van and several people came out. He ordered them to move to the back of the warehouse and to be seated against the wall. Most of the people looked Black or Latina. There were two armed guards. One with an assault rifle moved near those on the floor, the other got back in the truck and left. The door shut.

Ron and Joe looked at each other and knew they were in for something. "We need to figure out what we're going to do now that we have an armed guard," Joe whispered to Ron.

They kicked around a couple of ideas when they heard another vehicle.

Ron bolted across the road to take his spot in the woods, and no sooner was he hidden when they saw another very similar van, so similar that Joe thought it was the same one. It proceeded to do the exact same thing. More people were dropped off, and another armed man stayed with the first man who was guarding the initial group. They did the exact same thing and left right away. This time Joe noticed that Black and White individuals were in the group. He wondered if maybe Joette and Shanice might be here already or might be in another group yet to come.

1,500 miles away
The boss was pensive. "This seems to be working out well with the help we were able to get. I was a bit worried the fiasco with

that Wyatt guy might blow the whole northern system to pieces, but it didn't. Surprising what a little cash will do. You offer these guys ten grand, and they'll do anything."

His assistant said, "Yeah, I guess we need to keep looking for those who are struggling financially, but you know, most anyone will work for tax-free money. We've been able to hire anyone we want, especially politicians, although they want more money, but money is the easiest part. It's unending with the sources we have."

"Now we need to get the entire system working for us. We have almost built an army of volunteers who don't give a damn what happens. So great." He had a wry smile on his face as he sat at his desk. "You know we've got to inflict some kind of pain on Wyatt's parents. The northern sector is key to our operation. They gave us their word that he would work out. Wonder what we can do to make it hurt—but keep them on our side. His father is in the upper quarter of the one percent we go after, so we need to keep him happy at the same time."

"Don't worry, boss, we can take care of it. He'll be pissed, but he'll know that he screwed up."

"I'll leave it to you then. Plan it out and take care of it. That'll be all for now."

"Will check in with you when all is completed."

Tuesday afternoon
Joe wanted to do something since they had more than twenty individuals, but he knew better. They had to wait until dark unless something else happened. Then he heard another vehicle.

Ron was situated so he could see up the road, and as soon as he heard a vehicle, he turned to see if it was another van, and it was. This time a much bigger van. He could see the van do the same thing as the others. Again, two men had weapons, but this time the van did not pull into the warehouse, it parked and turned to back in next to the door.

What are they doing? Ron thought. Joe was thinking the same thing.

Joe was startled. In the group he saw someone who looked a lot like Joette! He could not be sure, since these women were all dressed the same and had stocking hats on. Maybe it was just wishful thinking. Another man got out and walked them into the building.

Ron saw too, but he was too far away for any real recognition. He wished Joe had a phone. Just then another van came down the road, even before this one had left. Again, they did the exact same thing. They unloaded the van with more people than any other vehicle had brought. All the individuals looked Black and, as far as Ron could tell, all of the victims were female. "What in hell are they planning to do with these people? They must have about one hundred."

Joe was close enough to see and he definitely saw a person who looked his way into the woods as if trying to make a run for it, but one of the guys with a gun grabbed her and pushed her into the building. He was startled and blurted out, "Shanice! That looked like Shanice! Oh, my God, are our wives here? What are they going to do to all these people?"

Again, one man stayed with these new captives. Now there were four men with assault rifles. The vans left and the garage door closed. One armed man, who looked like a sentry, stayed outside.

Joe needed to speak with Ron, so he moved east toward the back of the building where the two men were. It was tough going with the snow and his sore knee, and it took him more time than he wanted to get there. When he was close, he whistled so as not to startle the two since they were both armed. Then he whispered, "Hello, can you guys hear me?"

Both men were cautious, and raised their rifles in case they were being ambushed, but they answered quietly, "Yeah, who's there?"

"It's me, Joe. I need to call Ron and check in. You have the other phone, right?"

"Right here. Move over slowly so we can see you."

Joe did just that and moved as close as he could until they could see him. "You guys see anything here?"

"Not much. We've been hearing vehicles off and on for quite some time. We tried to peek around the building, but we couldn't see anything, so we just stayed put and tried to keep warm."

"Could I have the phone?"

"Here you go."

Joe dialed Ron, who had his phone on silent mode. He felt the vibration against his skin. He had put the phone in his pocket to keep it warm. "Yeah, who's this?"

"Ron, it's Joe. We've got to do something quickly. I thought Shanice was in that group from the big van. Not sure if I saw Joette as so many women were all dressed the same. We need a plan. We can't do anything during daylight, but maybe we could plan something for dusk. Hopefully there are no more vehicles—that could mess us up good."

"We could shoot the guy outside, but that would alert the other guys, and we should not hurt anyone if we can avoid it. What if I get his attention so he looks my way and then, since you are a lot closer, you might be able to get him from behind."

"Sounds good, but I'm not too sure I could with my knee. I'd have to drag my leg and it would take time."

"We could trade places."

"Why don't you come to the back of the building? Stay hidden. We're all back here."

Ron moved slowly through the snow until he reached the other three. They devised a plan in which Joe would walk in the woods until he could come out in the road. Then he would walk down the road toward the warehouse like he belonged. They would do it just before dusk. Ron would have Joe covered if anyone tried to do anything. As Ron moved to his position with his rifle and his 2x2x4, he asked, "Joe, do you think you can do that? Your knee seems bad right now."

"I'll give it a shot, but it might take some time."

"We have time but be careful."

Joe was able to make it quite easily to his spot, and soon Joe and Ron were both in position. The other men stayed in the back as before. Joe moved, but he was slower than ever now. His knee was throbbing. When he finally reached the spot in the road, he came out of the woods and began walking toward the man. When he was in the open, he began to speak, "Help me, help me."

The man raised his rifle and moved toward Joe. "Who the hell are you, anyway?"

Joe just kept saying, "Help me. Help me."

The man moved just enough so Ron had his chance. He was right near the building, and he stepped out and moved for the man. As he got close the man heard him and turned, but Ron let him have it on the side of his head and he was out. Ron took his assault rifle and began to drag the man to the woods. They needed to do something to incapacitate him should he wake, although that was not likely soon. Ron found the rope they had gotten earlier and used it to tie the guy's legs and hands, and he used the duct tape to gag him. He had to move quickly as Joe retrieved his weapon.

The plan was to raise the door and hope to get another man out in the open. They stood on each side of the door. It was dark now, but the light on the gable might hurt their plan, so they called the two guys in the back and told them to stay on the phone and open the door when they tell them and be ready to shoot if anyone drew a weapon. They were also supposed to stay on the ground, so they were not seen and would not be a target.

The garage door opened, and the back door opened just a crack at the same time. One of the armed men moved close to the garage door opening and yelled, "Close the damn door. It's cold, man! Hey, dude, close the door!" He walked past the opening close to where Ron was waiting. The two other guys had their weapons shouldered and were looking at the big door. They told the victims to remain seated against the walls around the room. Ron had his chance and clubbed the guy when he reached the outside.

The rest happened very rapidly when the guard was knocked to the ground and the door did not close. Joe yelled to the other two guards, "Drop your weapons and surrender and nobody will get hurt." That just brought a barrage of fire from inside. So, reluctantly, Ron took out one of the guards. There was a lot of screaming as the people were getting on the floor trying to avoid any stray bullets. It was chaos. Joe shot the other guard at the same time as Graybeard shot him, but he did not go down. Instead, he moved to the wall and grabbed a hostage off the floor.

Joe yelled, "Let her go and put the gun down!"

The guard just turned and fired, but, at the same time, he fell to the floor. He was out. Joe walked carefully toward him and kicked his weapon away.

They checked and secured the bodies, and told the hostages to remain inside, but the relief lasted only a moment because they saw lights from a vehicle coming down the road. Joe yelled, "Everyone stay where you are and don't move."

The two men in the truck saw the garage door open and all the hostages still sitting on the floor. They pulled up short of the door and stopped the truck, "What the…why's the door open?" the driver asked.

"Not sure. But it doesn't look right," said the other man. They weren't ready for what happened next.

Joe and Ron decided they would walk out and meet the truck. They knew enough to lift their ski masks, so they would look like the armed guards. Ron walked slowly, waving, and they waved back. Then Joe came out and waved. They walked up to the truck with guns in hand, and then Joe opened the door on the passenger's side and pulled the man out and clubbed him with his rifle. The driver wasn't quick enough because his door flew open and Ron pulled him out and shoved him to the ground.

Both men sat on the ground in a state of surprise and panic.

"What the hell are you guys going to do with these people?" Ron asked the driver.

Joe and Ron put their ski masks back on. They knew they could not let anyone know who they were, including their wives, for fear that someone might know them and be able to identify them later.

They interrogated the men for some time, and they found out that the drivers were to deliver the women to a place where they would then be assigned to another man. Joe, Ron, and Graybeard collected all the alive and dead bodies and put them in the warehouse. They loaded all the hostages in the truck, but there was utter confusion until Joe announced that they would free them when they could get to a safe place. Then it was time for them to leave.

Ron asked Graybeard, "Where's your buddy?"

"Don't know. I lost him during the fight. I think we're all in trouble. That guy is a problem. He knows this area better than anyone, and I know he has his cell phone. He bolted during the fight, and I looked around after, but he was gone. I'm afraid my son and I will have to get the hell out of here 'cause he's gonna be a problem. He never was one of us."

Joe and Ron knew they had no time to look for Redbeard, and they also knew this meant that all their trouble at keeping everyone from identifying them was over if Redbeard was on the loose. They told Graybeard to call his son who had their truck that would eventually pick him up. They also wished him luck and told him he definitely should hide out for a while.

Before they left, Joe and Ron explained to the women what was going on. Some were still quite upset, but they knew they could not stay there. Once they had everyone in agreement, they shut the place down, and drove out and headed for where, they were not sure, but it wasn't south.

CHAPTER 13: MISSING PROPERTY

The next day

When the truck did not arrive at its destination, the head man tried to communicate with the men in the large truck, but he was not able to make contact. He sent a team out to find the problem. He tried to get in touch with the three men who had been a part of the day: Graybeard, Redbeard, and the young guy. He figured they could go to the warehouse and find out what had happened.

They reached Redbeard who reported what had happened. He was afraid for his life, but he realized he had to give them all the details and hope they would believe he was on their side. Redbeard was at the warehouse, and he allowed the men who drove the large truck to give their version too. The boss was not happy. Who in the world would know about the place or even find it, and who would steal their property? A hunt was on to find the truck.

Joe and Ron knew they had to get rid of the truck and free the hostages. They drove north as far as they felt safe on Highway 23, then they hit the backroads. Joe thought they needed to free the women where they could escape without being detected. A lot were probably illegal immigrants. They stopped on a side road south of the Mackinac Bridge and opened the back. They told the hostages they were free to go—and where they were—but they said they had to get rid of the truck.

Ron said, "There's a town not far from here. You can go there and hopefully get help. Sorry, but we can't help you any more than that. We need to run and hide ourselves." Both men still had their ski masks on so they would not be given away.

At the word "free," the majority of the women ran for the town. Some lingered, but realized they needed to get away from the truck or they would be caught. They ran. Only two stayed: Shanice and Joette. "How did you ever find out we would be taken to that place?" both women exclaimed at the same time. They were overcome with joy and excitement. They had held everything in for so long. Both women had actually identified each other and their husbands earlier, but they did not say anything for fear of messing up whatever plan they might have.

Joe answered, "That's where we were taken, and we hoped it was a place they would take most hostages, so we waited because we had no other way of finding you."

Ron then said, "Let's get out of here. I stopped here because I know where I can find a vehicle. We might have to steal it, but it'll get us some distance from this place."

"We'll all have to hide out for a while until things cool off or we can figure something out. I'm sure that we're wanted by the law, but, hey, we're free right now, so lead the way," Joe said happily.

Joette verified what Joe had said, "The law has both of you in trouble, Joe for breaking bail and Ron for assisting Joe, so we have to move fast and avoid Colewin." Once they had secured a vehicle, Shanice and Joette told of their abductions and what had transpired since they last were together.

It took a few days, but the four found their way to the U.P. again. Joe thought they should hide for a time—and his brother had a very secluded cabin north of Ishpeming on forty acres, and he knew they could all stay there for a while. Their journey to the cabin took them past the National Ski Hall of Fame on U.S. 41 in Ishpeming, then north.

It wasn't the average cabin in the woods. It was a four-bedroom log cabin with a beautiful loft overlooking a large kitchen and living room. It had three huge picture windows to the front and was surrounded by very dense woods—a true hideaway. Years ago, Joe and his brothers had built it for his older brother who loved the U.P. woods, but who had a job in California, keeping him away most of the time. His older brother was very well off and kept supplies, a little cash, and even a four-wheeler that could be used by any of his other family members. He even had an above-ground gas tank that had a little gas in it. It was a beautiful place and very secluded. They welcomed the cash since none of them had any, nor did they have any identification.

The couples contacted their adult children to let them know what was going on. They enjoyed the cabin where they thought they would stay for a short time, but it ended up being quite a bit longer than that. They told their children what had occurred, and they stocked up for a while, but then the pandemic hit.

They also had their children turn some of Joe and Ron's belongings into cash. They sold Ron's corvette, Joe's pontoon boat, and an assortment of other high-profile belongings of Joette and Shanice's to make it look like they were really deceased. For all four, collecting their retirement money might take some doing. Once they settled in, they had Joe's brother get rid of the car that they had used to head north.

1,500 miles away

The weather in the mid-seventies in south Florida is pleasant in November, but for the boss, the day was anything but pleasant. "How could we lose about one-hundred hostages? We had plans for them. Did we find the truck yet?"

"Negative, sir, but I have the entire team out searching from the Bridge to the warehouse. We think they went north since they would be easy to spot the more they headed south, but we do have people scouring the area south too. We also have our police connections involved, so it won't take too long."

"It's already too long. Keep me updated on the progress."

"Will do, boss."

Several hours later

"We found the truck. It was about a mile from Cheboygan, Michigan, in the northern Lower Peninsula. We did not find any of the umm, guests."

"Keep searching; they can't be far away. It's only been four hours."

"Well, it's dark now, and we hope to have some luck during the day tomorrow, but we'll keep looking."

"Again, keep me abreast of the situation."

A few people had been found frozen to death in the woods near Cheboygan. No one knew who they were—and they had no identification. After searching for days in northern Michigan, no one else was ever found. How had they all disappeared?

CHAPTER 14: TIME FLIES

Six months later, May 2020

Time seems to fly the older one gets, but for the couples staying in the cabin in the woods, time seemed to stand still. It had been months since they had decided to hide this far north in the U.P., and they had not seen any vehicles they didn't recognize. A couple of Joe's brothers had visited on the sly, and his brothers were informed of the trouble they were all in. It had been a brutal winter, very cold and a lot of snow. At one point the road was so full of snow that it looked like they would never get out, although a week later when he could travel the back roads, along came Joe's brother who plowed the road.

The pandemic was a difficult time in everyone's lives, but out here, it was business as usual as they all got into a bit of hunting and snowmobiling. The only problem was that because of the virus, they really couldn't let any of Joe's brothers in the house. They usually visited from about six to ten feet away, but it was good to have some type of company.

Joe's younger brothers brought two of their Polaris snowmobiles out for them to use as needed, and every so often, they brought gas for them. Cross country skiing was a favorite pastime; first they made trails with the snowmobiles that they turned into classic ski trails. Evenings found them playing Scrabble, cribbage, or any variety of games, along, of course, with their favorite TV programs. The cabin was equipped with a great satellite dish, so the guys had watched some football in January and February. Other than being fugitives, they were actually enjoying the lack of job stress.

Eating was a joy since they all took turns making their specialties for the evening meal. They had wine and lots of beer, so life was good for a pandemic. They developed a taste for venison and rabbit stew. Most of the meat was fresh as they all liked to do some hunting. Joette was especially adept at bow hunting, using a compound bow she had acquired through barter with Joe's brother. She would sit out in a blind that they had designed about four feet off the ground. Deer were plentiful, and one time she picked off a beautiful twelve-point buck.

Money was tight, but they had a lot of help, and Joe's brother from California came through when he heard about the issues. He'd wire money to one of the brothers who would take it to Joe.

But it wasn't all fun and games as it seemed, especially on May 25 when George Floyd was murdered in Minneapolis. They all watched intently as the situation seemed to spark a national response. Ron was visibly upset. "That could have been me, or anyone of my Black or brown friends. When is this going to stop? How many more brothers and sisters have to die this way?"

Shanice was horrified watching the rerun of the nine minutes that the officer knelt on Floyd's neck. "What did the man do?" she kept asking.

"He tried to pass a counterfeit twenty-dollar bill, I guess," Ron said.

"For that a man dies? Are you kidding me? Did he know it was counterfeit?" Joette was mortified.

"This can't keep happening. What causes someone to kneel on someone's neck because he passed a counterfeit twenty, or, for that matter, any reason?" Joe questioned.

"Well, it's not the first. Have you been following the deaths lately? Did you see what happened to Breonna Taylor?" Shanice was upset. "Breonna was sleeping in bed and they shot her eight times!"

"There's going to be a protest, I'm sure," said Joe. "Something has to be done and some things have to change."

"Protests, sit-ins, and marches happen all the time, but what has changed? It just keeps happening. This will put some people over the edge if it doesn't end well." Ron was pensive, saying, "Something different has to happen."

"Right. Being Black in America. I'll never understand it as you do, Ron, but from the stories you have told me about profiling experiences you've had, I can see why you say that."

They watched all night as the city of Minneapolis marched and chanted and finally exploded.

"This will not help. Who in the world is setting fires to the community in which most Black people live? It's not the Black people who live there who are doing this." Ron was adamant.

"Do you think these bastards who are after us are responsible for some of the infiltration into the ranks of the protestors? Could they be getting people riled up to do these things—or are they doing them?"

"Could be, Joe. Something is going on that doesn't make any sense. Most peaceful protests end in violence. Why?"

"I don't know, but we've always tried to make a difference. Maybe we can do something this time that will spill over into, not only helping ourselves, but helping people like we used to."

Six months later, November 2020
Joe and Ron had completed a lot of research during their time at the cabin. They had purchased cell phones and used the cabin's computer that had excellent Wi-Fi north of Ishpeming. They had

seen few people during this time. A trapper had passed by, and a snowmobiler had gotten lost and passed through, but they did not stay. Joe was afraid of anyone knowing who they were and where they were, and with the pandemic still raging, they would not allow them within ten feet. They knew they would have to change identities to get back into civilization since they now knew that the forces that put them in this situation were very powerful.

Joe's son had acquired for them the equipment and the proper access for the Dark Web using TOR. Ron's son and his wife had come to stay for a while during the pandemic, and his knowledge of the web far outpaced any of the others. Shanice also had fair knowledge of the web and did her share. Their research led them to a site on the dark web that sold individuals, human trafficking for forced labor and sexual exploitation. It was engineered by the same group that was hiring people to join the force—the group that had changed both couples' lives.

They learned that the group was so rich they could buy and control people at will. They pay their laborers well and use others who would not join them as their indentured slaves, forcing them to work with the threat of killing their entire family. They have pictures and information about the families that prove to the captives that these people mean business. Very few try to escape, which made what Joe and Ron did a year ago a very special situation. They freed almost a hundred females who would probably have been sold into prostitution or slavery.

The couples knew they had few choices—and they also realized they did not have the resources to combat these people. Word had it that they were keeping both the far left and the far right at odds to keep the population uncertain of the future. Individuals have been planted in each group, and they send infiltrators to upend any demonstration by one or the other group. *Instability is the goal.* "You know, we have found a lot of information, but this last bit looks extremely evil," Joe said.

"I agree. It looks like they want to put doubt into the election," Ron exclaimed.

"For sure. The election is a done deal, but people are still arguing that the vote is false."

"Well, the Dark Web indicated that something serious is going to happen if the election is not overturned," Ron added.

"Joette and Shanice were listening to the exchange, and Joette said, "Is there anything we can do?""

Shanice agreed, "We can't just sit here and let all of this happen. We need to do something to stop the chaos that these people are causing."

"Sounds like something we would like to help change, but we have so few people we can really trust, and not much in financing to back us up," Ron said with a sense of defeat.

Joe was perplexed but was trying to stay positive. "So far, very little has happened, so we need to keep investigating and try to find out what the next big step will be for these people. We know they are not afraid to eliminate anyone, pay off anyone, or enslave people. We need to improve our search capacity and get people who know more about the Dark Web and other places where we can find current information."

"But because they want to keep both left and right at odds, it's bad for the country. Most people don't like the divisiveness, but when things get so muddled, it's difficult for anyone to see straight," Joette said, visibly worried.

1,500 miles away, December 2020
The boss exuded confidence, saying, "Well, things are playing into our hands. We need to keep this frustration going on both sides and make sure that we keep infiltrating the groups to keep

everyone on edge. The sooner we can get things to be *near chaos* is when we can step in."

"We have to come up with something really good for that to happen. What could set people off and confuse everyone into thinking that the other side is destroying the country?"

The boss continued, "I think I have a plan, but we'll have to get our politician friends involved and some of the police we have on the payroll. Let's find out how many we have in the National Guard and the active-duty military to see if we have enough to make a difference. Is the general still on the payroll—and is he on board with what we've been doing?"

"Not so certain anymore. He was visibly upset when I mentioned the plan you had last week. I know you've changed since, but he is for sure doubtful." The boss's right-hand man looked hesitant.

"We need him back on board. If we can keep the two factions fighting each other, we will need the military eventually because it will get bad, especially if I make the call that I've been considering."

"We'll get on it as soon as we can."

"No, get on it NOW!" the boss thundered. "We need every faction out there infiltrated, and we need more people overall, but, especially political, military, and the arm of the law!"

"Do you want our infiltrators involved soon? We have knowledge that the right is planning a huge gathering in D.C. come January. Would that be the time?"

The boss looked surprised. "You have read my mind. You understand the plan."

"Not sure, sir. I just thought you would take advantage of the situation and turn it into something."

Late December, 2020

Ron's son had come across some information while surfing the web late one night shortly after Christmas. He was alarmed and wanted his father and Joe to know. "There's chatter on the web that the group is going to make a mess this January to keep everyone on edge. They know that unrest will lead to their total control when they take over the government. They have people in high places now—and they will just step in and create the plutocracy they want. Of course, no one will understand that the country will be totally in the hands of this powerful, extremely rich group, and that they will be calling all the shots."

"Sounds about right," Ron and Joe both agreed.

"I found one other thing that was really alarming—a post that said something like 'the teacher from the northern sector and his friend have been located.' It didn't say your names, but this came up in a few posts, and I figured that someone knows that you are alive, and they are looking for you again. I'm not sure where it came from, but I saw it in three places."

"How could that be?" Joe jumped to his feet and stared at Ron. "Likely it is Redbeard as we figured. But located? How?"

"Redbeard must have turned on us for sure. I was hoping he wouldn't, but I guess that's what brought us here. Should have found him that night," Ron said.

"They probably figured we'd try to find a place up here in the U.P., don't you think?"

"Not sure, Joe. I really think they have all kinds of people looking for us. How they found out where we are is troubling. They probably looked at any places we've been in the last few years, and this is one of them, so I suppose, yes, they somehow found us here. My guess is they've checked my old hometown in Virginia too. We better contact our families."

1,500 miles away, New Year's Day, 2021

"Sir, I think we have a lead on the two guys who stole our truck back in 2019. Remember when we lost the women that we had rounded up for trading?"

"Yes, I recall. You don't mean women, you mean cargo that we purchased, right? I was very upset you never could find the cargo when we found out that the two gentlemen were still active, even after our man told us the events of that night. Those two have too much knowledge of the bunker, and they destroyed our delivery system. They will probably get help from the organization they used to work for. What type of information have you gathered so far?"

"It's not certain, but one of our informants lives in Michigan's central Upper Peninsula, and he said he heard a guy talk about a cabin up north that was being used by some people. He said the guy traps up there, and he has never seen some of those people previously. His description was similar to the one we put out on the web. We have men on the way up there to check it out; it should only take a few days before we'll know for sure."

"Good. That'll close a chapter we need closed. Hopefully, it is them. I'm getting sick and tired of the fact that we pay all these people, and they can't do better than they have with those guys."

"Also, we've got the northern sector set for delivery of the equipment you requested. May have to wait until spring, but the roads have been improved, the bunker increased in size, and the troops you requested are there and in place. A helipad has been set up for delivery of some of the equipment to travel over Lake Michigan and Superior. Some of the personnel are already there, so is the biological equipment. The other weapons you ordered for this coming week have also been delivered and are in transit to the people who will infiltrate the crowd."

"Sounds like all is going well. Have we had any more trouble with the people near the bunker?"

"None. The pandemic really slowed down the movement of people in the area, and most people just are not feeling safe yet. I'm sure it'll change soon, but right now, we are in great shape."

"How about the eastern sector near D.C.? Is it all set?"

"Yes, sir."

The boss rose from his chair, took a drink of his cocktail, and blew a big cloud of smoke from his Mayan sicar. "Good, our council meets tomorrow—and I'll give them the good news. They'll be happy to hear that their money is being used in the way they wanted."

January 2, 2021, 1 p.m.

It had been a long week, and the two couples had finally come to the conclusion that they needed to change their hiding place. A year is a long time to stay hidden in one place. If their names were coming up, then someone was on to them. They gathered the families and told them of their idea to move. All agreed that it was best. They also decided that their children should take extra precautions too, especially if anyone was snooping around trying to get information.

They all agreed that wherever the couples went, they should not let anyone know, not even anyone in the family. Ron and Joe talked about separating for a while and not contacting each other, but they finally agreed that they probably should stay together for protection.

It took some time to get everything back the way they had found the cabin. They had acquired a small van which they thought they would fill, but they really had not acquired that many things. They also had a small Honda Civic. When everything was packed and their adult children had left, Joe and Ron did everything they could to erase any tracks from vehicles and any footprints around the house. It was cold, very cold. It hit negative twenty at noon, so they moved as fast as they could. When they were satisfied, Joe and Ron jumped in the van and Shanice and Joette drove the Honda. They were to follow, but not close enough to be spotted as a pair on the road.

They had decided to head west where Joe and Joette had lived in a small town north of Duluth, Minnesota. It was very remote and a lot of small cabins and homes in the area had been abandoned when the mines moved out of the area. The houses would not be in good shape, but that was a chance they had to take. They would take U.S. 41 out of Ishpeming; then travel northwest to Duluth, and then north to Eveleth. Joe remembered the small town famous for the U.S. Hockey Hall of Fame Museum, but they would miss Hibbing, Minnesota, where Bob Dylan grew up. Then it was a trip as far north as possible past Virginia, Minnesota, to find someplace to stay for a while. It was a lot like the U.P. Mining was king, and many Yoopers moved to Minnesota when the mines around Negaunee failed in the U.P. Joe even had some relatives there, but he had never met them.

Joe and Joette also had some friends in Hibbing they had met when he and Joette were much younger, and they were hoping that that friendship would still be strong—if their friends were still alive! He and Joette used to hunt and fish, and spent a lot of time with several couples. Ron had been there too right after Joe left the army in '74. Ron took a leave from duty and visited Joe in Minnesota to introduce him to Shanice.

One often wonders how years pass and a person just keeps going on to the next thing. Joe, Ron, Joette, and Shanice did just that, but they were fortunate that they had been healthy throughout the years. Now, Joe was wondering if they would remain healthy with this unknown force after them. He knew how to get ahold of his old buddies in Hibbing, but he did not want to go there for fear of being recognized, and on top of that, the pandemic was still strong in many areas, so they wanted to avoid that too. None of them really wanted to move, but they agreed that it would be best. Yet, they all had lingering thoughts about staying—running just didn't suit them.

3:30 p.m.

They had gotten about ten minutes past Ishpeming when Ron said, "Joe, I don't want to go to Minnesota. If we do that, who knows where we'll have to go next if they keep hunting us."

"Ron, I agree. I had the same thought. We have to take a stand."

"We should. After all, we're going to be in our seventies soon. Who knows how long our health will hold out? Hopefully, a long time, but I want to stand for something."

"Like you say, 'If we don't stand for something....'"

"The hell with those bastards. Let's take a stand. Let's go back to your brother's cabin. It's a beautiful place even at twenty below zero. It has four bedrooms, bathrooms, a jacuzzi, and pleasant company. Do you think he'll mind?"

"He won't mind. He'd tell us to stay as long as we want."

"Besides, Joe, you have all kinds of relatives there who'll help us. We just have to let them in on what's happening."

"That's a good point. I have hundreds of friends and relatives there who'll pull together for us. We'll have to be careful, but most will spread the word to help."

"Let's see what the girls think," Ron said, happy to be doing something better than running.

"Give 'em a call."

Ron dialed the phone and got Shanice. Joette was driving. Before Ron could say anything, Shanice said, "We don't want to go to Minnesota. We want to go back to the cabin."

"Whoa, did you read our minds? We were thinking the same thing." Shanice sighed and then scolded the guys, "Couldn't you have thought of that before all the packing and preparation to leave!" They all had a little chuckle, but the four of them were relieved that they had come to this conclusion.

Joe heard the conversation and said, "We're going to turn around at Koski Corners. Do you know where that is?"

Shanice turned to Joette, "Do you know where Koski Corners is?"

Joette had a big smile on her face, "Yes, I do."

"They're turning around there."

"Sounds great."

Thirty minutes earlier

"That's the road we need to take to get to the place where they're staying," said the man sitting in the passenger seat of the Cadillac Escalade Platinum. Three others in the car were all holding AR-15s. Two Range Rover Sentinels followed with six armed men in each, with full military gear and camo.

"Man, this place is desolate. Who in their right mind would live up here and out this far? These guys must be some kind of lumberjacks or something."

"I hear you. It's damn cold up here. What's it say now? I think it got a little warmer. Only eighteen below, and, wow, it's beginning to snow a little."

"Can't. I heard that it can't snow when it gets this cold."

"Well, look. It's white stuff coming down."

"No shit, I hope we don't get caught in a snowstorm. That would be the pits. What if these guys aren't even there?"

"I don't know. You're the boss."

"According to the directions, we have to take a right turn up ahead. We got about a quarter mile to go."

"Got ya."

"Is this the road?"

"Must be."

"This is awful. I can't see anything."

"Turn on the damn lights."

A few chuckles came out of the back seat, and the leader turned and gave a sour look at the men in back. They quieted down quickly. The road was bendy and bumpy because of the snow that was falling, and it made it difficult to keep the vehicle moving smoothly. The forest was very dense, and it was already getting dark in the woods. It personified the shadows thrown by the head-lights and intensified the size of the snowflakes as they began to fall rapidly. There were no stars, moon, or lights other than the vehicle—and it was very, very eerie.

They came around a curve in the road at four p.m. where they saw the end of the road and what looked like a building up ahead.

4:00 p.m.

The two vehicles had turned around at Koski Corners and headed right back to the cabin. By four p.m. they were on the road leading north toward the cabin. In thirty minutes, they would be there if the snow held off a bit.

Shanice was concerned. "It wasn't snowing earlier. I hope it doesn't last, and we can get to the cabin."

"It's so slippery out here, and I can't see the road because of the snow. It's blinding."

Shanice reassured her, "Well, we can see the taillights of the van up ahead, so if we have trouble, they can help."

They drove a bit and then took the right turn onto the home stretch road. Relieved, Shanice said, "Thank God. We made it."

Just then, the van came to a stop up ahead. The girls looked at each other and wondered what now. Ron stepped out of the van and walked back to the Honda. Shanice rolled down the window.

"It looks like we have company. Did you notice the tracks in the snow?"

"Noticed your tracks. That's it," Shanice replied.

"We're less than a quarter mile away, so we turned off our lights. You should do the same. We're going to take a look, so you guys should back down the road where we took the right turn and get ready to run if we tell you."

"Sounds like a plan," Joette said in a shaky voice.

Ron told Joe to drive a little closer and to stop before the curve in the road. Then they proceeded on foot. When they got close, it was very dark, but they could see three vehicles and several men with guns outside. They also saw one light on in the cabin; then another. Somebody came out and said, "Search around the woods. Get your flashlights and check everything around here. We'll finish the inside." Then the light outside was turned on— and there on the deck was Redbeard.

Joe turned to Ron. "Let's get out of here. We should park up the road from the right turn and watch until they leave, then we'll go back and see if they leave anyone there before going in." They returned to the van and backed as quickly as they could, but it was tough going and right before they reached the turn, the van slipped into a dip in the road. "Damn it. Tell the girls to head up the road and take that first left and hide the Honda."

Ron thought otherwise and said, "We're going to need them to help get this thing out of here. If we can't, we'll give ourselves away if those guys decide to leave. I counted at least a dozen men." Ron retrieved the girls, and they had Joette drive and the others pushed the vehicle sideways, but nothing happened. They tried three more times before it finally dawned on Ron. "Now I know why that salesman said to take the van with the winch on the front!" He tied the cable to a tree and once they engaged it, the van bounced back on the road. After unhooking the wire, Joette backed it up and made the turn. They took the vehicles up the road—and decided they needed a new plan.

Ron got out and walked up the road close to the cabin and hid in the woods, hoping he might get a look at what they might do. It would not be long. As he remembered, at eighteen below zero a person could freeze in less than twenty minutes. They decided that the four of them would switch every fifteen minutes if necessary. It would be a bit of a walk from where he was to the road, but once he left the home-stretch road, it wasn't that far to the vehicles.

Back at the cabin, the men had torn the place apart, but after an hour of searching, they could not find anything that linked the two men to the place. Redbeard gave the order, "Everyone back in the vehicles. They aren't anywhere near here. If they had been, they are long gone, so false alarm. Let's check in with the boss to see what he wants us to do."

Soon all three vehicles were headed out. Most of the men were very happy to be back inside the warm SUV. Sometimes you can't seem to put on enough clothes when the temperature dips below zero, and for these guys that was the case. The vehicles were warm and cozy after being outside in the cold. They all smiled on the way back to Marquette where they were staying. Only Redbeard had a frown—and a phone call to make.

January 6, 2021

"Joe, girls, you have to see this." Watching TV news, Ron was excited and nervous at the same time.

"What is it?" Joette thought something serious had happened to one of them, or maybe those SUVs were back.

"Look, look at that. Oh, my God! What the hell? Where are the police? Look, those guys are just walking into the Capitol, and no one is stopping them."

Joe was mystified and pondered. *How could this be happening in our country? Where are the security forces that are always present during protests?*

They all watched in horror as the Capitol building was pillaged and overrun with individuals saying that the president told them to do it. Once again, Joe asked the important question, "Is this that rich group again infiltrating this group to cause it to turn into a rebellion?"

Ron just stood there and stared at the television. Shanice and Joette sat on the sofa with wide eyes. Their only thoughts were whether this could really be happening here? It seemed like hours before any sense of control was taken away from the mob. Joe had a knot in the pit of his stomach, and his fists were tightly clenched.

Ron just sat there and kept saying, "I knew this would happen! I knew this would happen! Too much negative rhetoric."

1,500 miles away

The number two man made a call, "Boss, are you watching the mob at the Capitol building?"

"I am. Maybe we've finally been successful. Did our people get to D.C. as we planned? It looks like they helped cause a mess there."

"Yes, our people are there to infiltrate and cause a disaster, but the left did not show up to counterprotest, so I think we won't get the effect we wanted."

"Oh, we're getting what we wanted. If they can overthrow those idiots inside, we'll move in as fast as we can and take over. This should be easy. Much better than what I had hoped for. What did our people do to help bring this about?"

"Not sure. Some of them were stuck on the outside of the group. The protest was much larger than they thought, plus they arrived much later than they should have. We had about three dozen people with Molotov cocktails, guns, and tear gas, but a lot of it never got used."

"Really, I guess we won't have to be as active as we thought. Maybe the left and right will take themselves down, or they will destroy the rule of law—that's good for us."

"Maybe so, boss."

"Keep me updated on our people and what they do and have done. This gives me some really good ideas to pass along to the committee."

"Will do."

Colewin, January 6, 2021

Charlie picked up his phone and called Don, "Are you watching this, Don?"

"Are you referring to what's going on at the Capitol?"

"Yes!" Charlie said.

"Sure am. I always thought that something like this was going to happen."

"What is going on? Are these the people who are trying to take over here? 'Cause if they are, I don't wanna have nothin' more to do with 'em. They're taking over the bunker. Got helicopters, troops, and all kinds of weapons pouring in."

"Yeah, I think you guys are in over your heads here."

"Our militia is nothing compared to these guys. They want ta take down the country and turn it into somethin' I don't agree with."

Don and Charlie had a long talk, and Charlie decided to tell those people that they were no longer welcome at his base—and they maybe should move their people and supplies elsewhere. He decided to contact the other bases in the U.P. to see what was happening there. Some of them had people in D.C., which surprised Charlie. Most knew little about the changes near Colewin. Some liked what was happening and thought that what they wanted would come quicker if they had help.

Charlie knew they were wrong. "These guys running our bunker are out of touch with us. They got money, and they don't understand us. It's worse than all the politicians put together. Course, some of them politicians are probably very rich too."

CHAPTER 15: THE FBI

The cabin, January 10, 2021

"What can we do next? This country seems to be spiraling out of control. What we've witnessed in the past year is unbelievable. We need to find out if this is all connected," Joe agonized.

"It's time we got law enforcement involved in this whole thing. We've been hiding out long enough," Joette responded.

"But how do we do that? We really can't trust anyone."

"Other than your brothers, we haven't seen any other people except the crew that got in here earlier this month," Ron said.

"There must be someone we can trust to help us out of this," Shanice added.

Joette had an idea. "What about that girl who joined the FBI years ago. Remember her? It was about twenty-plus years ago, I think."

"Yes, I remember her. She was a student of mine. Her name was Ann. The problem is we don't know who we can trust. Ron and I did work with her several times in the past, but...."

"But we need to trust somebody," Joette complained.

"She's right," Shanice agreed.

"I think we have to do something. This pandemic is still bad, but it seems to be letting up a bit in some places. It's been great being able to stay safe during it, but we won't want to keep hiding the rest of our lives."

"Well, as I said, Ron and I both know her from past work. We could trust her, that is if she is still in the bureau. I think we need to make a call." Joe was fed up and disgusted that he had not thought of her earlier and had not done something sooner.

Ron agreed, "We need to be proactive. Ann's a good start because we know her. We've been sitting around long enough. We should get my son on the web again and see if he can identify some of the leaders of this mess."

"That's good, get him on it right away, but I think we'll need more than one person searching. Let's give our friend a call. Since she's been in the FBI for more than twenty years, she knows a lot. Maybe she can get some help on the web too."

"Sounds good." Ron called his son and updated him on everything.

Joe searched for the person to call, hoping he would find that she was still in the FBI. It took some time, but he was able to identify a couple of individuals he thought might be her. He tried the first one, and, as luck would have it, she answered.

"Hello."

"Hello, is this Ann W.? It is? This is Joe DeLuca, your old high school English teacher. Do you remember me?"

"Yes, I do, but since you no longer are involved with the military, I've lost track of you."

"Ann, I'm in a real situation, and Ron too. Remember him?"

"Yes."

"I know we've worked together a lot, but that was a long time ago. Are you still in the FBI?"

"Why? Who wants to know?"

"We do. We wanted to call and touch base with you to see if you can help."

"How do I know for sure this is really you?"

"Well, let's see. We've worked together a lot, but how about something years ago, say from school. Can you remember your senior year, and the school play you were in? You played one of the old ladies. Remember in practice when you were struggling with the part? I told you to work with the women I brought in to help. One of them was my mother-in-law, and she had an expression you said you did not understand. Remember?"

"I do."

"Uff-da."

"So this is supposed to make me sure this is you?"

"Well, it's kind of lame, but it's the best I can do under the circumstances. I wanted to stay away from the legal aspects we worked on together since other people might know those, but not many people know about your high school years."

"OK, who did I play?"

"You were Mama."

"So, all right. For sure this has got to be you. No one else knows that story. Mr. DeLuca, what's the issue? Oh, and now that I know it's you, it's great to hear from you."

They spoke for a short time on the phone before Ann stopped him and said that she could not say much more over the phone. "Joe, I would like to talk to you because you and Ron have been on our radar for about a year. You used to be in the know with all this stuff, but since you and Ron left… Could you both meet me somewhere?"

"Really. Where would that be?"

"Let's make it a place where we don't have to worry about anyone listening in."

"You are in Detroit. We're nowhere near Detroit. I won't say where we are, but it would take some time for us to get there."

"All right. Are you in Michigan?"

"We're close." Joe did not want to give anything away, so he lied about being in Michigan.

"Could you meet near Bay City on I-75? There's the Bay City Rest Area. It's mostly closed during the winter, but you will still be able to pull in there. You won't be far from the Saginaw Valley Golf Course."

"Sure, we can be there. When?"

"Let's see, today is the tenth. I'll be near there on Wednesday. Could you make it then?"

"Sure. That's Wednesday, the thirteenth? What time and exact spot?" Joe asked.

"Right, the thirteenth. Let's say noon. Look for a black Cadillac. I'll try to find a spot with a table if any are there, otherwise we'll talk in my Caddy. Don't expose yourself until you see me exit the car. Don't be late because I won't be able to stay long."

"Lucky date. I hope it's lucky for us."

"I need to go, Mr. DeLuca. See you then."

"OK. Bye." Click.

It wasn't what Joe expected. He figured she could help him out and tell him about some of the people who had driven them into hiding, but she was being very guarded with her words.

"I guess we'll have to wait and see when we meet."

Joe explained to the others what he had just discussed, and they immediately began to plan their trip. They had a few days to get things ready, and they made lists of what they would need in the event that something would happen that they had not planned.

"I think we should be ready for anything," Ron noted.

"You're right. We should not take anything at face value when we meet, especially if she is on the payroll of these guys. Who knows?"

Colewin, January 10, 2021

Bates had been at the bunker now for quite some time. He had cleaned it out of any incriminating evidence that might hurt the group or him. The command center had told him to stay put and sent people to help improve the bunker. It was much bigger now, but he still had to operate the computer.

He had been at the computer for several hours and needed a break. There had been so much activity there recently that he had been asked to work long hours planning movements of personnel and equipment. The entire bunker had been reconfigured, so his office was now stuck in a small room straight ahead of where it had been. The rest of what had been his "home" was mostly used to bring equipment in and out of the bunker. It was just a huge storage area now with immense doors. Equipment would come in at all hours of the night barring any snow that might make it difficult.

Bates often thought of his friend Wyatt. He had few people he was close to, and Wyatt had been a lot of fun. They were not alike, but they liked to party. He wondered how Wyatt fit into this whole situation. Bates had made a lot of money working for these guys, but he knew there was a lot more to be had, and he wanted some of that action. What could he do to get there? He was getting tired of the people who constantly interrupted him and thought they were above him. These guys were just peons in a large movement that, at times, scared him, and it took a lot to scare Bates.

Next week, they were to get a visit from an important person who was going to plan some major event. Would he still have a job after that?

1,500 miles away, January 11, 2021

"Let's get this straight. We're going to meet to decide our big move." The boss was talking to a number of very key envoys that had been sent to him to get the official word. He was going to meet with the real committee members in the next couple of days—and he wanted everyone on the same page prior to making a big move. "Let's plan for somewhere that no one would expect us to be. We need a more desolate spot. Someplace that would be very nice, but would not give us away. This meeting may be the last prior to the event, so it is crucial that everything goes well. We'll need to be intelligent and stealthy to pull this off and take this democracy down or, at worst, be the ones who run it!"

The boss's assistant wasn't sure what he meant. "When you say desolate, what type of setting are you thinking about? You would still want all of the amenities that you always include, right? How do you want me to prepare for the language barriers that will exist, and do we know the people who will be there?"

"I'll fill you in later about the individuals and language problems, but, oh, yes, we will need to be comfortable and have time to play around."

January 12, 2021

Joe decided they needed to be prepared for anything if they drove downstate to meet Ann. He knew they would have to plan for a quick escape if anything went wrong. The two vehicles they had would not work for this, so they would need one of Joe's brother's help. He thought they would need two vehicles. One for their wives, who would stay hidden away from the meeting, but in a fast car if they needed to get out quickly.

He and Ron would drive something fast too, not too flashy, but something that might be expendable if necessary. They would be prepared to move out quickly and would have to hide weapons on their persons. For safety's sake, they would have to scope out the meeting spot first to know exactly where they would be. They didn't have much time to think about it, and they had to get the vehicles right away.

Joe's brother helped them trade in the van for a silver, 2018 Toyota Corolla, and Ron's son had access to a black, 2018 Chevrolet Camaro. Both were in great shape and would be perfect for what they thought they needed. The Corolla was not as fast as they hoped, but it would fit all four of them a bit more comfortably and still be fast enough.

It took all of the tenth and eleventh to get the Corolla, so they had less time to think about what they were doing. The Camaro they would pick up from Ron's son downstate. He would meet them in Clare, northwest of the Bay City Park, and their wives would transfer to it. They planned for a quick meeting and a quicker get-away if need be. Both cars would be fully gassed and ready for a long trip—equipped with numerous supplies in the trunks, everything from food, guns, knives, tools, zip ties, rope, chains, kitty litter (for tire traction in case they got stuck), and first aid kits. When they felt like they had everything ready, they left the cabin at three a.m. on a cold January day and headed south.

January 13, 2021

It was nine a.m. when Joe and Ron pulled into the rest area and surveyed the surroundings. Few people were there, and they noticed a picnic table where they could sit, but it was snow-covered and it was cold. "Brrr," Joe said as he scrutinized the area, seeing a restroom, but not much else. It was a quick on-and-off of I-75.

Joette and Shanice were already near the safe spot where they would wait for any indication from Joe and Ron if anything was amiss—and their escape car was compromised. The wives were parked on a street called Michigan Road on the west side of the park. Joette had earlier turned off at a fast-food place where they ate a quick breakfast. They had hoped to find something that they could call a good lunch, but at this stop it would be whatever they had on the menu. They had taken along an arsenal of weapons just in case, and both were packing hand guns. Shanice had her trusty Glock 19 because she liked the 15-shot capability. Joette had a Smith and Weston .380 Shanice had suggested. Both could easily back up Joe and Ron.

Joe and Ron drove to a spot where they could see all the incoming traffic. Ron took a walk around and purchased a few snacks at the rest area building. They waited. Not much was happening here on a cold January day. They were even surprised that this park was opened in January. Joe chuckled, "Too bad that it's the middle of winter. Otherwise, we could play a round of golf, something we did not get to do for a while."

The same day, 2021

Plans were galvanizing for the "committee" in a very secure and secluded location where they had all the amenities of the rich. You name it, they had it, including an 18-hole golf course, fine dining, gymnasium, massage parlor, and anything else one could imagine. The group was sitting at a round table with numbers at each seat. By choice, no one was identified, and a translator stood ready as needed, and all records of the event would never mention anyone by name. It was an interesting group of politicians, dictators, very rich men, and just plain old rich bullies who were used to getting their way. Numerous assistants were sitting nearby, and food was abundant. The current discussion was about the January 6 mob that stormed the capitol. The mediator, or the boss as he has become known, fielded most of the questions, and had help to pull up any statistics or other information he needed.

Mediator: "We were so close this time. It wouldn't have brought us to the place we want to be, but we were very close.

Additionally, if we can keep the ransomware accelerating, we can determine if we can take down the entire grid."

Seat 7: "Good, what else do we need to do?"

Mediator: "We need to keep the voting issue going to make sure we put doubt in all the elections. We have both sides taking a stand on the issue—that is the type of divisiveness we need."

Seat 9: "What about the military infiltration? Do we have any key players involved?"

Mediator: "We have one general who is on the fence. We cannot be sure we'll have him when needed. We have a few high-ranking navy personnel, but no one in a situation to make a huge difference."

Seat 9: "We need the navy involved to be able to launch a missile from offshore when the time comes."

Seat 1: "That's become a rather major issue. We need to work on that more. Offer more incentives. Whatever it takes. Maybe another country's navy could launch something, and we could blame it on the U.S. Navy."

Seat 5: "That could work, but it's used only if the event doesn't work. We have as much cash as we could ever want at this time, so let's see if it can buy us what we need."

Seat 4: "You can't get everything with cash. Sometimes we have to use other methods. Have we become soft? We can force some of these people through bribery, fraud, or taking them out."

Mediator: "We've tried to stay away from just taking individuals out, especially if they are well-known. We have made several people disappear, and we were able to do that because you have all provided money to throw around when and where needed."

Seat 7: "You mean to say we can't just take out some of the people we need, and blame it on either the left or the right? I'd like to see some big event very soon, bigger than January 6."

Mediator: "Maybe we can, but so far we have not been able to come up with the foolproof plan to keep our group out of the news. We have been successful staying in the background and letting both sides beat each other up. All we need to do is keep sending in infiltrators as we did in the past."

Seat 12: "I like how everything is going. I give my full confidence to the leader with the hope that he will get us where we want to be very soon—say by late next year or the year after."

Seat 8: "That sounds very good to me, but a bit overzealous. Possibly five years? We're in no hurry anyway. It looks to me like this will play out because both sides are getting so divisive. Who knows what will happen next—even without our help?"

Mediator: "Should we take a break for those who want to play the golf course here, and then come back tonight at seven?"

Seat 2: "Agreed, let's get the clubs and we can rehash some of this on the course."

Seat 3: "I'm game. Let's go."

A lot of loud YES replies were heard, and they all walked out intent on meeting at seven p.m.

January 13, 2021, shortly after noon

It was a few minutes after noon when a black Cadillac with Michigan plates pulled into the park. It took the upper road and came to a spot near the end of it, not far from where Joe and Ron were. They wondered if this was the car that was supposed to bring the FBI agent, Ann.

A man bundled in a heavy coat got out of the driver's seat, looked around, and walked to the back of the car, opened the door, and let Ann out. She looked like she was dressed for this time of year with black boots, long coat, gloves, and a stylish hat, and she was also wearing a mask, but she was not what one expects to see for an agent.

It was a cold January day, but in spite of the temperature, she walked to the nearest table, dusted off the small accumulation of snow from the top and seat, and sat down. Both Joe and Ron sat tight as they had planned for Joe to approach her as Ron sat back with his gun in hand to see what would transpire, hopefully just a meeting. Joe opened the door and watched as the man who let Ann out returned to the driver's seat and shut the door. When the door closed, Joe exited his vehicle and walked slowly toward Ann who was sitting with her hands folded like an elementary school child. Joe looked right and left and then at the Cadillac.

Nothing happened. Joe was also masked as he moved toward the table and asked, "Is everything good?"

Ann responded, "It's the same old Joe. You have always been cautious and careful. Good for you."

"Can't be too sure of anything after what we've been through this year," he quipped. Then he brushed the snow from the seat and sat across from Ann.

"True."

The table was situated such that Joe would have his back to Ron and his side to Ann's car. He sat at the table with one eye on the Cadillac and one on Ann. Then Joe quietly added, "Do you have any idea why we've had our lives taken from us?"

"Actually, Joe, as I've said, you and Ron have been on our radar for the past year or so. Your names have come up with a group that we have been investigating. I could not say much on the phone, and I can't tell you everything we have found, but I can put you in the know so you can protect yourselves."

"Really?"

"Yes, for some reason, you are on the wrong side of this group. We're not sure why, but the word is, you did something to mess up one of their money operations. You must have put them in slow motion for quite some time until they could get back up and running."

"What did you think when you saw our names?"

"Well, we started an investigation, but we were unable to find you guys because you quit your jobs and went into hiding, or something like that."

"Yeah, something like that. These guys tried to kill us and took our wives as hostages. We were extremely lucky to escape and find our wives in a group of women who were being herded by these guys for whatever reason, probably slavery, prostitution, or worse, death."

"Why? Joe, what did you guys do to deserve that?"

"Well, I got curious about the goings on of the militia in the eastern Upper Peninsula where I was teaching, and I brought Ron in to help me, but we really didn't find much. I do think something significant is going on there, and I think there are outside people involved, but I don't know what or who. I believe they thought that we were a threat based on our past involvement with these types of groups."

Ann was a bit puzzled. "We've been studying a group that we feel is pooling billions of dollars into an attempt to quietly overthrow the government, *not violently, but through stealth*. We think they might have had something to do with the January 6 attack at the capitol. We can't prove anything; however, we do have some people infiltrating their operations—but we have not been able to identify anyone in the top group who might be calling the shots. Nothing has led to anything in the U.P."

Joe half smiled. "Sure, that's exactly what they want. They must be diverting attention from the places they are doing most of their dirty work. I bet they have other places around the country, probably remote areas where you guys wouldn't think were viable places for things like this."

"Oh, they do. We know of two places where they are amassing weapons, military paraphernalia, and troops that would come in handy if they need to create a police state. We have our attention focused on one man, but so far nothing has surfaced that would put him at the top or in a position that we could arrest him."

Joe wasn't surprised at all based on what he had been through. He knew that the situation was a dire one—and that a lot of people were involved—but he had no idea that they were so spread out. "That's a bit scary."

"Yes, but it goes farther than that. We've had intel from the CIA that this goes overseas and extends to some countries that are on our list of bad guys. Furthermore, all these tax-exempt organizations that have been set up can pump money into the political process, and they don't even have to identify who's giving the donations, but they are heavily influencing our elections."

"So, this isn't just a domestic mess."

"Nope. Worldwide. It's a real problem, and we have some of our own people working for them—even high-ranking politicians who are dissatisfied with the way things are going. We had intel on individuals in the military who are involved too. No names yet, but a lot of insinuation."

"What can we do to help you and to help ourselves?"

"You need to stay out of this. Let the government handle it through us and a few other agencies we have working with us. You guys need to get back in hiding until this is over."

"Over! This isn't going to end in a few days or weeks or years by the looks of things, and we're not going to stay in hiding that long. Also, we're trying to figure out how I got in trouble at work. Who was behind that? I need to fix that too. We have children and grandchildren we seldom see. How about you tell me the name of the guy or guys you think are part of this?"

"Well, no. I can't do that."

"But Ron and I and our wives could work together in a clandestine way to assist."

"Ah, not so sure you understand the seriousness of these guys. Oh, yes, by the way, the ones we have identified so far, they are mostly men."

"Figures. We had a guy who tried to kill us. He works out of a warehouse somewhere in eastern lower Michigan, probably not real far from here. We escaped from the warehouse and drove up 23 toward Cheboygan to get out of there. We had about one hundred of their hostages, whom we freed when we reached a place where we felt they could get some help. Not really sure exactly where the warehouse is, and we don't know the guy's name, but he came after us where we were living last winter. Only identification is a red beard. Don't know much else. Two other guys were with him. One we called Graybeard and the other was just a young guy, maybe twenty or twenty-one. They could be dead by now because Redbeard separated from them when we had the other two help us."

"That might help. We can use any information you can give us. We'll send a group out to search for the warehouse and maybe locate your friend, Redbeard."

"Can you tell us any information about the guy you suspect might be involved at the top?" Joe asked.

"Can't."

Joe was adamant. "Come on, we were set up and almost killed by these guys. We have a favor to return. You know. Just give me an idea. No names. Your organization can't just step in and do what we could do. Your hands are tied, but theirs are not. They can do just about whatever they want to do, legal or illegal, because they can get away with it."

"I see your point, but we are making progress. We can work our way up the chain by finding the little guys who are only working for them for the money. There are a lot of them out there, and we're sure this is the right way to eliminate the oligarchy that is trying to change the way this country works."

"Just a name. That's it."

"Joe, it's confidential. I can't give you a name. I can tell you he works out of southern Florida. We think around Miami, but we could be wrong. It's only a guess."

"He must be one of the top guys, that is, he has a lot of money. Right?"

"Right. Billions. Oops, I shouldn't have said that. I think I better go, Joe. If you guys want our protection, just let us know. We can do a lot to help."

"Not right now, but thank you for the offer. We'll be in touch."

Just then the man in the car jumped out and motioned to Ann to get to the car. She moved hurriedly, and slipped out of the table as she yelled, "See you. Keep in touch." And they were gone.

Joe jumped up, turned, ran to the car, and hopped in. Ron was in the driver's seat and had the car running. Joe sent their wives a message to meet in ten minutes. They blasted out of the rest area as two black SUVs left the highway and entered it. Joe saw them as he and Ron pulled out onto I-75 and headed for a rendezvous spot with their wives.

Joe was worried. "Could those two SUVs be similar to the ones that came after us last winter? They sure look like them. Why were they there? Were they after us or Ann? I hope she is not in any trouble for meeting with us."

Ron turned to look at Joe. "Hey, man, look behind us. Those SUVs are moving fast. We've got to lose them." Ron put the metal down and the Corolla lurched ahead, losing them in a flash. "Wonder if we should have switched with the girls for the Camaro." Ron hit over one hundred mph before he even knew it. He knew where he wanted to get off the interstate, so at that speed he'd have to make sure he knew when he was close.

Joe felt the acceleration as the car sped down I-75, pulling him back into his seat and as he turned his head to look back, out of sight of the SUVs. He laughed and said, "Hope this isn't when the cops decide to show up."

Ron gave him a huge grin and laughed right along with him.

Not far behind doing about the same speed were the two black SUVs headed south and accelerating.

January 13, 2021

"Sorry about that, Charlie," Bates said indifferently, "but you guys are finished at this place, so pack up any stuff you have and get it out of here. Otherwise, you'll never get it. And don't think you can come back here ever. You guys crossed the line and made things worse for the takeover."

"Takeover? What takeover? And we will not get our stuff outta here 'cause this here is our base."

"I guess you want more trouble than you can handle then. You know they got Lane to confess everything. Luckily Sheriff Daryl was on it, and he kept your name out of it, but we could change that. He's on the payroll, you know."

"Payroll, what payroll?"

"Doesn't matter. Just forget this area ever existed."

"Won't. I'm getting a bit curious. Why da hell you need all these here vehicles with police written on them, and why all these guys here looking like police officers? What da hell?"

"You got five minutes to get your stuff and get out and don't come back."

"Says who?"

"You want me to call these guys here to take you out?" Bates was getting furious now. He had a job to do—and he did not want to screw it up.

Charlie grunted and fumed, but he knew he was dealing with people above his grade, and he figured he'd get his militia to handle anything from here on out. "This ain't the end of this here mess. You'll hear from me again."

"Better not, Charlie. They'll take you out."

"Aw, bullshit. You don't know nothing."

Charlie had shut down the base for some time, even longer than he had planned due to the pandemic. He had brought the troops back slowly with the hopes that he could have it up and running again, but the past six months had led to one problem after another. Now Bates said that the base was no longer the militia's, but it belonged to some rich guy.

Charlie was angry. "Well, we'll see about that."

Bates got back to work. He was tired of Charlie getting in his way all the time, acting like he owned the place. He was glad that the word had come down to get rid of any locals who were not on the payroll there. Since Lane's confession, a dark cloud had rested over the militia, and many people thought that they had planned and pulled off the big scheme. Without Daryl, the whole thing would have come crashing down. Bates knew the boss was watching, and if he wanted in on the big stuff, he had to deliver.

Charlie drove back to town with steam coming out of his hat. He moaned and groaned and cursed as he drove faster than he usually does on the backroads, but they had been improved and plowed by "someone," not his crew. He vowed to get his base back at whatever cost. The people who were there now did not belong, were not his kind of people, and were just in the way of his militia. "How the hell can they just take over our base? Those bastards will find out that they pushed out the wrong guy. This is the United States! You can't just take over someone's property."

Colewin, January 2021

Nothing had changed much in Colewin since Joe and Joette had made their forced exit, yet the place was changed. Tommy continued the business that had tragically fallen into his lap from his uncle. He and Wayne had spent some time trying to track down the whereabouts of Joe and Ron, and then Joette. They did not know about Shanice's disappearance from Lower Michigan, but they had not heard from her at all and did not know how to contact her.

After hearing from Joe, Wayne and Cathy made several calls to people investigating, and bothering the school's principal to get some answers, but she had none. Cathy was especially worried about Joette, but they were disgusted with the whole affair, and as their lives got busy, they soon had to leave things as they were, hoping that someday they would hear from them and know that they were safe. They had told Daryl about Sam and Charlie and the night at the bunker, but nothing came of it, and they were afraid to dig too far into the militia.

They kept an eye on the militia's base and hounded Daryl for a while, but then Daryl did not make an appearance as often in Colewin anymore. He had other important duties now that things were moving faster at the base. Wayne went back to his work and Cathy to her teaching job. They noticed when a "For Sale" sign went up at Joe and Joette's place, and wondered who might have done that. They investigated and found out that Joe's son had put the place up for sale sometime during the pandemic, yet they could not connect with him. They had only heard from Joe that one time a while ago, and they feared for the worst, but they were too afraid to continue any more investigating.

Tommy had spent time in the spring of 2020 working on his deceased uncle's place trying to help Sherry keep it up, and he worked on the cabin a bit so they could have a hunting season. With the pandemic, he wasn't quite sure what would happen, but it seemed that many people didn't think much about it—and still made appointments for the hunt in 2020. Tommy wasn't sure what to do, but Sherry needed some help. He knew that a few good hunts could help both him and her financially. Tommy was getting to that age that he needed his own place and was hoping to make enough to do that. He thought he might ask Sherry if he could live in the cabin during the off season, but he hadn't brought it up yet.

Tommy had several good hunts during the 2020 season, successful except that unknowingly, his hunts brought Covid-19 to Colewin. Tommy came down with it first and ended up in the hospital, first in Newberry and then he was transferred to Marquette. Several others in Colewin came down with it too, and a few deaths occurred. Tommy recovered after several weeks, and at his age he would probably be fine.

Early in 2021, Gunnar lost his farm to the bank even after his neighbors tried to help. Bud was living paycheck to paycheck, and almost had to sell his logging equipment, which would have been the end of his livelihood. The bar was doing fine, and Todd tried to hire Gunnar, but he would not bite, and before his farm was turned over to the bank, Gunnar was found dead in his barn.

During the pandemic, sometime in the spring of the year, students were back at school in person. Wendy was back too. This was her senior year as it was Paige's. Wendy hounded Paige, but Paige never faltered. She kept up her lies even after Lane could no longer keep things together and confessed. Paige was not a weak character. She was tough and she was going to carry on this charade as long as she could. It gave her some kind of status, although, not the best kind that most people wanted.

Wendy never let Paige rest. Several times the teachers had to intervene, and once Wendy was sent to the principal for her constant hounding of Paige, but shortly before graduation, Wendy got to her. Paige blew up in the hall in front of the principal's office. She screamed and yelled and cried and finally gave up. "Yes, yes, I lied. None of it happened, but you will never get me to say that to anyone, ever." But it was out, along with a tape that Wendy had made earlier of her admitting her lies. The principal had heard the whole thing and so had several students. In her breakdown, Paige had not realized that the halls around the corner were full of students and Elizabeth, the principal, was just outside her door with another teacher.

The principal's mouth dropped and her eyes bugged out like she had just been hit in the stomach really hard. What had she done? She took it on the word of two board members to immediately dismiss Joe, and she did not do any investigating. She left it all up to the police and Daryl. She felt horrible. There were calls for her resignation and threatening phone calls to board members, but nothing came of them. It took some time for the police to pull it all together because Daryl kept trying to force the issue, but eventually in late 2020, it all fell apart. Paige was eighteen now, and would have to face her destiny as an adult. She was allowed to graduate with her class since the law had not caught up with her yet, but that was the last that anyone in Colewin saw of her or any of her family who had left overnight.

Joette and Joe's cabin sold in a matter of months when a hunter from downstate came across it and bought it right away. Life goes on and Joe and Joette were soon forgotten in Colewin, but there were often stories about what might have happened to them. Were they dead or alive? Some thought they got a real bad deal, while others thought Joe got what he deserved, whatever that was.

Ron and Shanice had been renting, and their place had been put on the market right away, and new renters were in place in no time. They often wondered if they would ever get their belongings back but had a hunch that they had already been sold. Their son was taking care of their finances while they were in hiding and any other legal matters that needed to be taken care of. He took care of their savings, retirement funds, and stocks as Joe's children did for him and Joette.

Friday, January 15, 2021

Charlie got the militia together at his place on a January afternoon. Not much was happening in Colewin. It was cold and overcast— a good day to stay inside. Charlie had his meeting in his house as he had several times in the past. Thirty troop members showed up, and Charlie was happy. He decided to lay it out to them and explain what he knew was going on at the base. They had not really had any get togethers for quite some time, and Charlie was beginning to think that things were deteriorating.

"I called ya here to 'xplain what's been goin' on at the base. Not sure what you know about the whole thing. We been taken over by some rich guys. That Bates feller seems to be in charge out there now. They won't let us on the base, and they say now it's theirs."

Sam spoke up, "Who are these people anyway?"

"Well, you know, you got a taste of them last winter. I don't know much more'n that."

Betty was in the back of the room. She was angry with the events that had led up to Lane's arrest. She knew that if Lane ever opened up about the entire scheme, she too would be in trouble— as well as Charlie who deserved to be too. "You don't know nothing, do you? You're just guessin'. They took over and there is nothing you or any of us can do, and you know since January 6, I'm not sure I want anything to do with this group either."

Some nodded in agreement, and some were violently opposed to what she had said. Jim was one of those. "Hey, stop it right there. What happened on the sixth is what we're all about! We gotta keep doing this stuff until we can overthrow those bastards. I think whoever has the base is right on. They got all kinds of equipment to do what's got to be done, and if you don't like it, git out."

At that, Betty stood up and walked to the door followed by three or four others who felt the same way. Charlie yelled at Betty as she opened the door, "If you walk out o' here, you ain't never invited back, and you are in this militia deep, if you know what I mean."

Betty looked at him and stared him down. "No fool like you is ever going to scare me out of who I am and what I think. I'm outta here and glad of it. You wanna make somethin' of it, you try. You loser!" And Betty was gone. Several more people stood up and walked out with the ones who had followed Betty. No one said a word.

Charlie was left with about nineteen people counting himself. "And good riddance to all of ya anyway. Now we can git to work with people who want to have a strong militia here, and who want to get our base back."

Jim spoke again, "What do you mean, get our base back?"

Charlie looked surprised. "You know from those rich scoundrels that think they own us."

"Why do we need to do that?"

Charlie was perplexed. "'Cause they took our base and won't let up on it."

"Then we just join up with 'em. What's wrong with that? They got equipment and money and troops, everything we need to take down the government."

"We ain't taken down the government. We're just changing the way things are. What's wrong with you anyway?"

"Nothing's wrong with me. It's you. You've turned chicken, and you don't care anymore to do the things that got to be done."

Charlie was insistent. "We have a good group here. We could take back the base and develop into somethin' along with Escanaba, the Keweenaw, and the Lower. We'll be a force."

"Charlie, they are already a force. Didn't you see what happened last week? That was them. Now it's us too."

"No, no. This is wrong."

"What's wrong, Charlie, is you. You've lost your way and gotten weak, like I said."

"I'm tired o' you callin' me chicken and weak. Git outta my place."

"Happy to, Charlie. I'm gonna join up with the rich guy. Anyone else in?"

A group of people stood up and walked out with Jim, with fewer than ten people left—eight to be exact, and Charlie.

I-75 Southbound

It took Joe and Ron only a few minutes to exit and take the route to meet with their wives. It was slow going because now they were not on the interstate and the speed limit was much lower here, but they managed to find them sitting on the side of the road. Ron pulled alongside, to the west of, but not far from where they had met Ann. He lowered his window and was about to speak, when...

Shanice was facing the cars as they approached, and she saw them first and yelled to Ron to get out of the way. Two black SUVs were speeding toward them. Shanice pulled out her Glock and was ready as Ron bolted ahead and pulled a quick U-turn to face the SUVs. He was now directly behind Shanice and Joette and ready to back them up, and both he and Joe jumped out with pistols pulled and got in positions to respond, if need be.

The first SUV's window came down as they slowed and then sped past, but they did not do anything but stare. Shanice had her Glock pointed right at the man in the driver's seat. He only smiled. As the other SUV approached, it also slowed, and someone opened the window and got a good look; then both SUVs sped away.

"What was that?" Joette asked.

"Not sure," both Joe and Ron answered, breathing heavily and blowing clouds of cold air toward them.

Shanice spoke up, "I was ready for anything. One false move and that driver would have had some new holes to deal with. I guess he was lucky today."

"As were we," Joette noted.

Joe was excited. "So, they must know who we are. I thought they were after Ann when they first arrived. Not sure what they were doing unless they wanted to get a verification as to whether it was us. Damn, that could have been bad."

"I think we need to go somewhere and figure our next move," Ron said.

The women were hungry and knew they couldn't stop for long or in a fancy place. Shanice was hungry for lunch, which they had missed. "For sure. Should we check out some fast-food joint and talk it over?"

They found a small dive not far from where they had been earlier. Very wearily they got out and found a table where they could also keep an eye on the cars. The women ordered for all four of them and the guys sat at a table and watched the vehicles.

They realized that a search for a billionaire, possibly in Florida, was the old "needle in a haystack" idiom. They talked for about thirty minutes while eating a quick lunch and heading out. No decisions could be made, and they thought the best plan was to return to the U.P. and come up with something that was reasonable so they could get back to living their normal lives. Little did they know that Joe had been cleared of any wrongdoing in the case against him in Colewin. The word had not spread very far out of the area that both Lane and Paige were now the ones being investigated.

The decision to head to the U.P. came to an abrupt halt when they drove north and spotted two SUVs outside a building housing an excavating company, and standing near the driver's door of the nearest one were three guys—one who looked like Redbeard. Joe yelled suddenly to Ron and scared him so that he punched the pedal and they roared down the road. "Stop the car in that little grove of trees up ahead."

Ron did, asking, "What's going on, Joe?"

"Did you see those SUVs and those guys over there? I'm sure they're the ones that followed us today, and Redbeard was with them."

"What!"

"Let's go back and see what we can find. I'll call the girls to tell them what we're doing and to have them back us up. They're just a mile or two ahead."

Ron pulled into the grove while they waited for the girls to get back to them. Once they decided on how they were going to approach the situation, they were off down the road to the excavation company. When they arrived, no one was outside, so they decided to park and hide their vehicles, and each took a spot, so they had the vehicles surrounded. Ron and Joe snuck up to the vehicles, found they were open, popped the hoods and ripped out all the spark plugs. Joe got into the nearest one. Five minutes later Redbeard and two other guys came walking out of the building. They neared the car that Joe was in, and when the driver opened the door, Joe's Smith and Weston .44 Magnum was in his face. "Get on the ground now and have your buddies do the same."

Redbeard was headed for the passenger's side when Ron stuck his pistol in his neck. "Down, like the man said."

Shanice and Joette had their weapons out and had the third man covered as he tried to get in the back seat. "On the damn ground, man!" Shanice yelled. Joette gave the man a push and made him sit.

Joe asked Redbeard, "How many other men are with you?"

"Wouldn't you like to know? Good to see you again, old buddy. We knew you were on your way down, but we had to get a visual to make sure that it's you and your buddy."

Joe was not pleased. "Let's throw this guy in the back seat of our car. Ron, get the rope and zip ties out of the trunk of the Corolla, and tie these guys up, starting with Redbeard here. Girls, you cover these two."

It didn't take Ron long to get all three tied up. They threw the two guys in the SUV and decided that Redbeard should have a smooth ride in the trunk of their car. After transferring all their weapons, rope, food, and supplies to the back seat, they were off. Next stop would be later in the day somewhere near some cabins south of Cheboygan where Joe and Ron decided to interrogate Redbeard. The idea was to get him to release the names of others in the chain of command, hopefully leading to the boss. It would take a little over two hours to get to the cabins in the woods which they could rent for the day. They were not far from the area where Joe and Ron had been taken to the warehouse a year or so ago, and this was off the beaten path, so Joe felt comfortable with the spot.

He knew about these places from his many days of fishing and hunting.

They arrived around five-thirty p.m.; it was already dark and cold. Redbeard had been kicking and moving around for some time. He probably figured he could get someone's attention, but it was a quiet day and traffic was moving briskly. The women arrived first and secured a cabin for the night. They took one as far away from the office as was available, hidden in the woods. The guys pulled up about fifteen minutes later and their wives were already unpacking their things. It took a few minutes to find their car since it was concealed by the pine trees secluding the small cabin.

They backed up to the door and jumped out of the car. Ron popped the trunk and they grabbed Redbeard and threw him through the open door. It would be a long night. Joe and Ron were not happy with Redbeard. First of all, he chose to run away instead of helping them after they gave him a second chance, and second, he was sent to get rid of them.

They asked him a lot of questions about the people he worked for, but he did not know much. At least, that is what he said. Joe and Ron wanted the contact person for whom he worked, but he wasn't saying anything. After several hours, they took off his shoes and socks, cut off his shirt and his pants (he was still tied up) and set him outside in the snow. It was near zero degrees. They kept him there tied to a tree for a while despite the frigid temperatures. Once they thought he had enough, they brought him in and sat him in a chair and began an interrogation technique that they hoped would eventually lead to the person who dictates his moves.

"So, this guy is your contact," Joe insisted.

The snow and cold air had bitten into his flesh, but it didn't freeze his tongue. Once he was able to stop shivering, it loosened him up a bit. "Yes, yes, I meet him whenever he needs me. We work all over the place, but he mostly keeps us in Michigan."

"Where can we find this guy?" Ron was tired, but he wanted to get to the bottom of this.

"Don't know. You know if I tell you anything, I'm toast. Almost had it last time, but I saved myself, and they gave me a higher position. Now they'll just get rid of me."

"Too bad, think of what you've done to other people," Joe said.

Ron yelled in Redbeard's face, "Who are those other guys who were with you today, well, I guess yesterday now?"

"Just some flunkies who do what I say."

Joe was getting impatient. "How does this guy contact you?"

"I'm not saying anything else!"

Everyone was tired and needed sleep. Joe had suggested that the women sleep in the bedroom with the door closed, and he knew that he and Ron would need sleep soon.

Joe got up off his chair and said, "Let's tie him up to a tree again in the back. We'll gag him, and he can freeze to death."

"No. You can't do that. I'm not going back out there like this." The man was sitting there in his undershorts, and he had finally warmed up. "He'll send me a text on my burner, the one you took out of my pocket. He'll probably contact me tomorrow because I was supposed to report that we recognized you guys, but I never sent anything yet, and the other guys don't know him at all so they can't contact him."

"Sounds good," Ron said.

Joe agreed. "Let's tie him up really tight and hit the hay."

They added some rope to his hands and feet and gagged Redbeard. Ron took the first watch as Joe got a few hours of sleep. Then they switched and Ron got several hours. At ten-thirty a.m. a text came through for Redbeard. Joe had been watching for any contact, and he opened the message and read:

> Where are you? We need to meet.
> Three today, same place.

Joe kicked Redbeard who had also fallen asleep. "Hey, do you have to get back to this guy?"

Redbeard was groggy. "What? What did you say?"

"You got to get back to this guy?" Joe repeated.

"What, did he text?"

"Yes! He said: Three today, same place."

"Uh, just send a Y."

"You better be right, and this better work." Joe texted "Y."

CHAPTER 16: ON TO TRAVERSE CITY

Saturday, January 16, 2021

Ron and Joe were sitting on a side street just outside of Traverse City, Michigan, not far from the Grand Traverse Mall. They had taken Highway 31 out of Cheboygan and then South Airport Road to an Assembly of God Church parking lot where they had parked—and were ready for anything. Ron had positioned the car behind a tree, so it was completely hidden. Joe and Ron exited the car and decided they would hide in the trees since by now Redbeard's boss might know he'd been taken. They were hidden to anyone heading into the parking lot. They took their captive, still in his underwear, into the woods, and gave him a blanket and bound his feet to a tree.

Their wives had backed their car into some trees and were parked on the other end of the parking lot, facing the guys. Anyone who drove in had to pass Joe and Ron's car and would be between them and Joette and Shanice—they would be trapped. Redbeard said the man would come and park near the south end of the lot— which was where Joe and Ron had backed into some trees.

Before Redbeard was bound, he said, "He's not going to stop if he doesn't see my car."

"Don't need him to stop, just get in this parking lot. You're sure he'll be driving a black Dodge Ram 3500?"

"Always does."

Ron was doubtful. "Is he prompt? Will he be here right at three p.m.?"

"He's usually right on time, unless he suspects something—which he probably will 'cause you took me and disabled his SUVs."

"Joe, let's get the heavy artillery ready and tape that guy's mouth shut. Don't like the fact that we have to use these things outside of the military."

"Good point."

Joe went to the car, opened the trunk, and pulled out two old model M-16s similar to the ones that they had used in 'Nam, and he grabbed some duct tape which he used on Redbeard's mouth. Then he gave one of the M-16s to Ron and they both loaded them. The girls were also ready with their pistols and an over/under double-barreled shot gun and a Winchester .30-30.

At three p.m. two SUVs came down the South Airport Road. Sure enough, it was the two they had seen a day earlier.

"Ron, get ready, you see what I'm seeing?"

"Got it, Joe."

The two SUVs passed them and parked in the center of the lot. Two guys got out with submachine guns. The back door opened and a man got out. He had on a very stylish long black coat and sunglasses.

"That's got to be the man," Joe muttered.

The man looked around and did not see anything, no Redbeard, nothing. The other SUV had two men who were also standing near their vehicle, both armed.

"Might be too much firepower for us, Ron, and they must know we have Redbeard."

"Agreed. Let's just sit tight."

The boss looked around and did not see Redbeard. He motioned and then said, "He's not here. Something's up. Let's get out of here. I thought he had escaped when he answered yes. He must not have. Someone must have his burner." Then they carefully backed away, got in their vehicles, and left.

"We need to follow them. Ron, jump in the car. I'll get our man and throw him in the trunk."

"Right. Let's have the girls follow us, and we'll see what we can find out."

They almost lost the SUVs as they turned the corner out of South Airport Road, but they were not traveling fast, so it was easy to catch up. The SUVs separated and Joe had the women follow the one that headed east into town. They followed the other into Traverse City, but went in the opposite direction and shortly entered a parking garage. Joe and Ron followed at a distance. The SUV stopped on the third floor and the slick guy with the sunglasses got out. The SUV drove away, and the guy walked to a Dodge Ram just as Redbeard had described. They followed him to Underwood Ridge, a swanky, exclusive neighborhood with a view of the Bay.

Quite the place. The man pulled up to the house and entered the garage. No other people were around, and it was getting toward four p.m. Joe and Ron decided to drive down the street and check in with their wives, and then they were going to head back to the house and visit the slick-looking guy.

The phone rang in Joe's hand, and it was his wife, Joette. "Hey, we followed the SUV to a parking garage. They dropped the car and each went in separate directions. Should we follow either?"

"No. We were going to try to find you in case you needed backup. Head on over here. We're on Underwood Ridge. Where are you?"

"We're downtown just off East Front Street."

"You've been to Traverse City a lot, right? Do you know where Peninsula Drive is?"

"Yes. It heads out of town and up the peninsula."

"Good. Take Peninsula to Center Road, and you will run right into Underwood Ridge. We'll meet you there."

"All right. We'll be there in no time."

Shanice took a right and headed toward Peninsula. She and Joette had shopped in Traverse City many times, so they knew their way around. "Been here, done that," she said in a matter-of-fact tone. Joette just laughed.

The plan was to wait until dark when the four of them would enter the place. Joe was going to snoop around before dark to check for any security cameras or devices that might give them away. The other three stayed with the cars. When he returned, he said it looked like the guy was just moving in and he had a security system. He was probably in the process of getting everything set up in his new home.

Joe asked, "Do you know if we have any cutters in the tool box?"

Ron answered right away, "We have a pair of tin snips and a small wire cutter. We also have our hunting knives."

"Good. I'll take both and a knife and snip his service access to the security system."

It was getting dark as Joe went back to the house. He moved slowly and felt his way around to the back where he had seen the wires entering the house. He took a circuitous route so as not to leave too many tracks in the snow around the house. He found the wires and cut only the ones for the security system. When it was completed, he moved back to the vehicles, and now it was very dark.

Joe laid out the plan involving all four. Joette would stay in the wives' car until they called her, in case they had to retreat. Joe would enter from the front, Ron the garage, and Shanice the back. All three took their heavy artillery.

Ron was the first to enter. He was able to get in the side door of the garage. He tried to pick the lock, and got frustrated, but it gave easily when he kicked it in. Shanice tried the back door, but it was also locked. She saw some lights in the house, and she wasn't sure if the guy was nearby, so she decided to use her lock-picking skills instead of kicking in the door. It worked. Joe could not find any way to enter, so he decided to walk up to the side of the house avoiding the video doorbell in case it was still live and reached around with his M-16 and knocked on the door.

Joe did not hear anyone walk to the door, but someone said, "Yes, that you, Julie?"

Nothing happened and no one spoke, so the man opened the door and looked out. At that point, Shanice had her shotgun right in the middle of his back. When Joe heard her say, "You make any kind of move and you'll have a load of shot so big, it'll take four men to carry you to your grave," Joe jumped up on the porch and pointed his M-16 at the man.

"Whoa, what's going on here?"

"Don't say anything. Hands in the air, and just walk back slowly. No false moves or you're dead."

"OK, OK. Whatever you say."

"Where's Ron?" Joe asked Shanice.

"Haven't seen him yet."

Just then, Ron saw them as he walked in the front door. "Damn door to the house was like a fortress. Couldn't get in." Joe and Shanice smiled.

"You got a nice place here, man," Shanice said.

"Just moved in. Hope you guys didn't ruin anything."

"Naw, just a few broken doors," Ron laughed.

"And locks," added Shanice.

"Maybe a few other things, but they can all be fixed," Joe added with a grin.

It didn't take long for the guy to spill everything that they needed to know. He was scared shitless and didn't want to die. He loved his new home, and he thought they would let him stay there when they were finished. *Funny thought.*

Shanice had called Joette and told her to stay put—that they had the guy—and to be on the lookout for anyone going to the house. Then Shanice helped Ron and Joe bind the guy and set him in a chair.

They learned that he worked for a billionaire out of Chicago who was part of the committee for whom they all worked. He did not know his name. He only knew him as Mr. A., but he knew that he lived on the Gold Coast, but he wasn't sure exactly where on the Gold Coast it was. "I've never been there, and all of my contacts have been in strange places in Chicago and Detroit, but I've only seen him once—and he is old. Usually, I meet with someone who's working for him."

"We need more than that!" Joe screamed. This frightened the hell out of the guy, and he froze for a while. "More, you must know more."

"Really, please, let me go. I'm not sure what you need."

"Anything else you can think of?"

"I know he hasn't lived in Chicago that long. He's a new billionaire there, so you might be able to find out something that way. He's only there because of the committee. They needed someone in the Midwest that they could trust, and he's the guy."

Ron thought he would give his son a chance to locate this billionaire in Chicago. He knew that he could do it faster than they could. He turned to Shanice and said, "We should have our son get on this. He has all the equipment and could have this completed before we could even get started."

It was getting late so before she called, she told Joette to park the car and come in because this might take some time. Shanice then immediately pulled out her cell phone and gave her son a call.

Once her son was on it, it didn't take him long to figure out who the guy was. "Billionaires are kind of easy to follow," he said. "Looks like he lives near Lake Michigan on the Gold Coast. I'll see if I can get an address. His name is Adler. He has a wife and one son named Wyatt. Whoa! Looks like his son was recently deceased in the U.P. near Manistique."

"Oh, my gosh," Joette exclaimed, "that's the guy from the militia, and he was the one who murdered Tommy's uncle!"

"That must be Mr. Adler's son then, and for sure he is our guy," Joe said. They all agreed, and the next day they decided to take the two cars and drive to Chicago, always taking precautions, just in case.

Before they left, they bound their new hostage and threw him in the back seat. They called Ann and delivered the two hostages— this guy and Redbeard.

CHAPTER 17: CHICAGO

Monday, January 18, 2021

"Who lives like this?" Joe exclaimed. They were sitting in front of an opulent building, a single-family home they knew belonged to this billionaire. The place was quite lavish as one might expect. It had four or five stories and a rounded front, reminding Joe of an old castle, except it had reddish brick and was immaculately kept up. The trees were bare, but beautiful, the small lawn was blanketed with snow, and the shrubbery was covered with an ornate red material. The sidewalk led to a beautiful wide double front door accessed by four marble steps.

They wondered if they should just get up and walk to the front door and knock since it did not look like there were any personnel around. It was very quiet, almost too quiet. Joe decided that he would walk to the front door and ring the bell just to see what would happen. He did just that.

When the door opened slowly, a butler appeared. Joe said, "Hello, is Mr. Adler home?"

"He is not seeing anyone at the moment."

"Well, he'll see me. Tell him that Joe DeLuca is here—and that he knew Wyatt." Luckily, Ron's son had told them of the connection to Wyatt. This would be his parents' house. Joe knew that would get some kind of response. Hopefully, a good one.

"Just a moment, sir." Then the butler shut the door in Joe's face.

This did not surprise Joe. He thought: *This was the kind of treatment he expected, or thought he might expect. Rich is rich. They live their own lives and really, I guess they feel they are above most of us. They think they are smarter, work harder, play harder, and generally are better. I guess that's why they keep the rest of us from having anything easy, like health care, a savings account, time to enjoy life, even access to voting.*

The door opened and the butler let Joe in. The three in the cars outside were surprised, but very happy that Joe was able to see the man.

"Mr. Adler is in the study. You may go in, but, please, don't stay long. He's very tired and stressed."

"Sure, all right. Whatever you say," Joe responded. He took a right and walked straight to a room with very high ceilings, beautiful mahogany wood decorations and all kinds of souvenirs only a billionaire would have. His eyes moved to the left, and he saw a small man sitting in an enormous chair, his face was sallow, and his demeanor was forlorn. Was this the billionaire? "Hello, Mr. Adler, my name is Joe DeLuca. Nice place you have here."

"Oh, yes, it's okay. I prefer our other homes though. We only moved here temporarily. We prefer warmer climates and a more open area."

"I'm sure you do."

"This place isn't much. I have several other homes that are much nicer and in warmer climates. We prefer our, or I should say now, that I prefer my home on Capri, high on a cliff overlooking the Gulf. My wife and I really used to enjoy traveling on our yacht, but those days are gone."

"Yeah, must be nice, but come on…several homes and a yacht! Any idea how many people out there are homeless or live in shacks?"

"So, you knew my son?"

"Yes, not really well, but we met on occasion when he was in Colewin, Michigan."

"You knew him up there in the wilds of the Upper Peninsula? Colewin, right, oh my, we sent him there with the hope that he would get better. I especially thought he would improve after his time in Afghanistan. He just wasn't the same boy who left us years ago to join the Marines. He needed help, but he never got it."

"Oh, he left home."

"Yes, he wanted to go to the Upper Peninsula because he had this vision of a Utopia. Not sure where he got that, but we were more than happy to agree if he would improve. We made it tough for the boy. By we, I mean me and my wife, who passed recently. She died of a broken heart. She just withered away month after month, until...."

"Mr. Adler, I'm so sorry to hear that."

"That's all right. She was in so much pain after Wyatt's death. We just tried to do the best for him, but he rebelled, and he thought he would get back at us by running away and joining the military. He knew how to hurt us. He had so much going for him. He was smart, athletic, and he would have been very rich if he just stayed home, but he didn't want anything to do with us. When he came home from the military, he was different, angrier than he had ever been—and he got upset at everything."

"That can happen to people who serve in combat zones. Many suffer from PTSD and don't get the help they need when they need it."

"True, but we thought a change of scenery would be good for him, and we gave him an important job, but he just wasn't ready."

"No, but what do you mean, you gave him a job?"

"First, tell me what you knew of my son."

"I can't really say much. He was quite a party guy I hear, and he worked as a bear guide while trying to take over a militia post."

"Yes, that was his job. To keep an eye on what was happening there and to report back."

"Report what back?"

"I'm not at liberty to say. I've already said enough. If you don't have any other information about my son, then you should leave."

"That's not going to happen." At that, Joe hit send on his phone and a few minutes later, Ron and Shanice pushed their way into the home.

"What is going on? Who are these people?"

The butler heard the door and came running, and told them to leave, but Ron pulled out his pistol and told him to sit down. Shanice had her weapon out too and the man froze.

"Let's get the rope and tie this fellow up, so he doesn't plan anything while we're getting some information," Joe told Ron.

"You're lucky my staff isn't here today. Don't hurt my man now. I've been giving the others time off since the funeral. Sorry I didn't keep my security people on call today. It's unfortunate for me that the butler let you in."

Ron moved swiftly to the car and was back with several zip ties that were much quicker and more secure than using rope. "Here you go. Put your hands out and then the same with your feet." When the butler was tied up, they took him to the next room and tied him to a large oak bench. He was not going to go anywhere. They checked him for any tech that he might have, but they only found a cell phone and took that.

Joe continued as Mr. Adler argued about the civility of their visit, but he soon settled down and just looked forlorn. "So, what do you really want? Money? I can give you plenty, just don't hurt my friend and me. We've done nothing wrong."

"Right," Joe responded. "We're here because of what happened to us in Colewin." He explained the long story, and Mr. Adler said that had nothing to do with him.

"Your group is what we are here about. All you rich guys trying to control the country and take over the government. Power and control!"

"We do control the money and much of the country. It's what we do. You do realize that a handful of us control over fifty percent of all the wealth in this country, so good luck with trying to defeat us."

"We understand, but we want to know how and why your group is doing this—I mean trying to take over our democracy."

"I am involved in a group that has similar aspirations, but after my wife's death and my son's murder, I don't have the energy anymore. That group made our life a living hell after our son messed up. It took its toll, and my wife finally gave up and died of a broken heart and stress caused by this group. Everywhere we turned they were at us. Being rich is great, but when the other billionaires want revenge, it's a calamity."

"You are not in charge then?"

"In charge, by no means. I used to be very involved. We have amassed billions, now trillions of dollars and enlisted people from all over the world to achieve a plan that we created. Total domination—with power so raw that we were all very excited."

"You have a boss then?"

"We all have a boss, but at the same time, we are the bosses. I used to take orders from a man who works for the head guy, but I told them I wanted out. That didn't go so well."

"Can you tell us who it is?" Joe thought he was getting close to the top now, and he could turn over all the names to Ann to investigate.

"I really can't say. I have not attended meetings this year, and the head guy is not from here. I just never learned who it was. We do not use names when we have meetings."

"What about the guy who gives you orders then?"

"Well, he still contacts me, hoping to get me back in the fold. He usually contacts me once every two months to see where I stand. They like my money."

"We need his name then. Does he ever come here?"

"Sometimes. He is very unpredictable."

"When was the last time you spoke to him?"

"Just before my wife's death, late November."

"Hmmm, I think you're going to have company for a while until you hear from him."

Mr. Adler was not amused. "I don't want any trouble. I'm sick and I am still mourning my wife. If you really want to meet him, I can arrange it, but he seldom meets with anyone other than the boss, but if I can arrange it, you have to leave us alone—that is me and my help."

Joe, Ron, and Shanice were listening to this conversation, and Joe finally spoke up. "That could work. We don't need anything else, just get us a meeting."

Ron agreed immediately.

It took a little time, but Mr. Adler was able to arrange a meeting.

Joe decided they would leave the butler tied up, but they were not sure what to do with Mr. Adler, so they tied him to his favorite chair, knowing he would be found when all the help returned. They would report to Ann everything they had found with the exception of the meeting they would be attending. They knew they had other work to do.

CHAPTER 18: HEADING SOUTH

January 30, 2021

Joe, Ron, Joette, and Shanice all headed back to Michigan. They decided to give as much information to Ann as they could about Mr. Adler. Ann thought that what they had done was stupid, but she was glad the bureau would be able to find out as much as they could from all three people they had found, especially Mr. Adler.

Their meeting with the intermediary between the top man and Mr. Adler was to take place in February in Tampa, Florida. This they did not tell Ann. The time, date, and place would be sent to them a few days prior to the meeting. February in Florida did not sound bad to any of them, so once everything was completed with Ann, they made plans to go to Tampa.

They had not been among a lot of people for some time, and with the pandemic still raging in some areas, they decided to take as many precautions as they could. The first decision was to drive to Florida rather than fly. It would take some time, but they had that. The next decision was to take their cars to Ron's son's house and trade for a Suburban that would be much roomier for the four of them. They could take turns driving, and they would have room for everything that they might need for a short stay there. Luckily, they were able to book two rooms downtown, one with a kitchenette. Usually last-minute reservations, even during the pandemic did not work, but the place had a few cancellations so they were able to slip in.

Friday, February 12, 2021

The foursome was trying to stay low-key, but, at the same time, they were having a great time enjoying the easy life in Florida. The weather was gorgeous, and in addition to their own cooking, the food they had delivered was excellent—without mentioning the beverages. They kept a low profile, but they all sat outside and relaxed and enjoyed the weather, and then on February 12, as expected, Joe received a call on his cell phone at eight a.m. Ron and Joe were to meet with the man on Monday, February 15, at a local golf club. More information would come on Monday. This was it. They would finally get some answers, and maybe a chance to get these people off their backs, and hopefully get closer to the top people so the government could take these guys down, although Joe was not optimistic. Whoever called indicated that they would have everything arranged, and he added that they may bring along their spouses if they preferred. When Joe told everyone, they were astonished.

"How did he know that we were along?" Joette asked.

"Not really sure. It makes me a bit nervous that they knew."

"Maybe we should not all go. We could stay close by in case you need us or something crazy happens. Who knows what these guys want?" Shanice said.

Joette agreed, "That's really smart. We need to protect ourselves."

Ron was thinking out loud, "We have a few days, so let's come up with a plan to keep us all safe. Obviously, they must have eyes on us or something if they know that we are all here."

"Let's take some time to scope out the area and know where everything is, including where all the exits are. We need to learn as much as we can before Monday. Although we don't know how many people they have here, and they might have a number of armed guards. We do know that we will be having a meal with him, per his request. Who knows?"

A lot of strategizing went into the meeting, but it was all uncertain because they really did not know anything about this guy and what his real intentions were. A little bit of trepidation crept into the planning since they had been through so many close calls with these people, and they were in no mood to have to defend their lives again, but they also wanted to do some damage to their organization, so they knew they had to meet with this person. They came up with an idea that they thought might work.

Joe and Ron prepared and made sure they had their weapons ready. The women were going to go along, but they were going to stay out of the meeting and just spend time near or in the Club. They would keep in touch with each other and the guys using some technology that Joette had purchased—small, two-way earplugs that set her back over six hundred dollars, but would be worth it if something happened. Also, Joette and Shanice were going to separate, but they would keep in touch. Ron and Joe also needed one more item.

Monday, February 15, 2021

The call said they were to meet at the Club. They decided to wear masks even though it seemed most people were not taking this precaution. Joe expected that they would meet some thugs or bodyguards when they entered the foyer, but there were no signs of anyone who might fit that description. Everything looked calm and normal. They were to meet in the dining room, and a special table had been set up for them to have a very private conversation.

They approached a very upscale dining area, gave the maitre d' their names, and were seated promptly. Looking around, they saw only one man at the table which was filled with fine cheeses, caviar, bread, and an assortment of other very expensive appetizers, along with white and red wines. Five wine glasses had been placed along with the other dining implements. The host had a glass of red wine, and strangely, he had also poured four more glasses of wine which sat at the other four places. He was a middle-aged man with slightly graying hair. He had a wry smile, and his eyes were the piercing type that seem to look right through a person. He wore a very expensive, but casual golfing outfit. It looked like he was ready for a round. The table had five beautiful, comfortable chairs around it, probably because the man anticipated that their wives would join them. Joe and Ron looked the table over and took the seats right next to the man, one on his right; the other on his left.

"Well, hello gentlemen. It is great to finally get to meet both of you. It's been some kind of game trying to find you. By the way, you can lose the masks. We are very cautious and are tested all the time."

"We prefer the masks just the same, but you've found us," Joe said.

"Yes, we have. Oh, where are you wives? Are they going to join us?"

Ron grunted, "Probably not."

"That's too bad. I was hoping to get to know all of you this time. We've been tracking you for...umm...what is it almost two years now? You guys almost made a mess out of our operation in the north. You really caused us some concern, but now we have everything under control, and we know you aren't a threat anymore."

"A threat. What do you mean? We were never a threat."

"Yes, you were. Your past was a condition of concern for us. We had all kinds of trouble up there, and that Wyatt kid didn't make our operation any easier, but we took care of that. You know I never meet with anyone. I'm doing this because Adler asked me to, and he seemed quite troubled by you two. He just wants to be left alone now. I'd like to keep the man in the game, but I just don't know, and he will probably get voted out of the committee too, since he was such a problem."

Joe snickered, "I'm not sure of anything you just said, but I do know one thing. I don't think your group took care of Wyatt. The local and state police took care of him."

"Yes, that's what I mean."

Ron and Joe just looked at each other and shook their heads. The conversation had so far been short, but it had been very awkward for Joe and Ron. This guy was being an arrogant prig. It sounded like he owned them and the police the way he was talking, and it was strange how he dismissed Mr. Adler.

"So, what is the goal of this meeting that you were so insistent about having? I know you have turned some of our people over to the FBI. Why did you do that? It won't affect us at all, and I'll have those people back working for me in no time."

"You're sure about that?"

"Not sure. Positive."

"What makes you so arrogant? Is it that you're rich or are you just like that?" Joe was already tired of the man and could see that getting him out of the place and to the FBI would be impossible, but maybe they could get his name and face to them or do something else to slow him and his cohorts down.

"I can see you peons think you can make a difference here, but you cannot. We will soon be in power, and people like you will be harmless because we'll have control."

"Control?" Ron was aggravated too and he could see this guy must have bigger plans than they thought.

"Yes, control. We have so many people working for us. It's surprising how a little bit of money can sway people into changing their minds about almost anything."

"Apparently, you have a lot of that behind you. Money. I repeat, money," Joe stated.

"More than you can even imagine—and *money is power and power is control*. Yes, that's what we have. We have control of every sector of the country."

Frustrated, Ron once again asked, "You keep talking about *we*. Who do you mean?"

"That you will never know, but I can tell you. This is a worldwide movement of all the people who are tired of the U.S. getting involved in their business, so the best way to take care of that is not armed conflict with a superpower or even elections. The best way is to just take over—and that's what we're doing. We have a huge event that should take place early next year or the year after if all goes well, and it will be amazing."

Joe was not surprised, but he was confused a bit. "Event. What type of event are you talking about? And who do you mean when you say worldwide? If this is not an armed conflict, what is it?"

"I will not divulge any of our plans, but I can tell you this. We have infiltrated almost every political group, left- and right-wing groups, police, armed services, even supreme court justices. We have people everywhere who are making a difference. We make most protests violent by using our personnel in various ways. We even have conspiracy theories that get people on board with us. We don't really have to do much of anything, just put them out there. It is so easy to infiltrate groups and sway people!"

"You can't be serious about all of this. This country is stronger than a bunch of rich guys trying to take it down," Joe said.

"Think about it. Who controls most of the elections already? The rich. Our people are the ones who are on the ballot because we spend the money and have the influence. That's been the way in the U.S. since the beginning. Just check how many rich people have been and are in the government right now."

Ron was not surprised. "I know that. More than half of the members of Congress are millionaires, and the top ten percent own a lot more wealth than the rest of the members. Yeah, I guess we're run by the rich."

"Your country is a democracy, and you know that it has been viable for over two hundred and fifty years, but if you know any-thing about democracies, you know that they usually die because of internal problems or corruption. Even Socrates and Plato saw this a long time ago, and today many people see that other forms of government are better. You allow *anyone to vote*. That's ludicrous. When we take over that will change."

Ron and Joe were both getting a bit upset. They really wanted to take this guy down, but they knew it was beyond them.

"Furthermore, *we've a lot of people on our side who don't even know they are*. For example, those who feel that voting should be only for those who can prove they are competent. You can see the voting laws that are being passed even today. People don't want imbeciles selecting their leaders."

Joe was angry. "Blah, blah, blah, what you say is ridiculous. Through the vote, this democracy has given the largest number of people a good life. Many of those in charge are trying to make it a country for all people, like it was intended. We have problems, but we are a diverse country that offers all types of people a chance for a good life. The rich don't like that, but that's the direction of this nation."

"Well, Joe and Ron, take a look around you. Not here, of course, in this place. Isn't this a wonderful place! No. Look around you. There is poverty everywhere—and hate and misery. You live in a pipe dream. Your police can't even protect most people any-more because they are confused by the laws and actions of some politicians. They even kill some people just because. Your country is full of hate and despair."

"You can't be serious," Ron blurted.

"Oh yes, and as soon as we are in power, we'll get the Constitution changed or maybe thrown out, and we'll have a real ruling class of billionaires that will set things straight."

"What! That won't happen. You'll have more widespread poverty and chaos if you have billionaires in charge."

"We don't really care about that. As they say, 'Let them eat cake!'" and the man began to roar with laughter. "Anyway, you already have millionaires running the country; what's so different?"

"You don't care, do you?"

"It's not me. It's all of our committee who will take over and run this country so it is no longer this government that dominates other countries and uses them and throws them away as needed. We will eliminate all forms of democracy, beginning with the Statue of Liberty and that cute poem, the capitol building, maybe even the flag. Let's toast to the success of our silent revolution."

"Isn't that something." Joe stood quickly as planned and toppled his chair, which took long enough to let Ron do what they had planned. The man turned to see what had happened. Joe was still on his feet and bent to pick up his chair.

Suddenly, the man stood, "Shall we, as I've said, have a toast to our newfound glorious outlook?" As he stood, at the same time at the back of the dining hall, three large men in suits entered.

Joe was happy to toast with the man because he and Ron had been able to implement their plan. He might not be able to take down the whole organization, but he would take this jerk out of the picture and maybe slow them down a bit. They lowered their masks, and they toasted, but Ron and Joe knew enough not to eat or drink anything for fear of some stratagem that the man might have thought up, so they faked it. Joe and Ron then got up and politely said good-bye. "Have a nice day, and enjoy your lunch."

"You too," the man added. "And celebrate the little life you have left."

Joe looked at Ron, and they both shared a bit of a sneer.

However, as they left the dining area, they were met by two of the men who had walked in, and they told Joe and Ron to walk slowly out to the limousine parked in front. This was not part of the plan, but they knew they might encounter something like this.

"You think we'd really let you go free?" one of the men said. He was holding some type of handgun and had it jabbed into Joe's back. The man behind Ron had a similar gun in Ron's back. Both men were trying to be discreet and not make a scene, but Joe was not going to let that happen.

Joette and Shanice had gone shopping while the guys were meeting. Joette bought a Wilson nine iron and a putter, and Shanice bought a nice large Callaway driver, nothing too expensive. They had each been listening to the conversation and heard the last part.

While Shanice was listening to the conversation, she was also watching the entrance to the club and saw a limousine pull up. Three very large men exited, but the driver remained inside. She contacted Joette and told her to quickly meet her at the outside entrance to the dining hall. Shanice shared what she had seen, "I think these guys are a part of a setup. Let's go in and see what's up."

They saw Joe and Ron with two men and another big man blocking the entrance to the dining hall. Joe was arguing with one of the guys and making a scene that kept both men focused on him. Joette contacted both Joe and Ron to keep the two bullies occupied so they could help.

Joette and Shanice had a stun gun and some pepper spray. They approached the man in the entrance, and Joette said, "Hello, is this the entrance to the dining hall?" and as the man turned, Joette hit him with a full dose of her pepper spray. Shanice followed with a stun gun to his back and then, as he staggered around, she walloped him with the Calloway driver to the back of his knee. There was a loud whack and the man was in pain, and he went down like a three-hundred-pound sumo wrestler hitting the floor. Joette followed up with the handle of her nine-iron to the back of his head. He was out.

Joe continued to argue with the two men and had them turned toward him so they saw nothing of what happened, nor did the two thugs notice the women heading right for them.

Joette and Shanice slowly walked toward the four guys, and as they got near, they separated, taking a side. Joette yelled, "Dude," really loud to the guy on her left. He turned and she proceeded to flood his eyes with pepper spray, and as he bent over in pain, she took her nine iron and swung at his ankle. He howled in pain and went down like a defensive lineman getting chop-blocked. She followed up with the handle of her nine iron to the head; that guy was out cold. At the same time, Shanice took the stun gun and pushed it into the back of the other guy, and he staggered and turned around. As he did, she shot him with pepper spray. Shanice's guy tried to keep upright, but Ron threw a roundhouse to the chops.

Few people were around so they just left the guys on the ground and headed for the limousine. "Nice work, ladies," Joe said as they bolted through the doors. The maître d' saw what had happened and shouted, "Call an ambulance. I think these guys are hurt."

The four of them walked calmly out of the building so as not to cause any further scenes, and they approached the limousine from the back. Ron snuck around the driver's side of the limo and tapped on the window and when the driver rolled it down, Ron had a Glock in the back of the driver's neck before he knew what was happening. They threw him on the back seat, tied him up, and decided to take the limo. They had planned for a quick get-away, so everything was ready, but a limousine was a lot better than what they had decided earlier, and they were off to the airport where they had the Suburban packed and ready to go.

It would take about ten minutes to get there, but the diversion would be worth it. It was a pleasant ride in the limo, and they were at the airport in no time. When they arrived, they pulled up near their Suburban located in long-term parking, made sure their passenger was securely tied and gagged, and left him locked in the car. Someone would find him eventually.

They all just stood there for a few moments and looked at each other, wondering what had happened over the course of the last two years—and what was in store for them. They then moseyed to the Suburban and quietly piled in.

Shanice finally broke the silence. "How did it go at the meeting?"

"I would say *nicely*," said Joe.

Shanice and Joette were filled with excitement and the rush that comes when things go right, but they were also aware of the plight of the four people in the Suburban.

Ron added, "I had about two seconds to drop the drug in his drink, and it worked perfectly because he wanted to toast to the future, which we did, but as planned, neither of us drank or ate anything. We knew better."

They drove off with the hope of doing more to help Ann and the FBI to take this group down, yet they knew it would probably not be easy to evade the people who were after them. This trip to the airport should buy them some time to get away. They knew what they had accomplished was little that would affect this large organization, but it was a start.

Joe was pensive. "Yeah, I bet he's going to have a real bad time in a few minutes. I wonder how his three body guards and that driver are doing."

"Yes, could be a tough time for them. What do you think of the big event that he discussed? What could it be, and is it going to happen soon?"

"Not sure, Ron."

Joette spoke up from the back seat, "What big event? Is the event about us?"

"Not really, it's about all of us. I mean the country. They intend to take down the government."

Shanice was sick to her stomach. "It makes me ill to think that they could do that. From what we've seen so far, they must be very powerful. Think of what they did to the four of us."

Joette agreed, "Yes, they made us all disappear. We lost our jobs, homes, and our friends. What will they do next?"

They were moving down the highway and making good time. They had been driving for about an hour and their idea was to drive straight through to Ron's son's home. There they would plan for the future and make some calls to find out what type of trouble might lie ahead. They figured they would be on the road for over seventeen hours to reach their destination, so they were taking turns at the wheel.

Several hours later

Joe had taken the wheel and driven through most of Tennessee and part of Kentucky, but now he and Joette were snuggled and asleep in the back, and Ron had taken over the driving. Shanice was asleep in the passenger's seat.

Ron kept mulling over the event. What was it? Did it involve the country's financial status? Were they planning to storm the nation's capital again, this time doing some real damage? Were they... Who knows? He tried to clear his head and focus on the task of driving.

Joe woke and his first thoughts were *are we in the middle of the event?* He looked up and saw Ron and Shanice in the front seat. "Hey, Ron, how are you doing?

"Good. I'm good. I just can't get the thought of the event out of my mind. What in the world are they planning?"

Joe said, "I hear you. My head is in the same place." Ron was quiet and just kept thinking, and Joe dozed off again.

It was about four a.m. They had made good time, and they were just south of Ohio, only four hours from their destination. Suddenly, Ron startled everyone, "SHIT!" Behind the Suburban was a car lit up like a Christmas tree. "State cops. Wonder if he's on their payroll?"

By now they were all awake and looked at each other wondering if this was it.

Paranoia was running rampant in the quiet Suburban.

"Are we going to be taken again?" Joette said aloud.

"Everyone stay calm. Ron, pull over," Shanice said.

Ron did and drove to the side of the road.

The officer pulled up behind them and walked to the driver's side with flashlight in hand, peered in the window, and shook his head. "What are you all doing out here?"

"We're just heading back to Michigan," Joe said from the back seat.

"I'm not talking to you, sir."

Ron realized he had to say something. "Yes, we're just heading home from our trip."

"I need to see your license. And keep your hands where I can see them."

"But I need to get my license from my pocket."

"All right but do it slowly."

Ron complied and moved as slowly as he could. He gave his license to the officer who returned to his car.

Ron was nervous. "Is this where we get arrested? How will we get out of this, if…?"

The officer returned and handed Ron his license. Then he said, "Mr. Johnson, do you know you went over the center line back there?"

"I did? Sorry, officer, it must have been when I was talking to my friend in back."

"You need to be more careful. I'll let you go this time, but I've got your name and license number now, so drive carefully."

"Yes, sir."

The cop turned and left. They waited until he had pulled out before they resumed their trip. All four were visibly upset, and they all breathed a huge sigh as they got back on the road.

Ron was relieved. "Glad I named my son after me because this car is in his name!" He shook his head. "That was lucky, but what about the next police officer…will he be on their payroll?"

They traveled quietly for the next hour. Then Ron asked, "Hey, Joe, do you think we made a difference? I mean did we really do something to help here, to help stop these rich guys from taking advantage of people and destroying this country as we know it, and did we make it better for those who aren't as well off as even we are?"

"Well, Ron, a lot of what we did was for ourselves, but most of it was for the country and the people. We did the best we could. We might have done some things that we're not proud of, but we did what had to be done. People are suffering and dying because they have nothing, and they're being tricked into working for these people because they can't even get a respectable day's pay or earn a living wage, and these super rich people have everything and more. We did what we had to do."

Ron looked out at the sky and the dark clouds as they drove north on I-75 toward Michigan. "I guess you're right. We need to keep fighting, Joe."

Joe leaned back in his seat, closed his eyes and said, "Yep, and we will."

THE END

CPSIA information can be obtained
at www.ICGtesting.com
Printed in the USA
BVHW042118030322
630649BV00012B/442